KISS
AND
TELL

Center Point
Large Print

Also by Melanie Jacobson and available from Center Point Large Print:

Kiss Me Now
Kiss the Girl

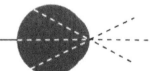

This Large Print Book carries the Seal of Approval of N.A.V.H.

KISS AND TELL

CREEKVILLE KISSES #3

MELANIE JACOBSON

CENTER POINT LARGE PRINT
THORNDIKE, MAINE

This Center Point Large Print edition
is published in the year 2024 by arrangement with
the author.

The text of this Large Print edition is unabridged.
In other aspects, this book may vary
from the original edition.
Printed in the United States of America
on permanent paper sourced using
environmentally responsible foresting methods.
Set in 16-point Times New Roman type.

ISBN: 979-8-89164-067-2

The Library of Congress has cataloged this record
under Library of Congress Control Number: 2023950453

CHAPTER ONE

PRESENT

Natalie's cheerful poster—complete with red hearts—waits for me as I exit the terminal into the airport baggage claim.

WELCOME HOME FROM PRISON!

I smile at my old friend. "It took me fifteen years to get to this point, but I'm definitely going to murder you now."

"I thought it'd draw less attention than writing WELCOME SUPER FAMOUS TABITHA WINTERS," she says. "Besides, what's a welcome back to Camp Oak Crest without a prank?"

"What's first aid for eye sprain from rolling them too hard?" I keep my tone dry, but there's something so reassuring, so *normal,* about Natalie's ridiculous poster that puts me at ease better than two hours of quiet affirmations on the plane had.

She tucks the poster under her arm and grabs me in a big hug, her honey curls tickling my nose. "It's good to see you, Tabs. How have you been?"

"Great?"

"Why is that a question? Cable show, best-selling cookbook. We're not worthy."

"One, stop with the famous stuff. Two, if my

oldest friends in the world aren't 'worthy,' who is?"

Natalie grins. "For real, thank you for coming out to kick off the grand reopening of the camp. Nothing like a celebrity chef to convince all the rich parents that they've put their kids in the best place."

"I can't wait to see the renovations." True. But also . . . not true? We'd spent three of the best summers of my life together as counselors at Camp Oak Crest, and I'm not ready to see it without its scruffiness from my memories. And that's my *least* stressful concern about coming.

Natalie promised Sawyer won't be here. But all the memories of him will. Did I mention two hours of affirmations?

"Let me grab your bags, and we'll hit the road. Ben is dying to see you, and you aren't going to believe how big Juniper is."

"Excuse me, but are you Tabitha Winters?" an unfamiliar voice behind me asks.

Natalie smothers a laugh, and I squeeze my eyes shut before putting on my public face and turning with a smile. "Hi, yes."

It's a woman in her mid-thirties, a middle-school-aged girl standing behind her with an expression suggesting she'd like to melt into the pavement, keeping her eyes on their luggage. "I knew it was you. Didn't I say it was her, Kayla?"

Kayla doesn't answer.

"I'm such a huge fan," the woman gushes. "I watched your YouTube cooking tutorials before you even went viral."

"Wow, you're an OG," I say, and Kayla cringes.

"Sure am," the lady says. "I don't want to bother you, but could we get a selfie with you? I'm dying. No one is going to believe we bumped into you in Roanoke, of all places."

"Sure," I say, even though the other half of her "we" looks like she'd rather die than be in this selfie.

"I can take it," Natalie offers.

When the lady and her tortured child leave, Natalie lifts an eyebrow at me. "Not famous, huh?"

"Shut up."

It's a short walk to the parking lot, and I whistle when she clicks the key fob to unlock a newer Tahoe. "If this camp 'van' is a sign of things to come, I'm prepared to be blown away."

"Nothing but the best for our star." She opens the passenger door and waves me in before grabbing my bags and throwing them in the back.

I ignore her and climb into the back seat.

"What are you doing?" she asks.

"If you're going to give me crap about being famous, I'm going to live the famous life. Drive, Jeeves."

She snorts. "Okay, Tabs. You are not super

famous. You are medium famous. Now sit in the front."

"Not even medium famous. I'm known only by kitchen nerds."

"Tabs, that lady—"

"Must be a kitchen nerd. Say it."

"All right, Tabitha. You're not famous at all."

I scramble out of the car and hop in the front seat.

She shuts the back door, then comes around and climbs behind the wheel and grins at me before merging us into the exiting airport traffic. Her hazel eyes show softer lines than the last time I saw her over dinner with her husband, Ben—another former camp counselor—in DC several months before.

"You look good," I say. "Rested."

She shakes her head. "Working harder than ever, but I'm happy. That's what you're seeing."

"Tell me about it, and start with this car. Major upgrade from the Rust Bucket." That's what we'd named the battered old Ford van that had chugged in and out of the camp all summer, doing runs into town.

"This is our personal vehicle, not the camp vehicle, if that clears things up for you. The Rust Bucket kicked the bucket a couple of years ago, we heard. Our campers will get a preowned ten-passenger van with air conditioning, so that's something."

"Air conditioning? Fancy," I tease.

"That's nothing. Wait until you see the kitchen. And your guest quarters. We should be charging people five-star hotel prices."

I love hearing the pride in her voice. Natalie and Ben's memories of Camp Oak Crest are uncomplicated, and they'll be perfect as the new owners. "I can't wait."

"You won't even recognize it. We've got big plans. I'm dying to give you a tour."

We talk easily all the way back to the camp. Natalie has always been that way, an undemanding presence who can sit with you quietly or keep up a conversation as the situation requires. She was doomed—um, destined—to become a therapist. Watching her face light up as she describes the activities she and Ben are planning make her look like the girl I met a million years ago when we'd both come to Oak Crest as nervous first-year campers.

It feels like old times already, so when we turn off for Camp Oak Crest an hour later, I'm not prepared for the pang in my chest at the sight of the updated camp sign.

"Like it?" Natalie asks. "Our investment partner has an in-house graphic designer, and she did it."

I don't like it, but it's not the designer's fault. It's larger than the old one, using the kitschy font from the national park signs on a silhouette of oaks. It's stylish but inviting . . . and nothing like the slightly crooked weather-beaten sign that had welcomed us back to camp every year.

"It looks great," I say. Which is true. I also don't ask point-blank about their "investment partner." It's Sawyer. I know it's Sawyer. I've google-stalked him enough over the last nine years to know that he's the only person who would have both the money and interest to fund their Oak Crest takeover. But we don't bring up Sawyer . . . ever. He's Ben's best friend, and I never want to make Natalie feel like she has to choose.

I brace myself to crunch onto the dirt road leading down to camp, but it's paved now, and the ride is smooth. That makes my chest feel weird too. Will my whole week here be me missing the way things used to be?

The view is the same, tall evergreens and oaks shutting out the late May sun except for a few spots where light dapples the road. A hush falls, quieting everything but the soft hum of the engine. As if she understands, Natalie doesn't say anything and lets me enjoy the forest as we wind farther into it. The gentle curves of the road carry us ever-so-slightly down until it opens into the familiar bowl of Camp Oak Crest.

"Wow." I peer through the windshield and try to take it all in. Everything is where I remembered it: the office off the parking lot, the mess hall behind it, the flagpole flying the American flag with the seal of the Virginia Commonwealth below it. But they're all glowed-up versions of themselves. Shiny green roofs gleam over freshly painted red doors, each building hewn from new lumber.

Natalie climbs down to get my bags from the back. I open my door and step out, taking in the fresh earth and pine smell of Oak Crest.

"Tabitha!"

I no sooner have my feet on the ground than Ben sweeps me into a giant hug. He's wearing their toddler daughter on his chest, so I get a two-fer as Juniper gives a happy squeak at being trapped between us. Ben's large, sturdy frame seems better suited to these woods than to the prestigious law office he quit anyway.

"Juniper! Squeezing you in real life is so much better than FaceTime," I croon, dropping a kiss on her brown curls. "You're even bigger than you were a week ago."

"I can't believe you're finally here." Natalie pulls me away from her husband for another hug. "Ben, will you grab her stuff? Come on, I'll show you to our guest cabins. You're going to *die*."

"Ben, it's okay, I can bring my bags."

"Nope." Natalie shakes her head as Ben pulls the baby out of her carrier and hands her off. She settles Juniper on her hip and heads away from the SUV. "We're going farther than you think we are. We need *bikes*." She leads me behind the office to a row of thick-tired beach cruisers, shiny paint jobs glinting in the sun. One of them has a baby seat attached, and Natalie pops Juniper into it without interrupting her own stream of chatter.

"The biggest change we've made is adding new guest cabins, but we put them on the far side of the lake. That way we can rent them to guests in the off-season. Corporate retreats, fall foliage tourists, stuff like that. It's about a half mile down, so we have bikes when people don't want to walk. Juniper loves the ride."

"How old is she now?" I ask as Juniper lifts her shirt to study her belly button.

"Fourteen months." Natalie clicks the last buckle into place on Juniper's seat. "Ready?"

I can't remember the last time I rode a bike, but breathing the Oak Crest air peels about ten years off my age. Suddenly, I'm nineteen again and ready for adventure. I sling my leg over the nearest bike, a shiny red one, and rest my foot on the pedal. "Ready."

Natalie sets an easy pace through the trees. The breeze against my cheeks is exhilarating. It smells like the start of summer and reminds me of every first day of camp I'd ever had here. As a camper, I came in each year as a bundle of nerves on the first day, hoping I'd make friends again. I'd met Natalie my first year and made new friends every summer after. By the time I was a counselor, I'd tumbled out of the Rust Bucket the week before the season opened, full of excitement, waiting to see my friends after a year apart at college. Summer never felt like it had started until I'd hugged Natalie, Ben, and Sawyer.

I'm glad for the time to process the absence of Sawyer while we bike. He'd been one of the best parts of camp until he was the worst. It's hard to feel that tug of nostalgia for him too—for who Tabitha and Sawyer were before he broke my heart into pieces no amount of duct tape or calamine lotion or any other camp remedies could fix.

It's an old scar, and I push Sawyer out of my mind and force myself to be present, to feel every sense, because all of them tingle. I can even taste a freshness in the air, something I haven't experienced since . . . well, since the last time I was at Oak Crest.

With a whoop and a laugh, I stand and pedal hard, passing Natalie and rattling out from the forest path to the lake a couple seconds before her. I stop my bike to take in the view. Eight new cabins stretch along this bank, ranging from cozy bungalows to two-story cabins.

Another rooftop—green, not red like these— pokes up farther on the slope rising into the forest. It's beyond the camp boundaries, and it makes me sad to think about the woods being developed, even for weekend homes. I wonder if Sawyer is behind it. His real estate projects are urban and commercial, not residential, but I hope he isn't trying to turn Camp Oak Crest into something it isn't.

A new dock for the guest quarters stretches out from the bank of the lake too. I glance back at the camp beach to reassure myself that the old one is still there, the one that had launched countless canoes over the last fifty years. It's hard to tell from a distance, but it looks as if it's been upgraded too.

"This is impressive," I say as Natalie stops beside me. "Smart to generate income during the off-season too."

"Yeah. Mr. Warren only liked kids and not the parents. He never wanted to expand the business, but that's part of what attracting the big dollar parents this weekend is about. We want to woo them into coming back for another family vacation later. Or think about us for corporate retreats and stuff." She waves at the cabins. "Anyway, pick one and it's yours for the week."

I point at the cottage farthest from the water and nearest the woods. "That one."

She slips a key from her back pocket and grins. "It's possible I knew exactly which one you would pick and only brought that key."

I laugh at her then cock my head at the distant whine of an engine.

"That's Ben on the ATV with your luggage. I

couldn't let you deprive him of an excuse to ride that thing."

"You're doing a fantastic job of making me feel like I'm on a Four Seasons property instead of my old summer camp. You kids have a bright future."

Her return smile holds a touch of anxiety. "You would know. This really matches up to the fancy-pants experience you have for other gigs?"

"It really does." I've flown all over the world, from London to Abu Dhabi, to cook for tycoons and sheikhs, but I'm already more comfortable here than I had been in any of their hotel luxury suites.

"Good." Her body relaxes. "It was a huge enough deal that you designed our camp menus. I can't say thank you enough for cooking for the opening gala."

"Are you kidding me? I wouldn't miss it, but I wish you'd let me donate my time."

She shakes her head. "No, ma'am. Your agent said it's five thousand a day, and that's what you're getting. That's one of the perks of having an investment group as our partner." She rubs her fingers together to indicate cash. "Deep corporate pockets. You could probably charge twice as much, and they wouldn't blink."

"Is that a dare?" Again, I don't comment on the fact that it's probably Sawyer paying my steep rates. Let him see how well I've done. I figured

15

out too late that money matters to him, so there's something . . . full circle about making his company write me a fat check.

"No, thank you! I'll never be dumb enough to give you a dare again."

Smart, given the number of dares I completed in our camp days. Eat an ant? Check. Pretend to be a cat for an entire day? Check. Introduce my pillow as my boyfriend for a week? Check.

She lets down her bike's kickstand, so I do too and follow her after she lifts Juniper out of the baby seat and heads toward the cabin. "Let's get you settled."

A squeal escapes me when we step into my new digs. "Natty! This is *amazing*. Pottery Barn threw up in here but in the best possible way."

She laughs. "That was the goal. Effortless, rustic chic. We hired a designer, and he made these places come to life."

"Courtesy of your partner again?"

"Our very silent partner. We make the choices and send in the invoices. It's a good dynamic."

The ATV grows louder outside, announcing Ben's arrival.

"Come on, I'll show you around while he gets your stuff unloaded."

The cabin is less than a thousand square feet, but it contains a full kitchen, a cozy living room with fireplace, and shelves stocked with board games and books but no TV in sight. The only bedroom is a master suite, the bathroom complete with an old-fashioned enamel tub that I already yearn to soak in while I stare at the trees through the picture window. Soft throw blankets and cozy wood leather furniture fill every room, along with pillows and rugs begging to be touched.

"It's perfect," I say. "I love that you don't even have TVs here."

"TD," Juniper chirps, the first non-babble word I've heard her say. "Mick Moush."

"The big cabins have TVs," Natalie says. "There's no cable, but we have a large library of DVDs."

"Mick Moush," Juniper insists. "TD."

Natalie smiles. "She loves watching Mickey's Clubhouse. On repeat. He's a good nanny when I need to get stuff done. Anyway, cell service is as bad as ever, and no internet out here either. If you need it, come up to the office anytime. You can use the internet there."

"That's great. I've felt so plugged into my life lately. It'll be good to have a reason why I can't return my agent's phone calls for a week."

"Or your mom's?" Natalie asks, a knowing look on her face.

"Don't you therapize me." I grab a pillow and shake it at her. Juniper claps and giggles. If there's anyone in the world I'd talk to about my hard things, it's Natalie, but that's not what I'm here for.

"Are you going to go see her?"

"I don't think so." I hold up my hands to fend off her next suggestion. "Only because I'll be busy this week helping you. I was home over Christmas, and it was . . . not terrible."

"That sounds encouraging."

"It was good, even. My dad's totally healthy again and he found a great assistant manager, so he's taking more time from the store to putter on personal projects. I met Grace's new man, and they're super happy. He's moving to Charleston with her soon, so they won't have to do long distance."

"Good. You didn't say anything about your mom."

"I gave her a dog."

Natalie watches me, waiting.

"She's happy with her dog?" I try.

"Is she happy about the show? Or the cookbook?"

It's complicated, so I pivot. "This week is about you. And Ben. And this place. Not my mom's weird hang ups. I'm already in love with everything you've done here. And you look happy. But are you okay about leaving your practice behind?" She'd had a thriving practice in suburban DC before they'd decided to buy Camp Oak Crest.

"I'm at peace," she says. "I spent so much time talking down campers and other counselors from emotional ledges when we were kids. It led me to my career. I'll have plenty of opportunities to do it again all summer."

"It's true. Camp never lacks for drama." Getting the lowdown on other people's drama was one of the fun parts of camp. It had been far less fun when I'd *become* the drama during my last summer. "You know, maybe I *do* need therapy. It's been more of a mind trip coming back here than I expected."

"You feeling okay?"

I pull at the tassel on a pillow while I think about this. "I don't know." Natalie and Ben had a front-row seat back then, so I don't have to fill in the details. But it's time for a confession. "I've kept up with him, you know. Not stalking level. But enough to know it's probably Sawyer backing you."

There's a long silence before she says, "Wow. I don't remember the last time I heard you say his name."

"That's not a denial."

"You're right. It's not." She meets my eyes, her expression calm. She's letting me decide how much information I want.

"I'm not going to randomly bump into him?" I absolutely need a warning for something like that. "And he won't be at the gala?"

"Honestly, he's almost never here. He lives in Chicago, and like I said, we run things, and he signs the checks between flights to supervise his different projects. He's super busy, plus he figured you'd probably prefer if he wasn't at the gala."

"He's right." Not that it would have been hard for him to guess. I'd rejected every call and deleted every message from him for months after everything went down. When he'd finally quit trying, I'd started breathing easier.

"We all figured you're a much bigger deal than him for the gala fundraiser. You still okay being here?" Her eye lines deepen like she's afraid I've changed my mind after setting foot in the camp.

"Yes. Totally. Or not totally. I knew I was going to have Sawyer flashbacks, but it's pretty weird having him pop up in every other memory I'm having right now."

"How does that feel?" Natalie asks. "Do you want to explore it or shut it down?"

"There's nothing to explore," I say. "I'm clear on what I felt then and now."

"For what it's worth, my advice is to sit with the memories and the feelings. It's when you try to push them out of the way that you run into trouble. They'll bubble up somewhere else in ways you don't want them to."

"Nah. I plan to keep myself so busy, I won't feel a thing."

"Very healthy." Her tone is dry. "I'll leave you to get settled." She heads toward the door. "The camp cook will handle dinner tonight so you can check out her skills. She's awesome. Or at least, I think she is? You're the expert."

"I'm sure she's great." I'm not worried about it. I earned a reputation for running a fun but tight ship early in my kitchen career, and I can get the staff where I need them to be by the gala dinner on Saturday.

"Head up to the office whenever you're ready for the rest of the tour. I know you won't relax until you know the schedule, so we'll review it, then you can take the rest of the day off before it gets crazy tomorrow."

Even though Natalie and I only talk every few weeks and see each other even less, the feeling of being seen—deep down in my core being seen—by someone who knows me and loves me for exactly who I am thrums up through my belly and chest. I throw my arms around her, catching Juniper in another hug that makes her squeak.

"It's so good to see you." I know I already said it, but I need to say it as my old self. As the goofy, unpolished "Tabby Cat" who'd shared a cabin with Natalie years before I was topping bestseller lists and getting my own show. Before people paid a premium for my time and talents. Before I had fooled the world into thinking I was cool. I need a hug from someone who knows the dork I still am deep down.

"I feel the same. But Tabs?" She draws back,

and a rare look of uncertainty flickers across her face.

"What?"

"I'm serious about you making peace with the ghosts. Do an exorcism, and maybe you won't feel like memories are waiting to pounce on you from every corner."

"I'll think about it," I say.

"I hope you do." She reaches for the door. "The new dock is open for all cabin guests. The trail behind the cabins leads to private property, so stay off that so we don't annoy the neighbor. Otherwise, do whatever you want. I'll see you later." She slips out and closes the door behind her with a final wave.

As soon as she's gone, I march into the bedroom and turn back the comforter. Sure enough, Ben short-sheeted the bed. I grin and remake it as I turn Natalie's advice over in my mind.

No summer camp is complete without a good ghost story, but mine is a bad one I don't want to resurrect. Yet every single one of my senses keeps pulling me back into the past, back to when I'd been happiest.

My mind dances away from the edges of the memories about Sawyer. There's an old, dull throb when I think about how we'd gone up in flames like old wood on the last-night-of-camp bonfire.

This isn't good. I can't keep avoiding these

memories of him or I'll make myself nuts. Natalie is right. I need to deal with them and clear a path to enjoy the rest of this week.

I fetch my bags from the porch and retrieve the clothes I need. As counselors, we'd taught the kids over and over that gear is king. You need to be dressed and equipped correctly for every activity for your own safety.

Which means I need to find the perfect outfit for a séance.

Fifteen minutes later, I'm back at the original dock in comfy shorts and a light sweatshirt. The wood that had inflicted multiple splinters every summer has been replaced with a non-wood composite. It's sturdier, but it looks almost identical to the one it replaced—same height, color, length—and I suspect it'll hold up far better than the old wood.

When I sit at the end of it, dangling my bare feet in the water, it's exactly like the countless times I'd hung out down here with Natalie, Sawyer, and Ben.

I close my eyes and go ghost hunting, searching for the spirit of memories past.

CHAPTER TWO
ELEVEN YEARS AGO

"Hey," a voice called.

I didn't recognize it, but it was a touch too deep and four days too early to be a camper.

I turned and spotted a guy standing on the bank near the start of the dock. A large duffel lay beside his feet, and he held his hand over his eyes like he was trying to see me better.

"Can I help you?" I withdrew my dangling feet from the water and stood.

"I hope so," he called. "Do you work here?"

"Yeah. Do you?"

"If I haven't been fired. I missed my flight, so I'm late."

Ah, he was the missing counselor. We'd had new counselor orientation this morning, and Director Warren had mentioned a latecomer.

"Where did you fly in from?" I asked as I walked down the dock.

"Boston," he said. "I flew into Roanoke, but there aren't that many flights, so when I missed mine, I had to wait until today. What about you? You from around here?"

"Pretty much. I'm from Creekville, which is only a couple hours by car. What made you want

24

to come here all the way from Boston? They don't have summer camps in Massachusetts?"

"I'm staying close to home for college, so I wanted an 'away from home' experience. Plus, I need a summer job, and my cousin came to this camp. It always sounded pretty cool, so I applied."

"Who's your cousin?"

"Becca Lewis. She's a couple years older than me."

"I remember her." She'd always been in the older camper group, so I never got to know her well, but I could picture her face. "You must be my age."

"Eighteen."

I nodded. "Just graduated from high school last week."

"Two weeks ago for me."

I'd reached the end of the dock. He was over six feet with dark, shaggy hair and dark eyes. His skin was pale enough to make me frown. He'd have to shellac himself in sunscreen the first couple of weeks until he built up some base color. On the upside, he looked my age. Older boys made me nervous, but guys my age didn't. Usually I made them nervous, honestly, probably because of my hair. It was long and curly and lightened to dark blonde in the summer, and all together, it made boys act kind of . . . dumb. Also, I had good boobs. Hmm. Could be that too.

"Did you check in at the office?" I asked.

"I poked my head in but there was no one there."

I rolled my eyes. "I'm sure Director Warren is 'checking on' Nurse Debbie." I gave the phrase the sarcastic air quotes it deserved.

"Sorry?" His forehead wrinkled.

"You'll see. What's your name?"

"Sawyer."

"I'm Tabitha. I'm a junior counselor. Came here as a camper forever, but this is my first time on this side of things." I held up the whistle on the string around my neck. All counselors got them.

"Shiny." His tone was uncertain, like he wasn't sure what response I wanted.

I let the whistle fall. "I hated the sound of these whistles when I was a kid, but part of me wants to use it immediately. Power really does corrupt."

A half smile peeked at me. He had a nice mouth, nicely full lips. "You a dictator in training?"

"Maybe? I guess I'll find out when the campers come."

When I stepped from the dock to the bank, I could see how tall he really was. I wasn't super short—5'5"—but I had to tilt my head slightly to look at him. "Come on, Stretch. I don't know too much counselor stuff, but I know where things are. I'll show you the boys' cabins."

"Stretch?"

"Camp names are a thing, and now you have one."

"Super original." His tone was dry.

I pointed at my chest. "Tabby Cat. Because I'm Tabitha. I didn't say we tried hard. The more obvious the name is, the better it sticks. Let's move it, *Stretch*."

When we reached the boys' cabins, I stopped and knocked on the first one. "Get out here, Ben."

Ben's head popped out. "What's good, Tab?"

"This is Sawyer, AKA Stretch, the guy who missed orientation this morning." Sawyer winced, but I ignored it. "We need to catch him up. Sawyer, this is Ben. We've been campers together since sixth grade, and now he's a counselor too."

"Old friends, huh?" Sawyer put the slightest emphasis on the word "friends," so slight I might have imagined it. Was he digging for relationship status info? My heart gave the tiniest skip. Summer romances were as much of a tradition as camp names at Oak Crest, but I'd sworn them off after Krish Varma broke my heart when we were fifteen. Still, it was good for my ego to think this pretty cute guy might be interested.

"Old friends," Ben confirmed. "Practically sib-lings." So it *wasn't* my imagination. Ben had heard Sawyer's unasked question and was setting him straight. "Nice to meet you, Stretch. I'd offer to give you the rest of the tour, but I'm trying to work out the archery schedule for the first session."

"Ben is a deadeye," I told Sawyer. "He won the archery competition every year, and he gets to run the range this year. Toss your bag in here for now, and I'll show you the rest of the camp."

He obliged, taking the only remaining open bed, which was closest to the door. It was the worst one because people always bumped it going in and out, especially to the bathroom at night. He might as well get used to it. Counselors were paired in twos and put in a cabin to sleep with eight campers, and we all had to sleep by the door to catch sleepwalkers or kids trying to sneak out. But until the campers showed up, the counselors all bunked together.

"It's nice here," he said as we wound through the cabins.

It was *perfect* here. Warm but not humid, with plenty of shady spots from the surrounding trees. All the facilities were comfortably worn so you didn't have to feel like they were too nice to drag in half the beach after sand volleyball. "Natalie—she's my bestie—says this place needs a remodel, but I disagree. The whole vibe here is scruffy hospitality, and that's how it should be."

"Got it," he said. "You love every splinter of this place, and you're going to judge me hard if I don't."

His tone was teasing, not snotty, but I narrowed my eyes at him. "Basically."

"Then I love it. Greatest sleepaway camp in the history of Virginia."

"The United States," I corrected him. "No, the whole world."

"Greatest sleepaway camp in the whole world." He made his expression as earnest as if he were giving testimony in court.

"Dang straight. Have you been to any other camps?"

"No."

I stopped. "Do you have any camping experience?"

"Not big sleepaway ones like this, but I did Boy Scout camp every summer until high school."

I thought about it for a second. "That's probably enough for you to be okay here."

"Is there anything I need to watch out for or worry about?" He gazed ahead to the girls' cabins, situated on the other side of the main camp restrooms and showers.

"Not really. No snakes. The staff is cool." I considered the question. "Poison oak and eighth graders. That's about it."

"Eighth graders?" His lips twitched like he wasn't sure if I was being funny.

"Yeah. Worse than snakes. By far the most dangerous critters at Oak Crest. They kind of suck. But don't worry; they always give the eighth-grade cabins to the older counselors. You'll get a bunch of the young, homesick, crying ones."

His eyes widen. "That does not sound better."

"They're sweet. If you'd been there this morning," I said with a pointed sidelong glance that made him smile, "they told us to figure out how to distract them, and that's it. They'll forget they're homesick every time you give them a new activity. Like puppies."

"Camp Oak Crest is perfect except for poison oak, eighth graders, and crying first-year campers."

"You're catching on, Stretch. Oh, and watch out for pranks. But only if they're being pulled on you."

"Does that happen a lot?"

"Sometimes. That's also tradition." I didn't tell him I was the reigning prank queen of Oak Crest. In fact, I was already cooking up a welcome for him to help him feel right at home.

"Are we talking short-sheeting and itching powder or what?" he asked. "That was scout camp level."

I suppressed a snort. Amateur. "There are only a few ground rules. Style matters. No physical harm to the victim, no damage to their property. But if you can cause them massive inconvenience, public humiliation, or both, you're doing it right."

"Great."

He did not sound like he thought it was great. Well, he'd get over it. It was eat or be eaten in the prank wars around here. He'd see for himself soon enough.

I led him past the archery range, the ropes course, and our two main trailheads. "This one goes up to Moon Rock." I pointed to the well-worn path. "The campers aren't supposed to come up here without their leaders, but they always do. Especially the—"

"Eighth graders?" he guessed.

I shot him a cheesy finger gun. "You're catching on. It's like they finish seventh grade, and suddenly the only thing they can think about is kissing."

"Moon Rock is basically the make out spot?"

My cheeks warm from talking about make outs with the cute new guy. "Exactly. And the eighth graders are . . ." I couldn't think of a non-crass way to say it.

"I remember," he said. "You don't have to explain."

It came out slightly awkward, and I studied him with a side glance as I led him toward the lodge. He was cute, but not the cocky kind of cute like the boys who always sign up to lifeguard at the Creekville pool. Sawyer hadn't grown all the way into his looks yet, so his eyebrows were too stark, and his arms too gawky, and his hair too messy, like he hadn't learned to tame it yet. He

31

was hesitant and slightly serious. But cute.

Not that it mattered to me. Krish Varma hadn't actually broken my heart, but I *had* learned camp romances were messy when he kissed Lexi Burke the next night. Plus, being a counselor would make me too busy to try to fit in stolen moments with a boy when our campers would be keeping us on our toes, day and night. Plus, I wasn't in the market for a summer boyfriend, especially not one who lived all the way in Massachusetts. Plus, my mom had a near-anxiety attack any time she thought Grace or I was in danger of getting a boyfriend.

But I did love a good project, and my mind was already buzzing with ways to break in my new friend Stretch and loosen him up. I'd caught a few half smiles from him, and I wanted to see what happened when he smiled for real. For curiosity, of course.

No other reason.

Definitely not because those half smiles made my stomach do a tiny flip. Nope. Definitely not because of that.

CHAPTER THREE
PRESENT

A bird swoops close to my end of the dock and chitters, startling me out of the memory of my first day as a counselor. Of meeting Sawyer, completely oblivious to how much he would matter to me by the time we were done.

It seems like when someone is going to be a big deal in your life, you should know the first time you see them. Like when you're watching a show and an actor comes on in a minor part at first, but they're so famous you know they're going to end up being a major character.

Sawyer should have come with that kind of warning.

I'd had no idea when I walked him over to the boys' cabins that he and Ben would be some of my best friends by September.

I'd had no idea we'd become the most legendary pranksters in Oak Crest history, or that my story with Ben and Natalie would burn for years with a bright steady glow while my story with Sawyer flamed out.

Like a shooting star?

No. Like a car explosion in a movie, where some poor idiot is about to get into his vehicle right before a hidden bomb sends it sky high in a fireball.

Exactly like that.

The sun had slid a bit farther below the mountains while I wandered down memory lane. I stand and brush the seat of my shorts. Time to put the memories aside and focus on the job Ben and Natalie hired me to do.

I make my way up to the office, noting the interior has gotten the same glow up as the rest of the camp.

"Hey." Natalie smiles from behind the front desk. "Did you get a nap in?"

"No, but I don't need one. Remember, I'm used to a kitchen pace. I'm good to go. I sat on the old dock and tried to honor my feelings."

Natalie's dimple flashes at me. That's one of her phrases. "Honoring feelings" means acknowledging our emotions and letting them be instead of trying to make them go away. "Were they hard feelings?"

I shake my head. "Not really. Old memories. My first day as a counselor."

"Meeting Sawyer?"

"Yeah."

"Does he still feel like the Ghost of Summer Camp Past?"

"Kind of. But it's fine. I'm sure I'll be in a groove soon, and I won't keep tripping over memories left and right." I don't want to talk about this anymore, about how Sawyer feels like a nearly tangible presence. I haven't seen him in nine years. It shouldn't be so easy to recall every angle of his face, every plane of his body. I change the subject. "Where's Juniper?"

"Helping Ben. By which I mean Ben is trying to get things done while keeping Juniper from eating dirt and rocks. But it's his turn." She gives me a shrug like, *Them's the breaks.* "Want a tour of the rest of the place?"

"Of course. But I'm telling you, if the kid cabins have gotten the royal treatment, I might burn everything down."

"Right. Because they should live in the same crappy conditions we did," she says wryly.

"You get me."

"We made some improvements, but I think you'll be okay with them."

She walks me over to the girls' cabins first, and I poke my head in and turn to face her, my eyes wide. "Why is this so perfect?"

"I know, right?"

The old metal bunkbeds with squeaky springs have given way to sturdy pine berths built into the slanted walls of the A-frames. There are no windows, but each triangular hut has a big glass screen door, a vast improvement over the cheap hollow-core doors that had warped and sagged worse every year. The screen doors let in lots of light, and the floors have been refinished, years of scuff marks and camp grime sanded away. Two counselor beds flank the door.

"It's almost the same, but somehow better," I say. "How did you do this?"

"That's what we were going for. We think the kids need to have a pared-down experience but didn't think they needed to feel like they were living in converted army barracks."

"Converted Soviet army barracks," I say, and she laughs.

"Exactly. And there's going to be a lot of wear and tear. Kids are kids, so we didn't get too fancy, but I hope it feels more welcoming than *our* first summer here."

"It'll probably help with the first couple days of homesickness." By about day four, even the most homesick campers had figured out that beneath the no-frills accommodations seethed a hive of adventure and warmth and fun, but more welcoming cabins might get them there faster.

"Prepare to have your mind truly blown," Natalie says, pointing to the floor near the back wall.

"Holy . . ." This time I don't even finish the thought, just walk over and touch the compact air conditioner.

"I know it's tempting to worship it as a god but pull yourself together."

I look over my shoulder, unwilling to let it

go. "What I wouldn't have given back in our counselor days."

"Believe me, I know. That's why we put them in. Come on and I'll show you the grounds."

She tells me about other upgrades and improvements, but she only has half my attention at best. Sawyer memories take over again.

There's the field where I'd led my cabin of girls to victory over his boys in the color wars. And there's the old fire ring where the counselors spent the last night together after a long day of cleaning up and packing to leave in the morning. Ben would play his guitar, and it would always take Sawyer two to three songs before he'd relax enough to join in with his steady baritone.

There's the flagpole, of course, the site of the most epic prank in camp history, and *I'd* come out the winner that time. And there's the Moon Rock trailhead.

For the trail no one was supposed to know about or use, it had always been the most well-beaten one.

I tear my eyes away. I'm not ready for that memory yet.

"Anyway," Natalie says, "I think you'll be pleased, and so far, everything you've ordered has come in without a problem."

I blink at her, trying to catch up. "Sorry?"

"All the food? It came in without a problem."

"Oh, right." I give myself a slight shake.

"I'm saving the kitchen for last, but what do you think of the rest?" Natalie asks. "Be honest. I can tell when you're lying anyway."

"It looks amazing." It's the truth. "I can't believe what you've done with the place. It's exactly what I would want summer camp to be if I was coming here for the first time."

"Thanks." Pride tinges her smile. "We've worked hard on it."

I hesitate but decide to plunge ahead. "About Sawyer . . ."

She gives me a questioning look.

I slide my hands into the pockets of my shorts. "I sat on the dock and chased out old memories. It went okay."

"Yeah?" It's an invitation to share more.

"Yeah. I've made that last day with him bigger than it needed to be. I thought he'd broken my heart past fixing but check me out." I wave a hand to indicate my whole body. "I'm at the scene of his emotional hit-and-run, and I'm doing fine. Feeling good, even. Don't worry about it anymore this week, okay? I want you to enjoy it. Out with the old memories and in with new ones."

Her eyes twinkle. "Fire ceremony?"

I laugh. We'd held those during the last week of every session for the campers, a chance to symbolically throw whatever they wanted in the fire: fears, grudges, misbeliefs. It was an empowering experience for them, but for the counselors, it was a shorthand where we joked about throwing in every small annoyance. Cook Marge snapped at you? Throw it into the fire. The one tween girl giving you enough attitude to choke a moose? Throw her into the fire. "I've got a few things I could burn," I admit, grinning.

"Let's do one after dinner for old times' sake."

"Sounds perfect."

She fist pumps. "Now let's go survey your new kingdom!"

Chapter Four
TEN YEARS AGO

Sawyer managed to catch his flight for his second summer at Oak Crest. My sister, Grace, drove me to the Roanoke airport, where local counselors met up with the handful flying in to take the Rust Bucket to camp.

I spotted him standing at the Ground Transportation shuttle stop, the same old duffel bag by his feet, but he looked different now. He'd grown into his features more, and while his dark hair still swooped over his forehead, he'd tamed it.

He saw me at nearly the exact same moment, a grin breaking over his face, and it transformed the severe eyebrows and dark eyes, giving him an animation it had taken nearly our entire first summer to pull out of him.

Grace drew in a breath. "Nice," she said. "Very nice. You think they could use more counselors this summer?"

The way she stared at Sawyer, unblinking, bugged me, and I opened my door to let myself out at the curb before she was technically at a complete stop. "Staff's full," I tossed over my shoulder.

"Hey, Tab," Sawyer said, still grinning, and I

ran to him for a hug, glad summer was officially underway.

He caught me easily, and for the few seconds our bodies pressed together, a tingle I hadn't felt last year when we hugged goodbye danced along every point where we connected. Startled, I stepped back and hid my confusion by giving him a light punch on the arm.

"How are you, you old son of a gun?"

Sawyer laughed at Director Warren's favorite phrase. "Same old, same old."

"Uh, Tab?" Grace called from the car, and she sounded amused.

"Bye, Grace. I'm set. See you in August."

She grinned and shook her head, pulling away from the curb.

"Was that your sister?" Sawyer asked. "She didn't want to be a counselor too?"

"Nah. She liked being a camper, but she prefers working in my dad's hardware store. She wants to go into mechanical engineering, so it's a good job for that."

I was still trying to catalog the differences in Sawyer. Did he smell different? I didn't remember noticing his smell last year, but now it was tickling the inside of my nose even though it wasn't strong. Just clean, warm cotton and a hint of spice, maybe from his deodorant or soap.

I felt hyperaware of him in an uncomfortable way. Goosebumpy. It made me nervous, so I turned to talk to the other counselors waiting for the shuttle, catching up on college or whatever else they'd had going on since last summer.

Whatever this weird feeling was, it would settle down by the time we got to camp, and we could go back to being Stretch and Tab. When I couldn't avoid him anymore, I tried to shove us into more comfortable territory.

"Did you develop any game this year?" I asked.

"Game?"

"Pranks." He'd been a sitting duck last year as I'd initiated him with all the camp classics: red Kool-Aid powder in his showerhead, frog in his bunk, Saran Wrapping the boys' toilets.

He reached into his back pocket and pulled out a paperback, turning it to show me the cover. *101 Pranks to Fool Your Friends.*

I tsked and shook my head at him. "Aw, Sawyer. That's sad."

But he only gave me an unreadable smile. "We'll see."

I wanted to sit by him in the Rust Bucket when it rattled up to see if I could catch the light scent again. When the clunky van door slid open, I forced myself to sit with Merrilee instead, a counselor a year ahead of me, climbing into the far back with her where we ended up chatting about our summer goals.

The only problem was Sawyer sitting two rows ahead of me. It meant my eyes fell on him every

42

three seconds if I wasn't careful. I forced my gaze back to Merrilee and squinted with the effort of keeping it there. After about fifteen minutes, she began fidgeting from my attention.

It was creepy. I knew it was creepy. But I didn't know why I was feeling such a weird vibe toward Sawyer, and I only had an hour to get my head right before we got back to camp. I made my smile brighter, listened to Merrilee more intently, and—if the speed she flung herself from the Rust Bucket at camp was anything to go by—skeeved her out even worse.

Natalie and Ben were waiting by the parking lot for the van, and Natalie pounced on me as soon as I set foot on the ground, sweeping me into a giant hug before turning and giving Sawyer the same squealing welcome. I watched her carefully, but she didn't seem to be suffering from unexplained tingling.

She let go of Sawyer to grab me by my wrist again. "Let's get your stuff and go or you're going to end up by the door." She grabbed my backpack from the rear of the van, and I hurried after her with my bulging duffel bag, huffing as I tried to keep up.

"What did you pack? Bricks?" she asked when I dropped it on the last cot *not* by the door.

"Some kitchen stuff," I said. "I wanted to try a few things this summer."

She shook her head. "You did get the foil

dinners to passable last year, but you're tempting fate to ask for more kitchen luck."

"Wasn't luck," I said. "It was seasoning salt and sautéing the onions ahead of time. I've got a few ideas."

"You think Cook Marge will let you try them?"

I grinned. "Maybe I won't tell her."

Nat laughed but it trailed off, and her face grew serious as she bit her lower lip.

"Don't worry," I said. "I'm not going to tick her off."

"It's not that. There's something I need to tell you, and I don't want you to be mad at me. Promise?"

"No," I said. "How can I promise when I have no idea what you're going to say?"

"I've been talking to someone from camp all year. A guy," she clarified.

A knot of anxiety formed in my stomach, small but definitely there. Was she about to tell me she and Sawyer were a thing? The knot got tighter.

What in the—

Why would I care? I wasn't into Sawyer like that. He and Natalie would be cute together. But now my chest was starting to hurt.

"We've been messaging then FaceTiming. And I like him so much."

I tried to take a deep breath without her noticing, hoping it would neutralize the irrational wave of acid rolling through my stomach.

"—and he's so cute and funny, which I already knew, but I had no idea Ben was so deep, and—"

"Ben?" She was talking about Ben? She thought Ben was cute? I mean, he was pretty average-looking, although he did have a great smile. He wasn't nearly as cute as Sawy—

Ugh. I wanted to punch my own face. He was my friend. He had only ever been my friend. *Knock it off.*

"Yeah, Ben," she said. "You're not mad, are you?"

"Why would I be mad? Do you think I like him or something?"

She shook her head. "No, but we're all pretty tight, us plus Sawyer. Ben's talking to Sawyer right now because we want you both to know *nothing* is going to change."

I snorted. I wasn't upset, but those were famous last words every girl heard from a friend who got a boyfriend.

"I'm being for real." Natalie knelt on the bed and grabbed my hands, looking into my eyes with so much Natalie sincerity, I could only laugh. "You know there's no PDA at camp, and we'll do all the same stuff as last year. Sundays off in town, group hikes, all that."

She looked at me like she was waiting for a verdict, maybe even dreading one, but so much relief flooded through me that she'd meant Ben and not Sawyer that it was easy to give her a comforting smile.

"I'm not upset," I promised. "Surprised. When did this happen?"

"He messaged me after one of our Instagram group chats to crack a joke about what I said. It evolved from there." We'd all kept up with each other casually—I thought—through a group chat every week or so. I had no idea they'd gone private. (If Sawyer and I had done the same thing, maybe my reaction to him at the airport would have made more sense?) But I'd thought we were all just touching base every once in a while.

Touching base . . .

I narrowed my eyes at Natalie. "I'm going to need details, girl. What does 'evolved' mean? And why did you mention PDA? Have you guys made out yet?"

She blushed. "No, nothing like that."

"Yet?" I prompted again.

Her cheeks turned pinker. "Yet."

I grinned. "The rules are that I don't want to see any smooching all up in my face, but I better hear every single detail about it afterward."

A smile peeked back at me. "You don't mind?"

"Nope."

"I thought you and Sawyer might worry it would change the vibe."

I shook my head. "If you say it won't, I believe you."

"Good." Her face relaxed, the lines softening. "Speaking of you and Sawyer . . ."

"Yeah?" I kept my voice casual. Super casual. *So* casual.

"Is there anything going on between you two?"

Okay, not casual enough. "No," I said. "No private chats or face sucking."

She pinked again, and I laughed. She made it so easy. This was going to be fun.

"Okay," she said. "I thought . . ."

I'd started unzipping my duffel, but I glanced over at her. "You thought what?"

"I sensed a vibe between you two last summer."

"No vibe." I went back to unpacking my duffel, in search of my favorite sneakers for running around camp.

"Ben also thought . . ."

She had my attention again. "No. You're doing the thing where now that you're all loved up, you think everyone else should be loved up. And you promised nothing would change." I shook my finger like I was scolding a camper. "No camp romances. Camp romances are a dumb idea." Her face fell. *Oops.* "I mean, not you and Ben. Everybody else. Me especially."

She held her hands up to fend me off. "Okay, okay, there's nothing going on. It just would have been so perfect—" She broke off when she saw my expression. "Right. Nothing going on. Nothing changes."

It wasn't true. Things would definitely change. I could only hope it wasn't too much. Last summer had been perfect, and I'd been looking forward to topping it. I stifled a sigh. Maybe it wouldn't be the summer I'd imagined, but we'd make it truly epic anyway.

I was wrong.

Annoyingly, tragically wrong.

Okay, "tragic" was strong. But definitely annoyingly wrong.

The four of us still ran around and did almost everything together, and Ben and Natalie were good about not doing any public displays of affection in front of the campers. But when it was our time off, all bets were off. Natalie had dragged me out of the cabin on her second morning to report they had finally kissed at Moon Rock, and it was *the best.* I'd have guessed from her glowy eyes and the way she kept touching her lips even if she hadn't told me.

Sawyer and I even exchanged amused glances and rolled eyes at breakfast as they fussed over each other.

It wasn't so bad after a couple of weeks. I went out of my way to make sure Sawyer didn't get any "vibes" from me. Gave him the hardcore friend treatment, calling, "Hey, buddy," across the camp when I saw him, or making sure Ben and Natalie sat together between us instead of sitting side by side, like two couples.

If Sawyer had sensed anything in our airport hug, there was no evidence of it now. I kept getting twinges if he brushed against me, or if our eyes met as we laughed at camper antics. There were times I could have sworn he rearranged his cabin's schedule so our campers did the same activities at the same time. But I never acted any differently, and pretty soon, I was convinced we were back on the same footing as last summer.

By the end of camp, I was sure of it, and I walked down to the lakeside final campfire as relaxed as usual at this point of the summer. The final session campers left by noon; all that was left to do was hang out, get up early to clean up and winterize the camp, and say our goodbyes.

I didn't know what it was about the closing counselor campfire, but it smelled better and the s'mores tasted more delicious than any other campfire we'd had that summer. It had been like that last summer too.

I glanced over to where Sawyer struggled with his s'more. He never roasted the marshmallow enough, so it didn't do its job of melting the chocolate and sticking the graham crackers together.

I grimaced and sat beside him. "Let me do it."

He scowled. "You burn them."

"Let's call it flambé. I do it because it's the right way to make a s'more." He grumbled but handed it over, and in a few minutes, I returned a perfectly gooey s'more to him.

He bit into it, and a satisfied smile flickered over his mouth. It was such a good mouth. Full lips without being too thick—

Anyway. I set about making another one, distracting myself.

"You ready to go home tomorrow?" he asked.

"Sure," I said. "I only have to be there a few days before I head back to campus." I went to the University of Virginia, Arlington, majoring in marketing.

"Sounds like you don't want to be home for long. You don't like it there?"

We'd never talked about our families much. Annoying campers, yes. Counselor gossip, yes. The number of times we caught Director Warren and Nurse Debbie making eyes at each other when they thought no one else was watching, definitely.

"I like home," I said. "Mostly. Grace and I fight sometimes, but it's not a huge deal. I get along great with my dad."

"What about your mom?"

I sighed, barely conscious I was doing it.

"I guess that's a no."

"She's . . ." I tried to think of how to explain my mom. "She didn't want me to go to school in state. She had big plans for herself, and she gave them up when she and my dad got married. They love each other, but she's always on our case to get out of Creekville. Out of *Virginia*. She wants us to be astronauts and doctors." It was also why she got anxious if either of us dated a guy more than twice.

"She's not thrilled you're going into advertising?" he guessed.

I shrugged. "I'm not either, honestly. I don't know if anyone grows up and says they want to go into marketing. But I'm good at it, and I can get a good job when I graduate. It's not enough for her. My ambitions aren't big enough. I'm not good *enough* at marketing, and she thinks I won't get a good *enough* job."

"She sounds intense."

I snapped and pointed at him. "Bingo. What about you? You ready to go back?"

His eyes met mine for a couple of seconds. "No."

It was a simple answer, and he didn't follow it up with anything, but I suppressed a shiver when he looked away. *What was that?!* That had *meaning* and stuff in it.

Right then, Brinley Wexler stood up and swayed the tiniest bit on her feet.

"Looks like she got more booze," I whispered to Sawyer.

"Legendary," he said, but he didn't sound impressed. There were a handful of counselors who were legally old enough to drink, but it was against camp rules. They did it anyway, and always offered it to the rest of us, but most

51

of us never took them up on it. I didn't have any practice holding my liquor, and the last thing I wanted to do was get sent home by Director Warren for being too blitzed to do my job. Plus, dealing with nine-year-olds in the heat all day while nursing a hangover sounded brutal.

"Guys, I have an announcement," Brinley said, her S sounds slightly squishy.

"She found the lake monster," I guessed in a low voice.

Sawyer shook his head. "She's changing her name to Jackie Daniels because she loves it so much she wants to marry it."

That made me laugh, and Brinley squinted in our direction, but the campfire flames seemed to confuse her, and she weaved a tiny bit. "We're playing a game," she said.

"Great." That was Ben. He didn't mean it.

Natalie shushed him. "Give her a second. Could be fun." Raising her voice she asked, "What game, Brinley?"

"Truth or Dare," Brinley announced triumphantly.

This met with groans around the circle.

"Guys?" Brinley's voice wavered like we were about to deal with impending tears. "We're all going to be adults in the real world soon—"

"Or in rehab," Sawyer muttered. I nudged his knee with mine to shut him up and regretted it when the hair on his leg tickled my bare skin.

"—and we won't have many chances like this to just be goofy."

"You're right," Natalie said, always encouraging. "I'm down for Truth or Dare."

This time, there was a softer grumble, but no one flatly rejected the idea.

"I'll start," Brinley said, her voice happy again. "Merrilee, truth or dare?"

I was almost positive I heard Merrilee sigh before she said, "Truth."

Brinley pouted for a second, then brightened. "How many times have you made out at Moon Rock?"

"Counting as a camper too?" Merrilee asked, and everyone laughed. "Seven."

"Wow," Natalie said to us beneath the noise of the crackling fire. "Go, Merrilee. I didn't know she had it in her."

I squinted at her through the flames, and a small smile played on her plain face. *Get it, Merrilee.*

Merrilee challenged the next counselor, and the next four rounds were more truths. The only half-interesting one came when Deandre Wilson revealed he'd caught the director and Nurse Debbie skinny-dipping one night and hid their clothes before running away.

"I'm glad I didn't see that." I rubbed my eyes, trying to banish even imagining the pale, pale scene.

Ben chose truth, which elicited boos and

another pout from Brinley, but he didn't back down.

"Fine," Deandre said. "Tell us what's up with you and Natalie."

Another softball question, but instead of answering, Ben looked over at Natalie and laced his fingers through hers. "I'm going to need a minute to consult." He pulled her to her feet, keeping a firm grip on her hand amid catcalls from the circle.

They vanished beyond the reach of the campfire light, and Sawyer and I exchanged glances.

"What's that about?" he asked.

I had no idea. A couple of minutes passed, then a couple more before they reappeared, this time Natalie tucked tightly against Ben's side.

"What's up with me and Natalie is that I love this girl," Ben said, "and I thought she should hear it from me before you did."

We erupted in cheers, and my heart squeezed at the look they exchanged, full of happiness and promise. I'd have to get the rest of the story from her tonight in our cabin.

"A Camp Oak Crest love match," Merrilee called. "We've had a few marriages come out of here, you know."

It was true. I could remember two different sets of counselors from when I was a kid who were married now. Maybe that was why I was skittish about camp romances. My mom had fallen in love at twenty and never let us forget that she should have waited.

"Whoa." Natalie held her hand up in a "simmer down" gesture. "Getting ahead of yourselves there."

But I studied her smile, and I wasn't so sure. These two were gone on each other.

"Your turn, Sawyer," Ben said.

The circle broke into a chant. "Dare, dare, dare, dare!"

I didn't think Sawyer would go for it. He wasn't the kind of guy who cared much about peer pressure, always keeping his own steady course. But he cracked a smile and said, "Fine. Dare."

Maybe in stronger light, I would have noticed an evil gleam in Ben's eye. Maybe I could have done something to derail him. But I was waiting for him to dare Sawyer to jump in the lake fully clothed or something, so I wasn't at all prepared to hear him say, "I dare you to kiss Tabitha."

My eyes flew to Natalie first. Did she have something to do with this? But her eyes were wide too. Then I looked at Sawyer. His expression hadn't changed at all. Sometimes, if he was embarrassed, the tips of his ears went red, but in the firelight, I couldn't tell if they were or not.

"You don't have to do it," he said, quietly. "Ben's being . . ."

What? A jerk? That wasn't usually Ben's thing.

But Sawyer didn't finish the sentence. Instead, he cleared his throat, and I had a feeling he was about to tell Ben to shove it.

I didn't know what came over me. Last night of camp magic? The same vibe that had caught me off guard when I'd seen him at the airport? Whatever it was, it took over now.

"It's okay. I'll do it," I said before he could speak. Sawyer's eyes widened as everyone hooted and whistled.

"Yesssh," Brinley cheered, and I hoped someone had taken away her bottle.

"You sure?" Sawyer asked.

"Why not? It's just a stupid game, right?"

"Right, yeah."

I leaned toward him, but he jerked back. A couple of the guys said, "Oooh," like he'd blocked my shot, but right as a wave of mortification crested to swallow me alive, he took my hand and pulled me to my feet.

"Not here." He towed me in the direction of the woods.

"No fair," someone called. "How will we know you went through with it?"

"You'll have to trust us," he called over his shoulder.

He stopped behind the dock house and turned to face me, still holding my hand. "You don't have to do this. Ben was out of line."

If I thought he was trying to get out of this, I

would have turned around and headed right back to the fire. But instinct told me he didn't want to get out of this. He just didn't want me to feel trapped. Something about him saying Ben was out of line, like . . . like Ben knew something I didn't. Like Ben was trying to help Sawyer out because . . .

Why not do it? It was the last night of camp. It wasn't like it could complicate the summer. It was a kiss—one that could satisfy my curiosity—not a relationship. We'd have a whole school year to forget about it. I tangled my free hand in his hoodie strings. "I never back down from a dare."

He hesitated for another full second before a soft curse escaped him, then he leaned down and his lips met mine.

They felt as good as they looked, but I was caught off guard by the spark. No, straight-up shocked. We taught campers to build fires using lots of tinder, highly flammable bits that would catch and burn quickly so they'd feel successful. I went up exactly like that, like his mouth had lit me on fire, all my senses suddenly tuned to the sensation of heat. Just heat. So hot, I gave a tiny gasp.

He tensed like he would draw back, but I pulled on the hoodie strings. He kissed me harder, his lips parting the seam of mine, deepening the kiss until I had to slide my hand around the back of his neck and lean into him for support.

What was happening?!?!

I did not know. I did not care. And it did not stop for a long time. I wasn't even sure how long it was before faint catcalls from the fire ring reached us, and Sawyer pulled away and straightened.

We looked at each other. Or tried to as best we could in the dark. I thought he blinked a few times.

"Um, I'm—"

If he said he was sorry, I'd . . . I'd . . . knee him in the crotch. I did *not* want to hear that he regretted it.

"We'd better get back." I turned to the lake.

"Right. Let's go."

"Don't worry, I'll tell them you were great."

"Thanks." He sounded bemused. "Wait, what do you mean you'll *tell*—"

But a clamor of "So? How was it? Did you do it? What happened?" questions poured out as the other counselors caught sight of us.

"Tell usssh," Brinley said.

"She won't," Natalie said as I was about to answer. "I've known her for years, and she doesn't kiss and tell. Good luck getting anything out of her."

"Boo!" Brinley said. "Then you tell us, Sawyer."

He only shrugged, and we took our seats again, but I noticed he sat a couple of inches farther away than before.

Oh no. Was I bad at kissing? I was nineteen; he wasn't my first kiss. I hadn't had gobs of practice, but I thought I knew what I was doing.

"Your turn, Sawyer," Ben said.

Sawyer dared Natalie to sing the camp song while standing on her head, but I barely paid attention to the rest of the game. The fire was starting to burn down to embers, and I stared into them, trying to divine the truth: did I suck at kissing?

Soon the group broke up, everyone leaving to grab at least a few hours of sleep before the next day of cleanup and traveling home.

I walked beside Natalie to our cabin in silence, thinking over that kiss.

As soon as the door closed behind us, she whirled on me and grabbed my arms, giving me a shake. "So? Kiss and tell, right now. How was it?"

"I . . . don't know?"

Her jaw dropped. "You didn't kiss?"

"We did."

She squealed. "And?"

"And it was amazing?" Another squeal. "Maybe? I'm not sure what he thought. I think he almost apologized for doing it, and when we got back to the fire, he sat farther away from me."

Maybe guys didn't notice details like that, but girls did. Natalie would take it seriously. She tapped her lips, her expression thoughtful. Then she snapped her fingers. "He was too turned on. He couldn't risk sitting too close to you."

My cheeks warmed. "You think?"

She tilted her head. "You could always ask him."

"Yeah, right."

"Then my ruling stands. I'm sure you're not a bad kisser. Not that I'm going to verify. No shade to those who experiment, but these lips are for Ben."

"I'm wounded but I get it," I said.

"You still haven't told me the most important thing. Do you like him?"

I looked at her like she'd grown another head. "Because of one kiss?"

"Yes."

"YES."

That got the loudest squeal of all. "Yay! I knew it. I *knew* it. Too bad you dummies waited until the last day of camp to figure it out."

"What do you mean?"

"I told you on the first day that there's always a vibe with you guys."

True. I could see it now—with my perfect hindsight. "What do I do?"

She grinned. "I don't know, but you have nine months to figure it out before you see him again."

CHAPTER FIVE

Natalie and I walk into the camp kitchen. Before I say a word, I hug the fridge. I can't help it.

"Honey, you may have bigger voids in your life than I realized," Natalie says.

I press my face against the stainless-steel door. "You don't understand. This is a KoolMore."

"But do you need to hug it?"

"I do. What I wouldn't have given for this fridge back in the day. Your cook gets it."

The woman wearing a chef's smock makes a noise of agreement. So far, she hasn't spoken any actual words.

"See?"

"No, and now I'm worried about how you're going to react to the rest of this kitchen. Come on," Natalie says. "There's more to see."

I step away from the KoolMore but leave it with a love pat. "I'll be back for you, cutie. Don't worry."

"She's not normally like this," Natalie reassures Lisa, the cook, after she introduces us.

"Yes, I am," I inform her.

Natalie sighs. "Okay, yes, she is."

Lisa gives me a smile, but it trembles at the edges. I see this look on people's faces sometimes at book signings. Lisa is a true fan, bless her heart. I mostly don't mind unless they get pushy about selfies when I'm on my private time. But if Lisa is a shy fan, it'll take extra work to pull her out of her shell while we prep for the gala this weekend.

"Why don't you show me through the kitchen, Lisa? I don't know if Natalie cares much about the nuances of burner size and roasting capacity."

"Um, sure." But her eyes are darting from side to side.

Maybe giving her something specific to talk about will get her mind off her nerves. "Let's start with the range."

It seems to work as she blinks and tells me about it. We used this model in the second restaurant I worked in, but I listen like it's new information. By the time we've moved on to the wall ovens, she's speaking more naturally, her enthusiasm for the ovens shining through.

Honestly, I don't blame her. They're gorgeous, and they get a love pat too.

The tour takes fifteen minutes as she explains the finer points of her pantry system and demonstrates the state-of-the-art dishwasher setup.

"I can't believe the upgrades, Nat. You guys did good. It'll be a pleasure to work in here this week."

Confusion ripples across Lisa's face, and she turns to Natalie, but Natalie is already looping her arm through mine. "You guys can get into the nitty-gritty details tomorrow. You need to see the dining hall."

Like everything else at the camp, their make-over has worked wonders. And like everything else I've seen, I experience a pang for the old version of it. I let myself feel it then release it. Upgraded tables sporting durable vinyl tops have replaced scarred wooden trestle tables in here. It makes sense. They have to withstand a lot during the summer, from kids banging silverware during camp songs to rainy day crafts.

After Natalie walks me through the other changes—a new PA system, a slightly raised stage, roller shades so the late afternoon sun doesn't blind the kids at dinner—we walk outside, and she checks her watch.

"I need to call a parent who's trying to get a solo bunk for their child because she's sensitive to other people's auras."

"Um . . ."

"I know. But Lisa usually cooks dinner for us, so how about if we meet back here in an hour to eat, then Ben will put Juniper down for bed, and we can do our fire ceremony?"

"Sounds great."

I pedal my bike to the cottage, enjoying the late afternoon warmth, gentle in late May. It will become heavier as the summer wears on, but right now, it's perfect. I remember this so well. Even with the sun up, I can almost feel the gathering dusk, and I'm surprised I'm still calibrated to the rhythms of this place. I guess nine years away wasn't enough to overwrite the nine years I spent coming here as a camper then counselor.

There's nothing I need to do for the next hour before dinner and our fire ceremony, so I want to check out the private trail behind the cottages. I know Natalie said not to, but ten years ago, this had been part of the camp's property, left undeveloped so the kids could have land to range in and practice their nature skills. I need to reassure myself it's not turning into a horrific subdivision back there.

I park the bike and fetch a flashlight from my cabin. I haven't forgotten my woodcraft, and I'm too smart to head out to a new trail without one. I won't be going far, but it's better to plan as if I am. Lack of preparation is a breeding ground for emergencies, in restaurant kitchens and summer camps.

No warning or trespassing signs tell me to stay off the trail, so I don't. I'll give it twenty minutes before I turn around and get ready for dinner.

It takes about ten minutes before the path lightens ahead and leads me to a clearing. I peer through the trees and stifle a gasp. Did I get the wrong kind of mushrooms in my omelet this morning?

Because I had expected to find a house standing there.

I just didn't expect to find Sawyer Reed sitting on its deck.

CHAPTER SIX

TEN YEARS AGO

Sawyer's kiss—our Truth or Dare kiss—stuck with me for days after I got home from camp.

I relived it multiple times an hour, trying to remember every detail. Where had his hands been? And mine? What sounds had he made? Did I make any noises? Did they sound stupid? Was he really into me?

As if it wasn't bad enough that I was torturing myself this way, I seemed to be the only one doing it. Our Instagram group chat was the same as it ever was, complaining about the days we were stuck at home with nothing to do before we could go back to school.

Why was he not suffering? He should be suffering.

I was suffering.

Everyone must suffer.

I might not have said this aloud, but my dad for sure picked up on my vibes because he stuck me in the stockroom to do inventory where I couldn't interact with other humans. I counted screws with a vengeance, because screw them. Honestly. Stupid screws.

Then the third day after camp dawned with a

bright and glorious message. In my DMs. From Sawyer.

It had come in around 3 AM, and before I read it, I knew that was even better. It meant I was on his mind in the middle of the night. I fumbled my phone to the floor trying to swipe open the message, then squinted and read it three times.

SAWYER: So. I'm not sorry I kissed you. I'm sorry I kissed you that way.

Okay.
Okay, this wasn't . . . bad?
Or good.
It was . . .
I didn't know what it was. If I asked him to explain, would I sound stupid for not getting it?

Maybe. But I'd feel dumber if I tried to play it off and got it wrong.

After agonizing for half an hour and trying to squeeze every ounce of meaning out of every single word, I gave up.

TABITHA: Explain . . . ?

English majors, eat your hearts out.

SAWYER: I wanted to do that all summer. Ben knew. He thought he

66

was helping. I shouldn't have done it on a dare. Kissing is better when both people are into it.

Oh. My. Gosh.
Ohmygosh.
OHMYGOSHOHMYGOSHOHMYGOSH.
Natalie was right: he was into me.
I needed to say something quick after a confession like that.

> **TABITHA:** My bad. I thought both people WERE into it.

I read over the message, considered deleting it for reasons of total dumbness, then doubled down instead and sent a winky emoji.
A WINKY EMOJI.
I dropped my phone and pulled my covers over my head with a groan.
My phone buzzed almost immediately, and I couldn't have resisted checking it any more than peanut butter could resist jelly.

> **SAWYER:** Damn. I definitely should have done it sooner.

Swoooooooon.
That was the beginning of our DMs. At first, it was a few times a week, catching up on school as

we each got back to campus, or talking about a movie we'd both seen.

Then it became every day.

It never grew to phone calls. Neither of us suggested it, and I wondered if Sawyer's reasons were the same as mine. He'd already become a high point of each day. Keeping it to messages made it manageable, like he was inside an efficient boundary, a section that belonged to a different part of my life.

Even so, I dated less my sophomore year than I had my freshman year. The boys I met . . . it was different. They weren't as funny as Sawyer. Or as cute. Or if they were cute, they were also too cocky. And mostly boring.

The next summer, I made Grace drive me all the way into Camp Oak Crest. She complained bitterly until I gave her twenty bucks to shut up. But I couldn't meet the Rust Bucket at the airport. I couldn't. I was a hot mess and trying not to look like it because I didn't know what to do when I saw Sawyer.

In a normal year, I couldn't wait to run and fling myself at Natalie and Ben *and* Sawyer, giving back huge hugs, all of us talking at once as we caught up.

But that third summer . . . I didn't know if I wanted to puke, run away, or jump on Sawyer and kiss his face off. The urge to do the last one was so overwhelming, I wasn't sure I could fight it, which is why I wanted to escape to the safety of my cabin before I had to face him. I needed time to pull myself together. Because even though I couldn't name my feelings—I wasn't sure yet what they were—I could feel them written all over my face.

Grace dropped me off, and I got first dibs in the counselor cabin, dropping my stuff on the back corner bunk. I sat and gave myself a pep talk about being normal when Sawyer got to camp.

You can do this, Tab. You are twenty, not a baby. But every time I imagined seeing him again, I felt like I was coming out of my skin. And to have that happen at Camp Oak Crest? The one place in the world where I'd always felt so completely me? To feel like I was a canoe bobbing on the lake, no paddles, no pilot?

I didn't like it.

I tensed at the sound of every slamming car door in the distance. Any minute now it could be Natalie arriving, wanting to know what I was going to do about Sawyer, and I *didn't freaking know.* It could be Sawyer arriving, wondering the same thing.

Another car door slammed, and I jumped, then pressed my lips together to keep in a frustrated grunt. I poked my head out of the cabin, and when I verified it wasn't the Rust Bucket, I decided enough was enough. Time to take control of this situation. I needed to set the terms for seeing Sawyer. I needed the upper hand when I saw Sawyer, or I wouldn't be able to shake the coming-out-of-my-skin feeling.

I jogged over to the office.

"Hey, Tabitha. Welcome back," Director Warren said when I walked in. He was a nice guy with an unfortunate ferret-y mouth and nose. Slightly too small eyes. A bristly moustache. His voice even had a tendency to squeak when he got excited. But he was fair, and the counselors liked him.

"Hey, Director Warren," I said. "When is the next shuttle due from Roanoke?"

He smiled and glanced at his watch. "Anxious to see your friends?"

Anxious was putting it mildly. "You know it. Always feels like forever."

"About forty-five minutes," he said.

"Great," I said, already backing out. Nothing put people—even me—off-balance like a prank. I brainstormed and dismissed several. They were either too elaborate to pull off in a very short time, or too broad to really throw Sawyer off. I needed something specific, something that would push his buttons specifically. Something that would discombobulate him and bring him down to my level.

Finally, I thought of a plan, but I was going to have to work fast. I stood on the stump next to the office, the only place to get cell reception reliably—and called Grace. "I need you to turn around and come back."

"What? No. I'm already on the highway."

"Come back right now or I'll tell Mom you answered your phone while you were driving."

"You suck."

"See you in a few." I didn't feel guilty. I had a vision, and Grace would fall in line.

When she turned into the parking lot fifteen minutes later, I was waiting for her with an armful of bed linens and a soccer ball.

"What's going on?" she demanded.

"I'm starting the prank game early."

Her face wavered, like she was torn between protesting . . . and there it was: her smile won out. "Okay, what's the plan?"

"I need to get Sawyer. Let's start driving and I'll explain along the way." I was already climbing into the passenger seat.

"Spill," she said as she pulled onto the highway.

"Ben is terrified of bears. Natalie hates small spaces. I have my shark thing—"

"Which is so stupid," she interrupted. "You never have to go in a shark's house if you don't want to."

"Shut up," I said crankily because she was right. "Sawyer's thing is ghosts." It took me a while to figure it out. The whole first summer, I would have sworn he had no phobias at all.

But last summer, maybe because of my heightened awareness of him, I'd noticed the only time he acted remotely squirrelly was when we told ghost stories. And we had a ghost story night during every session. It had taken me until the third session of camp to notice and the fourth to confirm it, but he definitely acted differently on ghost story night. Tense. Looking over his shoulder. Flinching. Very slightly, but it was there.

I'd been planning to play on that at some point this summer, but I'd never catch him more off guard than if I did it right now.

"The Rust Bucket should be coming in about twenty minutes. We'll drive a mile or two then pull over to the side of the road. You'll flag down the Rust Bucket, and when it stops, you're going to say we were on the way to Oak Crest when you swerved to avoid a dog, but we saw it limp into the woods. I was worried it was hurt by another car, so I went looking for it, but you're scared of dogs, and it was big, and you want someone to check on me."

"I am *not* scared of dogs."

I rolled my eyes. "Then say it's big, and I've been gone for a while, and you're worried I need help with it."

"Okay, but what about the sheets and the soccer ball?"

I stuck the ball under the sheet and cinched the fabric beneath it. "Meet Tragic Claire. Sawyer is going to find her when he runs into the woods."

72

Grace smirked. We told the story of Tragic Claire every year precisely because she was our creepiest legend, the spirit of a pregnant young bride who'd been shot by a Union deserter and left to die when she wouldn't give up the last of her cornmeal when he demanded it. She was said to wander the nearby woods, calling the name of her Confederate husband, John Willis, always followed by the high, thin cry of the child she'd never held.

Someone had shifted on their log while Merrilee told the story last summer, and I swear, Sawyer had jumped a foot at the sound, even if no one else noticed. I was playing a hunch here, but I was sure I was right.

I had Grace pull off the side of the road at a place where it was easy to slip into the trees. I picked my way through the woods until I was about fifty yards from the highway. It only took a few minutes to get myself situated, wrapping the sheet around me like a cloak and securing the soccer ball beneath my T-shirt to become poor, pregnant Claire.

I settled behind a thick oak and waited. It was almost fifteen minutes before I heard the sound of a vehicle from the direction of the highway, then Grace's asking for help.

A couple of minutes later, someone entered the woods running, and Sawyer shouted my name.

The woods were dark enough to be dim even

in midday, and when he paused, trying to figure out where he was, I called his name, making my voice sound confused.

"Tab? Tabitha? Is that you? Are you okay? I'm coming!"

He started running again, toward me this time, and when he was about twenty yards away, I let out my best thin, ghost baby wail.

Sawyer froze. "Tabitha?"

"Here," I said in my own voice, trying to sound confused.

"Are you crying?"

"No. I'm turned around. Sawyer? Is that you?"

"Yeah, it's—"

But I let out another ghost baby wail.

"Did you hear it that time?" he asked.

Now I injected some stress into my voice. "Hear what? How come I can't find you?"

"Coming."

He sounded freaked out but resolved, and my conscience pricked at me. He had to know there was no ghost baby out here, didn't he? I decided not to keep the joke going any longer, and I stepped around the tree to show myself. But I was still in my ghost stuff, and before I could say anything, instead of grinning, he yelped and stumbled backward, tripping over a branch and hitting the ground with a loud *whumpf*.

"Sawyer! It's me! Oh, no." I ran over to him and dropped to my knees beside him. His eyes were closed, a grimace of pain contorting his face. "Are you okay? Did you hurt yourself?" My years of first aid training kicked in, and I reached for his head to check it for injury.

He struck lightning fast, snatching my wrist and toppling me onto his chest.

"Well, hey, Tragic Claire."

I blinked at him, his face inches away, his dark eyes fixed on mine. "You broke the baby," I said. The ball had popped out from beneath my shirt and bounced to the ground.

He didn't look. "I'm sure it's fine."

"But—"

"Hey, Tab. It's good to see you."

I sighed. "Did I scare you at all?"

His pupils flared for the tiniest microsecond. I would have missed it if I wasn't staring right in his face when he said, "No." But I did see it. He'd been scared for a second, and I suddenly felt better about this summer now that I'd wrestled back the upper hand. "Is there a dog?"

"No."

"Help me up," he said.

I stood and reached down to pull him to his feet, but when he was standing, instead of letting go, he leaned down like he was going to kiss me. I froze, mesmerized as I watched his head lowering to mine, but he swerved at the last second and whispered in my ear instead. "I can't wait to pay you back."

An electric zing shot down my spine as he turned and sauntered toward the car.

I stared after him, not sure I'd gotten the upper hand at all.

CHAPTER SEVEN
PRESENT

I squint at the deck, not sure I trust my eyes. Sawyer Reed is here. At Camp Oak Crest. Or right next to it. Sawyer Reed, in the flesh.

I scuttle behind the nearest tree. The trail opens to the side of his house—a house as big as the largest cabin down on my beach—and the front faces the lake. It has a wraparound deck, and the side where Sawyer works at a patio table also boasts a hot tub. He's in shorts and a tank top, his laptop open in front of him as he types furiously. The slightest turn of his head will give him a clear view of the trail. I barely breathe even though there's no way he could hear me. It's at least forty yards to the edge of the deck.

He's broader through the shoulders, bigger in the way boys become when they grow into their bodies, but the set of them is so familiar, my palms go sweaty.

Even at a distance, I can tell he's a hotter version of the Sawyer I knew.

Dang it, Sawyer.

And all of that aside, *why is he here?*

Ben and Natalie must know about this. Why did they lie and say he wouldn't be?

I review every mention of Sawyer in my mind, but all Natalie had specifically said was "He's hardly ever here," not that he wasn't here now. And that he wouldn't be at the gala, and I wouldn't bump into him. But she hadn't flat out said Sawyer was not at Oak Crest.

But I've bumped into him. Or nearly have. He just doesn't know it yet.

In a way, it's almost not surprising. I've been so immersed in memories from the minute I landed in Virginia that I can almost believe I've manifested him in the flesh.

He pauses his typing to stretch his neck and limber his fingers, two more parts of him I'd gotten to know well our last summer. A blur of senses and snatches of memory crashes over me in an intense wave of nostalgia. For a few breathless seconds, I'm nine years in the past, feeling every glance from Sawyer like a touch, sneaking in time to press so tightly together that I don't know where my breaths end and his begin.

I lean back against the tree, resting my head against the trunk as I process the wash of feelings and consider this new development. My chest is tight, my palms sweating. What would Therapist Jane tell me to do?

Breathe.

I do, starting the circular pattern she taught me when anxiety strikes, deep breaths I hold and release while I count.

Describe the situation to yourself exactly as it's happening.

Okay. The first boy I ever loved has grown into a super-hot human and he's back to haunt me. But I can almost hear Jane redirecting me, so I do it myself, describing the situation for real. The first boy I ever loved is back, and I don't know why, but I think it has to do with me. Nat and Ben are in on this.

Name the fear.

I don't know why he's here or why they're hiding him, and it stresses me out when I don't understand what's happening.

Are you catastrophizing?

Catastrophizing? Worst-case scenario, Sawyer is here to somehow humiliate me, and I end up having to cut Ben and Natalie out of my life. I definitely don't think that's why he's here. So no, not catastrophizing.

Can anything in this situation realistically hurt you physically or emotionally?

I consider this carefully. There have only been two times in my life where I felt like I might break: when my dad was sick, and before that, when Sawyer left me. But my dad got better. And Sawyer . . . that was a rough breakup, but I'm over it. So no. Nothing in this situation can hurt me.

When you strip out fear and anger, what feelings do you still have?

79

Um, bafflement? A tummy flutter I don't want to name.

And . . . curiosity. What is the endgame here?

It smells like the complicated shenanigans that mark the best pranks.

But Ben and Natalie would never prank me over something to do with Sawyer, which means this has to be Sawyer's doing. Maybe they have to go along with this because he controls the purse strings? And what is "this"? If it's a prank, I don't love being the butt of it, especially when I don't understand the point. There's no way Natalie would try to embarrass me. I'm positive she has a good reason for not mentioning Sawyer's here.

But Sawyer . . .

I peer around the tree again, watching him, noticing new details. His hair is shorter, but he still has a flop of bangs that don't quite touch his eyebrows. He's also got a light tan instead of the pasty complexion that always marked the beginning of camp. I wonder if I would see lines around his eyes if I were closer, or notice new scars.

He pauses and looks toward the woods, his body motionless and alert. A buck waiting, sensing a change in his environment. I freeze and hold my breath until he looks down at his laptop and goes back to work.

After a couple of minutes, I risk retreat down the trail, moving quietly until I'm far enough away to break into a jog, determined to get out of range so we don't run into each other before I'm ready.

I suspect I won't see him around camp at all. They've gone to great lengths to keep him hidden. What do I want to do with this information? I want to make sense of all my racing thoughts, organize them, and figure out what to do next.

I let myself into my cabin, fingers itching for the large Crayola markers and tempura paints that had marked so many poster- and banner-making projects from summer camps past. I could raid the lodge for that stuff, but I can make this work with notebook and paper.

A few minutes later, I have a glass of wine, a notebook, and a fresh pen in front of me at my cabin's small dining table, the title of my first list written across the top of the page.

Why Is Sawyer Reed Here and Why Did No One Tell Me?

1. He is here for the grand re-opening.
2. But Natalie doesn't lie, so . . .
3. They thought I would freak out.
4. They thought I wouldn't come.
5. It's really stupid no one told me.

Then again, after we broke up, I was the one who had changed the subject every time his name came up until Natalie and Ben got the hint and didn't bring him up anymore. Can't blame them for following my unspoken Sawyer protocol.

I draw a line beneath that list and start another one.

How Do I Feel About Sawyer Being Here?
1. Bad
2. Not good
3. Bad

I stare at the list before I tear the whole sheet out and crumple it, tossing it into the woodburning stove in the corner for a future visitor to use as tinder.

I need to confront Natalie about this, but . . .

Seeing Sawyer didn't hurt like I'd always feared it would.

Every time I'd thought about him over the years, when one of the happier memories would creep in, it was always followed by the memory of that last morning. I'd learned to quit thinking about him, to push away every memory so the painful ones couldn't sneak in on the tail end of the good ones. When I remembered fun times with Ben and Natalie, I'd make Sawyer a faceless blur to avoid the sharp jab in my chest at the memory of the way his eyes crinkled when he laughed, or the pricking even closer to my heart when I thought about the way they would soften as he watched me when he thought no one was looking.

The Sawyer on the deck has grown up. It isn't the same soft face anymore.

"I've grown up too." I say it aloud, letting it sink in.

The kid inside me who had been holding on to her hurt? She was over it. It's time to let go. And at Camp Oak Crest, if I'd learned nothing else, it was the power of ridiculous rituals.

I start a new list.

How to Lay the Ghost of Old Sawyer to Rest and Also Make Natalie and Ben Sorry They Didn't Tell Me What Was Up

1. Campfire ritual: lay old hurts to rest
2. Do lots of sneaking and spying to gather intel
3. The Ghost of Summer Camps Past pranks Sawyer
4. The Ghost of Summer Camp Present pranks Ben. Natalie is going to have to be collateral damage.

I don't even feel bad about that. At the very least, she's guilty of a cover-up.

I scan the list, satisfied. It's right on the money, and it's time to get some of the old camp magic going.

I didn't bring a backpack, but I have a tote bag that will do. I'd meant to use it for the lake beach, but I'm giving it an even better job as I pack to meet Natalie for dinner. My notebook and pen go inside, and my flashlight too. Outside, I refresh my bug spray then head for my bike.

It's much closer to dark when I reach the main camp, and Natalie waves to me from the lodge where I park and join her in the dining hall. Ben and Juniper are already there.

Lisa serves a delicious dinner, even if she can't meet my eyes as she sets it in front of me. After we enjoy the roast chicken and grilled spring veggies, I push back from the table. "I need to pay my compliments to the chef."

Natalie shakes her head. "You'd probably make her pee her pants. You have an interesting effect on people for someone who isn't a 'celebrity.' Let Ben pass it along while we go down to the fire ring."

"Fine, but I'll push you in it if you say celebrity again."

The kindling is already stacked in the regulation teepee shape to achieve best burn, bits of dry bark and dry grass inside it, neatly stacked fuel logs ready to add.

"You ready?" she asks, crouching down with a matchbook.

So innocent sounding. Not at all like someone who has told some big old lies of omission. But I keep my face relaxed. "Ready." I heft my tote bag to demonstrate.

At the fire ceremony we used to do for the

kids, we'd give a speech about the transformative nature of fire: while it could destroy good things, like houses and forests if we weren't careful, we had the power to harness it for good, to use it to burn things out of our lives that we didn't want anymore. Each counselor would make a big production of writing down what they wanted to burn out of their lives; most of us wrote the same thing for every ceremony since it was more about modeling what to do for the kids and making it okay for them to do the same thing.

Each counselor would step forward and read theirs aloud. I'd always put "I will throw away the pressure of other people's expectations." It sounded deep without being too specific. Then I'd let my paper fall into the fire. Sawyer would always step forward and say, "Mine is private," but later he told me his were blank. He'd wanted the kids to know they didn't have to share if it was too personal.

Natalie had always put something different for each fire ceremony. She was already majoring in psychology, and her sincere efforts to fulfill the spirit of the activity during every session had foreshadowed the stellar therapist she would become.

It was a corny activity the way most camp activities are if you don't look at them through a lens specific to the time and place, but it had always had a profound effect on the campers.

Over the years, Natalie told me about different kids who had sought her out on Instagram or through her website to let her know what a turning point the ceremony had been for them.

This time, I have every intention of leaning into this ceremony as much as Natalie always had.

"I'm glad you're keeping this tradition," I say. "I think of all the kids who have reached out to you about it since. That's pretty special."

"It can be, if you let it." She tilts her head. "You used to say the same thing every time. The thing about other people's expectations."

I shrug. "I wasn't taking it super seriously. I didn't feel like putting myself out there for a bunch of little kids."

"And now?"

"Now I want to embrace it. Truly let go of some things. I can't believe I've only been here a day, and I already have so much clarity." *A ton of it, my friend. Enough clarity to see the trap y'all are laying for me. You'll have to be much sneakier to outprank me.*

I sit on one of the rough-hewn benches surrounding the fire pit and draw out my notebook and pen. "See? Supplies. I even have extras if you need them."

"I'm impressed. You *are* taking this seriously."

"Of course. Being here gives me a great measuring stick to see how much I've grown in ten years. I'm ready now."

"You're being a good sport, but I know you had to look past old hurts to do this for us, and I'm grateful."

She's so sincere. It almost makes me feel bad about everything I have planned tomorrow. Then I remember Sawyer diving from the dock this afternoon, and sitting on his deck, relaxed, while I skulked in the woods, freaking out. The guilt passes. "I'd do anything for you. You know that."

"It's good for me to do the fire ceremony tonight too, so I can release some fears I have before the opening. So now we write them down."

I settle my notebook on my knees and get to work. Natalie's pencil scrapes softly on her paper, but while she's done in less than a minute, I'm still writing. I write. And I write. And I write.

Natalie shifts on her seat, and I stifle a smile. We used to tell the campers to pick a word or write a sentence at most. I'm sure that's what Natalie did, but I keep writing until I'm positive she's uncomfortable. Mainly emotionally, but I won't mind if a sliver pokes her in the butt either.

"I'm finished," I announce after several minutes.

She tears a page from her notebook and walks to the fire, looking it over before reading it aloud. "I release my fear that we will meet emergencies we can't handle. I release my fear we won't succeed this summer. I release my fear we can't do this as well as Director Warren did." She lets the paper flutter into the flames, and when it catches, she turns to me with a smile. "It still feels good to do that."

I rise and walk to the fire while she takes her seat. At the edge, I clear my throat.

"You're going to read it aloud."

I give her a patient look. "Told you, I'm a changed woman."

"If that paper says you're releasing the weight of other people's expectations, I'm not going to believe you."

I stick my tongue out and clear my throat again. Then I read what I wrote, louder than I need to, because there's no telling who might be listening.

"Sawyer was a young, dumb kid. So dumb. The dumbest. Super, super dumb. And I was an overly romantic one. I can forgive him for being twenty, and I can forgive myself for it too. Coming back here is a gift. I will let myself have it and enjoy every minute of it. I will live in the present in a way I haven't since that summer. I release the past and the future. None of it matters as much as right now. Not even how extremely, super dumb Sawyer was." I hope with all my heart he's lurking nearby.

Natalie says nothing as I drop the paper into the fire. The flames turn it to ashes slowly dancing toward the lake.

As I watch the words burn away, I'm more moved than I expect to be. I'd written it to lull

Natalie into a false sense of security, but in finding the right words for this show I'm putting on, I've given these words to myself too. And it does feel good to release them into the fire.

But she's still going to pay.

I hear her sniffle, and I fight a smile, but I keep my face thoughtful as I take my seat next to her.

"You really think you're ready to let it all go?" she asks, her voice quiet.

"It's been nine years. Shouldn't I be? Wouldn't you worry if I weren't?"

"Yes," she admits. "But yes, I've been hoping this week would give you closure."

Is that a clue about why she's hiding Sawyer? I dart a glance at the woods, half expecting Sawyer to jump out and yell, "Surprise!" But the forest stays quiet.

Natalie follows my glance. "Something wrong?"

"Thought I heard an owl. Now tell me about what you have planned for your fancy guests while I labor thanklessly in your kitchen this week."

She snorts but tells me about the mini-camp they're throwing for these donors. "All of them have already donated to secure their reservation this weekend, but Ben and I are hoping we can conjure enough of the Camp Oak Crest magic to entice them into donating even more."

"You won't need the old magic," I tell her. "You're going to make new magic, and it will be even more special."

She rests her head on my shoulder. "Thank you again for being part of it. I haven't been able to find the right words to say how much it means to us."

"Anything for you." *Even—no, especially—my arsenal of greatest pranks*. But I keep my same relaxed expression as our conversation drifts to other counselors from years past.

Finally, she yawns, and I stand and make a shooing motion. "You need your sleep, Director Natalie. I know Juniper gets you up early."

"She's better—or maybe worse—than a rooster," she says on another yawn. "See you at break-fast?"

"Wouldn't miss it."

She walks me to my bike before we part ways, but while she goes back to their cabin, I head for a different trail, one that will not take me home.

I stop at the foot of it, debating. This place had held some of my best memories until it had all gone wrong. It's felt okay—better than I expected—to confront some of the more painful ones. But am I ready to relive the best ones with Sawyer?

"You need to do this," I say aloud.

This is where it had started all those years ago, and if I'm going to put it behind me, I have to start at the beginning now too.

With one last deep breath, I park the bike and head up to Moon Rock.

CHAPTER EIGHT
NINE YEARS AGO

"How many kids have we busted over the years for trying to sneak up here?" I asked Sawyer, as he towed me up the trail behind him.

"At least twenty this summer." He didn't let go of my hand.

"So now we're going to be camp outlaws?" I demanded.

He stopped and turned to face me on the trail. "Yeah. You got a problem with that?"

I grinned back. "Not even a little one."

He grabbed my hand, hustling us up the trail, and my heart raced faster than my feet. He hadn't told me what we were doing up here, but kids only snuck up to Moon Rock for one reason. It had been the scene of a thousand first kisses over the years, and when the counselors were cheering for a particular couple, we always gave them a fifteen-minute head start before we went up to bust them.

"You ever come here as a camper?" Sawyer asked as we stepped out to the tiny clearing at the end of the trail. A knee-high boulder sat near the end of a small bluff, and as promised, the view of the moon over the lake was excellent.

"A time or two," I confessed.

"Why, Tabitha Winters, I'm shocked." He glanced down at me, and I could barely make out the glint of his eyes in the light of the half-moon. "Was it everything you dreamed it would be?" he teased.

"Is any kiss at fifteen what you dream it will be? Krish Varma cut my lip with his braces, so it was kind of a bust."

"But you said a time or *two*," Sawyer reminded me.

"The second time was better."

"I think I'm jealous."

My heart was pounding so loudly I couldn't believe he was buying my cool act. It wasn't over fear of being discovered. The campers weren't due for four more days. It was nerves over making a bolder move than I'd ever made before. But I'd been wanting to do this since I'd scared him in the woods this afternoon, and it wasn't a big stretch to think this is what Sawyer wanted too. It was exactly why he'd brought me up here.

I turned to face him fully. "You're the second time."

"Is that so?" His voice had grown soft and low, and he pulled me closer with the hand he held, drawing it around his waist while he slid his other hand beneath my jaw and gently nudged my chin up.

"That's so," I breathed. "I'll let you know how it goes."

"I've learned some things since last summer."

"About kissing?" I didn't want to think about him practicing while he was at school.

"About timing," he said. "Like not to wait until the end of the summer. And to pick my moment so no one else tries to pick it for me."

"You've picked pretty well."

And then he kissed me. I was almost twenty-one, and I'd had plenty of kisses since the last one with Krish at Moon Rock. There'd been a handful in high school and double that in college, because it turned out kissing was fun, and I made a point of being good at it.

But none of those kisses—not even the dare last summer—had prepared me for this one with Sawyer, who kissed me like he'd been born to do it. It started gently at first, a soft seeking of permission of his lips against mine, but when the warm slide of his mouth sent sparks shooting through my stomach, I made a soft moan. I'd be embarrassed by it except it gave Sawyer all the encouragement he needed to take it deeper. He tasted like all the pent-up looks and touches from the previous summer, all the flirty texts and IMs through the school year, all of it pulsing between us in a honeyed heat of need and wanting like I had never felt before.

I had no idea how long we'd been completely

lost in each other, and who knew how much more lost we'd have gotten if it hadn't been for the sound of cracking branches and muffled laughter coming from the trail.

Sawyer pulled away from me, blinking to reorient himself. "Probably Ben and Nat. I'll kick them out. They hog this place all summer."

But I recognized the perfect opportunity for the second prank of summer.

"Wait," I said, plucking at his sleeve. "Prisoner protocol."

He paused and I caught the quick flash of his grin. "Prisoner protocol," he confirmed.

We hurried behind the closest bushes and waited for Ben and Natalie so we could scare the pants off them at the worst possible time. A bubble of laughter threatened to escape me as I imagined their faces before they figured out what was going on, but I didn't feel remotely guilty. They were interrupting the most incredible moment of my life. Payback was fair.

This was an old routine every counselor knew, one we did during the second week of camp. By then, we had the kids' trust enough to thrill them with a campfire story about an escaped convict in the woods without sending any of them into a breakdown before the "convict" revealed themselves and gave them all highly coveted pudding cups.

But when the gigglers stumbled into the

clearing, I clapped my hand over my mouth. It was Director Warren and Nurse Debbie! Face-sucking sounds began, and I exchanged horrified looks with Sawyer. Please let my moan have sounded cute and not like . . . whatever noise Nurse Debbie had just made.

"Oh, Warren," she said. "You're so bad."

I was thankful for the dark so Sawyer couldn't see how bright red her words had turned my face. A choked laugh came from Sawyer, but they didn't hear him over the sound of their own make out.

"We're practically married, Debbie. Nothing bad about it."

"I can't wait until Thanksgiving," she murmured.

"We should announce it. I don't want to sneak around with you."

Her voice sounded less addled this time. "No way, Warren. The last thing I want to do is put up with a camp full of little pukes making kissy faces or singing kissing songs all summer. We get married at Thanksgiving, and when everyone shows up next summer, it'll be a done deal and not even worth talking about."

"Aw, sugar, I didn't mean to upset you," Director Warren said in a voice so syrupy it made me want to barf. "It's just hard for me to hide how I feel about you."

"Oh, honey, I know," she said, followed by loud slurping.

Next to me, Sawyer shook with laughter, and I yanked him by the sleeve to get him out of there before he set me off too. We had to slink through the trees and back to the trail several yards down the hill. It was a poor display of our ninja skills as we navigated the loud underbrush in the dark, but the camp director and the camp nurse were way too wrapped up in each other to notice.

At the bottom of the trail, Sawyer slipped his small Maglite from his pocket and shone it in my face. Whatever he saw on it made him lose it again, and soon we were both laughing so hard we were bent double.

"I can't breathe," he gasped. "Make it stop."

"Oh, Warren," I said in my Sexy Nurse Debbie voice, and set him off again. We staggered over to a nearby picnic table and did our Director and Nurse impressions—made worse because we flipped roles and I played Warren while he played Debbie—until I was crying, and I got an actual stitch in my side.

"Ow, okay, cramp. We have to stop," I begged. "I swear if you say 'Warren' one more time, you're dead to me."

He was quiet for a full five seconds, then, breathily, "Oh, Warren."

When we finally pulled ourselves together, he grinned at me across the picnic table. The lights running through the grounds cast a dim yellow light over us, but his eyes still shone. "They literally went up there for the exact same reason we did, so why was that so gross?"

"I don't know, but it isssss," I wailed, which set him off again.

"Is it because they're old? That must be it."

"That's definitely it," I agreed. "Nurse Debbie is at least forty, and I bet Director Warren is even older. Ew."

"So gross," he agreed. "Old people need to not make out. Or kiss. Why are they even getting married? Weddings are for young people."

"Definitely. If I'm not married by thirty, then . . ." I trailed off, not able to think of anything drastic enough to finish the sentence.

"You'll get married by the time you're thirty. You're too awesome not to."

Coming on the heels of the best kiss of my life, it made me flush with happiness. "Maybe I'll have the opposite problem. Maybe people will want to marry me, but I won't want to marry them."

He nodded as if I had a good point. "It's true. We may never find people awesome enough to marry. But I'd marry you if I was old enough to get married."

"You are old enough, dummy. We're old enough to vote, go to war, almost old enough to drink. We are definitely old enough to get married. Not that I want to!" I rushed to make that *real* clear.

He shrugged. "That's what it says on paper, but I don't believe it."

"When is old enough to get married?"

He thought about it. "Twenty-seven. You should definitely not be able to get married if you aren't old enough to rent a car."

"Twenty-seven sounds good. But now I'm stressed I won't find anyone cool enough to marry when I'm twenty-seven."

"Let's make a deal. If we aren't married by the time we're thirty, we'll marry each other and save each other from being Director Warren and *Nurse Debbie*." The last part he said in his fake sexy voice, and I gave him a light punch on the arm.

"A backup plan. I like it. But only if you promise never to do that voice again."

"Deal," he said. "And now we have to seal it with a kiss." Then he dragged me behind the nearest empty cabin and made me forget all about the director and the nurse.

CHAPTER NINE
PRESENT

I step into the scruffy clearing of Moon Rock. It's almost full dark, and I need the flashlight as I study the space, smaller now than in memory. This is the only place I've still been nervous to come back to because this is where I fell for Sawyer first, and later, where I fell even deeper.

My words at the fire ceremony had felt true, but this is where I'll find out if I meant them. If I can stare down the memories here, then I can let the last of them go. Turn the page on all of this. Or better yet, close the book entirely and start a new one.

I walk the perimeter of the clearing, my shoes scuffing the dirt. I don't need any kind of ceremony here. I only need to prove to myself that it doesn't matter like it used to.

The memories do come back, and I climb on top of the medium-sized boulder and sit with my arms around my knees and let them. I remember how it felt to be with Sawyer, so excited to see him, every moment breathless as I waited for whatever might happen between us next. The next touch. Or kiss. Or confession. All of it was so . . .

Young.

I look out at the lake and a smile sneaks out. I try to name the feeling behind it. It's a feeling of ... affection? For twenty-year-old Tabitha, young and smitten, sure of what comes next in life, giddy about her boy. She didn't know, couldn't know, how fast things can change. That change is the only constant. That it's always survivable, no matter what it is. And that Sawyer's rejection isn't going to shape or define her. That she'll go on to a bright future. She'll even become good friends with Grace one day.

It's affection for my old self's innocence and naivete. And forgiveness too, for not seeing what was coming next with Sawyer and bailing before it all crashed and burned. I feel forgiveness too for twenty-year-old Sawyer, who was only a kid. It's impossible to sit here at twenty-nine and resent the behavior of a boy who had been barely out of his teens.

I think about the ashes from the fire ceremony swirling over the lake. By now, they'll have drifted down to its surface and disappeared beneath it. They're gone. Out there. And inside me.

I stand and stretch, reaching my arms as high as I can, as if I could touch the moon and pull it down. It's a way of stepping into my full self, the one who doesn't carry around the petty hurts of childhood.

Then I sit down and reach for my tote bag,

because I may have let go of the petty hurts, but pranks are pretty good for the soul too. And I owe some people.

It takes a minute to figure out my lighting situation, but making a weird side bun in my hair and tucking my small Maglite in it for an improvised headlamp works well enough. I open my notebook to a new page: How to Get Natalie and Ben to Crack.

This is going to take finesse to pull off, because there's an art to the perfect prank. Not hurting people or property is a baseline. Truly great pranks go beyond that. They require creativity, a knowledge of the victim, excellent timing, and a deep, deep well of patience.

It takes me a while to figure out how to set up all the different threads and weave them together, but an hour later, I put down my pen, stretch my back, read over my plan, and . . .

Cackle. Evilly.

No regrets.

The woodland gods of Camp Oak Crest smile on me the very next morning when I wake before dawn, not even needing my alarm. I slip into shorts and a tank top and grab the bottle of bubble bath from beside the tub.

Ten swift minutes through the forest later, and I reach the edge of Sawyer's property. Or the property where he's staying, anyway. The windows are all dark, and there's enough predawn light to see that no steam rises from the hot tub in the cool morning air, which means it isn't running. Perfect.

It won't be enough to get Ben and Natalie to confess they're hiding him. Sawyer's in on whatever this is, so he's sealed his own fate.

I run across the clearing to the stairs leading up to the hot tub and reach into my bag for my first tool: the bottle of rose-scented bubble bath from my cottage bathroom. Then I pull out the extra one from the small bathroom cupboard and add it too. It will lay there, dormant, until the next time Sawyer decides to use the hot tub, and then . . . Sud City.

He gave me the idea, after all. Year Two, his cabin of boys had poured liquid dish soap into the dishwasher when my girls had KP duty, generating an enormous flood of bubbles in the kitchen and an extra hour of cleanup for my annoyed campers.

Then quick as a squirrel, I run back to the woods and off to do my spying. Entire empires have been brought down by people listening at doors. It won't be hard to figure out what Ben and Natalie are up to now that I know they're up to something. They're both terrible liars if you know what to look for.

I start at the office. Natalie gave me a key in case I wanted to get in and use the landline or computer. Cell service is as spotty as ever out here, but they're keeping in touch with Sawyer somehow, or we'd have crossed paths already. I'd checked for wires leading to his place and hadn't seen any, so either there's a Wi-Fi set up I can't see or they're doing it some other way. At this point, I wouldn't put carrier pigeons or smoke signals past them.

The computer is cold, and it takes a minute to boot up and rumble to life, but getting in is no problem. Natalie also gave me her password, explaining it's only protected to keep homesick campers from sneaking in and inundating their parents with messages. I don't feel a twinge of guilt that Natalie had not expected me to go into her and Ben's emails. All's fair in war and pranks when two of your oldest friends are hiding your ex at camp and not telling you.

Natalie's email doesn't yield much when I search for Sawyer's name, only a message from a couple of months before, RSVP-ing for Juniper's first birthday. She'd invited me too, but my shooting schedule wouldn't allow it, so I'd sent her a giant unicorn piñata for the party.

Ben's, however, is the motherlode. There's an email from five days ago informing Sawyer that Jared and Kylie had gotten the house ready, and another from two days ago letting Sawyer know what time Natalie was supposed to pick me up the following day. "Watch for the bike," he said.

"She'll pick the red one. If it's not in front of her cabin, the coast is clear."

Ah. First mystery solved. Now I know how we've avoided crossing paths so far. I can't decide if I'm impressed or bothered that they guessed I'd pick the red bike.

If it were anyone but Ben and Natalie, I'd find this whole thing incredibly creepy, but the two of them are good down to their bones. Whatever their intentions are, they aren't trying to hurt me. But what *are* they up to?

Jared and Kylie. They're the next key. I'd met them in passing the previous night when Natalie introduced me to the kitchen staff. They're aides-de-camp, she'd explained. Which basically means they're the senior counselors, and after breakfast today, they'll spend all morning shuttling the new counselors from the airport as the camp buzzes to life. We'd always just had four days to get the camp ready for summer, but this year, with a whole new slate of counselors, Ben wants to do extra training with them.

I'll have to catch Jared and Kylie before they disappear into the madness of the day. I lock the office behind me and head straight for the mess hall where a light shines through the kitchen window. That would be Lisa, no doubt.

She glances up at me, startled. "Miss Winters," she says, then corrects herself when I hold up my hand. "I mean, Tabitha." She swallows like it hadn't been comfortable to say. "You're earlier than I expected. I'm sorry. I was planning on breakfast at eight, but I can whip up something for you. Here, let me—"

"Lisa, it's fine. I know it's weird to have other cooks in your space, but how about if I make us a frittata, and we can visit before we have to dive into business?"

She looks at me like it's the most baffling idea she's ever heard.

"You . . . don't like frittatas?" I guess.

"No, um, I love them. I just . . . I don't know what to do while you're making me breakfast?" It comes out as almost a squeak.

"How about if you prep lunch and keep me company while I work? If there's one thing I remember about running this kitchen, it's that there's no such thing as getting too far ahead on food prep."

"Sure, okay." She glances at me, still uncertain, and I give her an encouraging nod. "I'm, um, going to get chickpeas? For hummus? For the lunches," she adds. "Take whatever you need from the cold locker."

I fetch the eggs and all the veggies I want, deciding to go with Tuscan flavors. She meets me at the prep table with a number ten can of chickpeas. It looks comically large until you consider how much a staff of hungry college kids can put away.

"You've already been cooking this morning?" I nod toward the skillet on the stove, which has very recently been frying bacon. The question is where it went. There are already broken eggshells in the garbage can when I drop my six empty shells to join them. "Are Ben and Natalie up already?"

"Oh, this isn't for them." I know that. Natalie is vegetarian and Ben doesn't eat first thing in the morning. But Sawyer loves bacon. "This is for, um. A guest?"

"You don't sound sure."

"It's for a guest," she says firmly.

"Like . . . Sawyer Reed? And he asked for extra bacon."

Her mouth falls open. "You're . . . you're not supposed to know that."

"Well, I do. And Ben and Natalie can't know that I know, so now you're keeping a double secret. Can you do that?" She looks torn, and I realize I'm asking her to be loyal to me over her bosses. "Only until tonight," I promise. "Then you don't have to keep any more secrets."

"Okay," she agrees. "But not after tonight."

"Deal. Now, do you want to learn the trick to making the best frittata in the world? I learned it from Giada herself."

"Giada?" she whispers reverently.

"Giada."

I walk her through making the frittata, including my secret (fresh thyme), and when we slide the skillet into the oven to bake, I lean against the counter and adopt a casual pose. "Hey, where can I find a screwdriver? I want to tighten the seat on my bike while the frittata cooks."

"Oh, the toolshed behind the office has whatever you need, but I keep a basic toolbox in here. Check the mop closet, you'll see it right on the shelf. I can clean up while you do that?"

"Thanks," I say, walking toward the mop closet. I'd normally never make someone else clean up after me, but I need fifteen minutes to get the next phase of my plan underway. I hurry back to the office with my screwdriver in hand, and after placing a quick Amazon order from the front desk computer, I spend the next several minutes loosening every single screw in the two office chairs until they're almost but not *quite* ready to fall out.

I make it back to find Lisa staring at the frittata on the stove top like she's not sure what she should do with it next.

I glance down at my watch. "Perfect, it's almost eight o'clock. Let's dig in." I serve us each a piece and we eat in the kitchen.

She nods when she takes her first bite. "This is legit."

"Right? It's all about the thyme." I'm almost done when I hear Juniper's chatter out in the mess hall, which means Natalie and Ben will be here in a second.

"Whew, I'm full," I say, scraping my remaining bites into the garbage. "I hear the Mendozas. Can you tell them I went for a quick canoe out on the lake?"

"Sure thing."

I wave her a cheerful goodbye and head out the back kitchen door and detour to the shed first. I hadn't noticed it attached to the back of the main office. It's a new addition, but I'm betting the key Natalie gave me for the office is probably a master. Sure enough, it opens the shed door too, and thanks to Ben's meticulous nature, the tools hang neatly on pegboard with labels so people know where to return them. I take down the cordless drill and give it a whir, smiling when it proves the battery is fully charged, but expecting nothing less. Ben and Natalie are going to be great camp owners.

Now off to manage more mischief.

CHAPTER TEN
NINE YEARS AGO

"Tabby Cat?" Natalie poked her head through our cabin door. I had it to myself, and I'd been lying in my bunk for an hour, enjoying the quiet. The campers had left this morning, and we were off until early Monday.

"Hey, Natty. What's up?"

"Do you have plans today?"

"Probably. I'm sure Sawyer and I will do something."

"But nothing definite yet?"

"Nope. What's up?"

She came in and sat at the foot of my bed, gnawing her bottom lip. "Do you think we could talk?"

"Am I in trouble?" My pulse started hammering. Had I said something I shouldn't have? Forgotten to do something I should have?

"What? No. Why do you always think you're in trouble?"

I relaxed against my pillow. "Just have a fun brain, I guess."

"I want advice," she said. "That's all. Except it's a pretty big thing, and I want plenty of time to talk it all through. Could we go on a walk or something? I think better when I move."

"Sure." I was already climbing off the bed. "Have you eaten lunch yet? Let's do that then hike the lake. Let me tell Sawyer so he doesn't wonder where I disappeared to."

We didn't even have to go as far as the boys' cabins on the other side of the camp to find him. He and Ben were down by the lake playing horseshoes.

"Join us, girls?" Ben called.

"He means *ladies,*" Sawyer said with an elbow to Ben's ribs.

"No thanks either way," Natalie answered. "We're going to grab lunch and go on a hike."

"Sounds fun. We'll come too," Ben said, starting to set down his horseshoe.

"We're doing girl time," Natalie said. Her voice had the faintest stress in it.

Ben paused and straightened. "Right. Got it. Have fun." He sounded way too casual.

We turned toward the mess hall, and I waited until we were out of earshot before I grabbed Natalie's arm. "If you're pregnant, tell me right now."

"What?" It was almost a yelp. "No! We haven't even . . . you know."

I breathed a sigh of relief. If that wasn't it, whatever was coming, I could handle.

"Man, your mind goes extreme places," she said, opening the mess hall door for me.

We each grabbed a bag lunch from the table

110

by the door. Camp meals weren't very involved on the weekend with the paying campers gone. We generally felt lucky to get sandwiches and packaged chips instead of weird concoctions made of ingredients Marge wanted to use up before they expired, like the Cottage Cheese Ground Beef Crumble Surprise we got two weekends ago.

I waited until we were out of the hall, away from the other counselors, before I prompted her. "Well?"

Before she could answer, Ben called to us. "Why not canoe?"

"What?" Natalie called back, sounding confused.

He waved us over, he and Sawyer standing beside one of the canoes now. "It's going to be cooler on the water today. You should take the boat out. It'll be nice not to have any rug rats splashing you."

"I don't know," she said, looking from it to the water. "I'd already decided on hiking."

"Right, but I thought you might like even *more* peace and quiet for, uh, talking?"

He obviously knew what Natalie wanted to discuss, and now I was more anxious than ever to know what it was. Besides, the worst part of canoeing was wrestling the stupid things down to the dock, and they'd done the dirty work for us.

"Canoeing sounds good, Nat. Let's do it."

"Safety first," Sawyer said, handing us each a life jacket.

"Have fun." Ben waved and they turned toward the mess hall.

As we put in the canoe, I fixed Natalie with a stare. "Tell me."

"Ben wants to transfer to Lafayette, so we're not long-distance anymore."

"Okay." Lafayette was her university, and it was two hours from his.

"What do you think?" she asked as I climbed into the bow and settled myself on the seat.

"I said okay."

"Okay, he should transfer?" She shoved off from the dock and we started paddling.

"Yeah."

We sent the canoe gliding forward for a couple of minutes in silence.

She broke it halfway to the middle of the lake. "You didn't even think about it."

I looked at her over my shoulder. "Seriously? This feels like a no-brainer."

"But this is huge."

"Yes, but it's still a no-brainer."

"You, the queen of overthinking, think this is a no-brainer? What is even happening?"

"Can he afford it?"

"Yes. It's less than his tuition right now."

"Do you love him?"

"Yes."

I turned in my seat to face her. I'd meant to splash her with a paddle, but when my feet touched the canoe again, I scowled instead.

"It's bad that I love him?" she guessed, looking at my face.

"Right now it is." I pointed to the bottom of the canoe. "It's got a leak." It was a pretty big crack too. No way those two had missed this.

She stared down at it and growled. "I'm sure this was Sawyer's idea."

I shot her a look.

"Fine, it doesn't matter. They're both idiots."

"Yep."

"Let's go."

We turned the canoe, and once we were pointed toward camp, I spotted Dumb and Dumber on the shore. Even from a distance, their posture was cocky.

"I bet Sawyer is so pleased with himself right now," I grumbled.

"It *is* the first time he's gotten ahead."

We kept a very official unofficial tally of who owed whom payback for shenanigans.

"I changed my mind. Ben should not transfer." I had to set down my paddle to start bailing. Those idiots hadn't even left us a mercy bucket, so I was scooping and tossing out handfuls of water and not keeping up as the canoe filled.

Natalie was paddling hard, but as I checked

113

the distance to shore to see if we could make it, I spotted Sawyer bent double, Ben slapping his back.

"I'm going to kill them," I said, scooping faster. "Ben should not transfer, and when we get back to the dock, you should definitely dump him. In the water. Literally. Then dump him figuratively too."

"I can't," she said, and her tone was regretful. "I really do love him."

I heaved an exasperated sigh. "Fine. You don't have to dump him literally. And he can transfer. But we're making them pay."

"Hundred percent. Because this canoe is going to sink."

I yelled a curse I would never say in front of the campers and reached for my paddle. We were going to have to abandon the canoe and flip it before it got any more swamped and sank.

"I'm going to kill them, Nat. For real." I dropped into the water and reached for the side of the canoe, holding on to the paddle with the other hand to stay stable.

"I'll help," she said before dropping in beside me.

"But you *looooove* him," I said.

"Sure. But I don't like him right now. He's dead meat."

"Yessss."

We flipped the canoe and swam it back to the

114

dock. Ben and Sawyer sat at the end of it, legs swinging, grinning.

"Looks like you had trouble out there, ladies." Sawyer didn't even pretend to be concerned.

"Imagine that," I said, my voice drier than Marge's toast.

"We'd help you out, but . . ." Ben trailed off, grinning.

"But you know we'd pull you guys in, head-first? Good guess," Natalie said. "But we don't want your help."

We swam past them to the point where we could touch and walk the rest the way to the shore where we banked the canoe and dragged ourselves up next to it, collapsing and breathing hard.

"Bold move when I had big things to consider," Natalie called to Ben.

"Are you saying you don't want me to transfer?" he called back, not sounding stressed.

"I'm saying I don't like you taking that answer for granted," she called up to the sky, too tired to prop herself up anymore.

The sound of running footsteps echoed from the dock, then Ben's face appeared above us right before he dropped to his knees beside her.

"I knew you'd say yes, but not because I'm taking you for granted the way you think."

She struggled up to her elbows again. "Is there more than one kind of taking for granted?"

"It's just that I knew if you felt even a tenth for

me of what I do for you, there's no way you'd say no."

All right, that was pretty sweet. But I wouldn't admit it out loud.

Natalie must have thought so too because even though she tried for a full three seconds to hold onto her scowl, a smile broke free anyway, and she recovered enough to launch herself at him and cover him with kisses.

Sawyer had come up the dock at a normal pace, and he stepped onto the bank now. "Gross."

"Super gross. I'm getting a cavity."

"Want to go run away into the woods and do some of that ourselves?"

"Definitely." I held out a hand so he could pull me to my feet. "Bye, lovebirds."

They paid no attention to us. Sawyer walked me to my cabin and waited while I changed. When I came out in dry shorts and a tank top, he crooked his head toward the Moon Rock trail. "Want to go see if it's as fun in the daytime too?"

"Race you," I called behind me, already running for the trailhead. We laughed and wrestled all the way up the trail, and when I beat him to the top of the rock, I looped my arms around his neck and smiled down at him standing below me. "Just so you know, none of this is going to spare you from payback." And I swallowed his groan with a kiss.

CHAPTER ELEVEN
PRESENT

By four o'clock, I'm exhausted, but it's the good kind where my muscles and brain have been doing fun work.

I'd laid my traps for Natalie, Ben, and Sawyer and still had the whole day stretching ahead of me, so I'd gone to my happy place and joined Lisa in the kitchen.

She and I spent the day planning and prepping for upcoming meals. Once she'd gotten over her initial shyness with me, a little praise had gone a long way, and she'd proven to be a competent and skilled chef. She ordered her assistants around firmly but kindly, explaining counselors would work in the kitchen this week, but next week as the first campers arrived, they'd begin rotating in for KP duty. It was exactly how we'd done it in the old days, and I'd loved it. I'd even traded lifeguard shifts for KP supervision some nights, preferring the bustle of the kitchen to breaking up water fights.

But I have two more meals to prep before I can call it good for the day. "Lisa, I noticed a picnic hamper in the mudroom at my cabin. You wouldn't happen to have an extra one around here, would you?"

"Oh, sure. I'll grab it for you. Going on a picnic tomorrow?"

"Putting something together for tonight. I'm going to raid the pantry if you don't mind."

"Go right ahead," she says. "But I can't believe you want to cook for yourself after spending all day in here. I never want to make dinner when I get home. I promise, Kylie will put a great dinner together for you."

"Is there anything she and Jared can't do?"

"I haven't found it yet," Lisa says. "The Mendozas did good hiring them."

"You too, Lisa. They did good with you too." She turns a deep red, and I distract her to save her dignity. "Let's give Kylie a night off. I don't mind. You all need to pace yourselves. You have no idea how exhausting the first week of camp can be."

Lisa shrugs and fetches the hamper for me, and I fill it with the ingredients I need from the pantry and fridge. "Thanks, Lisa. See you tomorrow!" I give her a cheerful wave and head out to put the last piece of my plan in place. Next stop: the office.

"Hey, Ben." I poke my head in. "I have a surprise for you and Natalie. Will you meet me by the dock in an hour? And bring Juniper."

"Uh, sure, but that's getting awfully close to dinner."

"Trust me." I bat my lashes at him, and he rolls his eyes.

"All right. Get out of here, dork." He shifts on his chair and frowns, then shifts again.

"Something wrong?" I ask sweetly.

"No, it's just—nothing. See you at the dock in an hour."

I close the door behind me, but instead of heading to my cottage, I wait inside of Girls Cabin 1, the closest one to the office, and watch until he leaves fifteen minutes later. As soon as he's out of sight, I dart into his office and hack into his email one last time.

> *Hey, Sawyer.*
> *Nat and I wanted to use the hot tub after dinner tonight, around 6:30. Would you mind warming it up for us?*
> *Thanks*

It's strange to type Sawyer's name after all these years. To communicate with him so directly—if it even counts as communicating when I'm impersonating Ben, not reaching out as myself.

But the idea of talking to Sawyer doesn't feel impossible anymore. If all my plotting works, we'll be face to face shortly, and instead of dreading it, I'm . . .

I wouldn't go as far as to say I welcome it. But I'm okay with it.

It feels pretty good to feel okay.

I reread my forged email "from" Ben, and satisfied it's as low-key as Ben is, send it. I'm banking on Sawyer not finding it a super weird request, given that his is the only hot tub I've spotted on the grounds so far.

I scoop up the hamper and meander down to the dock, content to spend a half hour in the late afternoon sun waiting for my victims to arrive.

I hear Juniper before I see them, and I turn to wave at them as they make their way down to me.

"What's this?" Natalie asks, smiling as she takes in the sight of me standing next to one of their new canoes and a picnic basket.

"I've been watching this place get busier and busier all day with the new counselors, and I have a feeling you won't get any quiet time from now until Labor Day, so I figured I'd claim godmother privileges and sweep my goddaughter away while you get time together. So, I've planned a mini-date for you. A late afternoon canoe on the lake, complete with a canoe-friendly dinner I made. It's not fancy, but it should taste pretty good while you're out there drifting on the water."

"Oh, Tabby Cat, you didn't have to do that! You're already doing us such a huge favor by being here this week."

"Turns out I'm a full-service celebrity chef." I wink. "And honestly, you've done me a favor, bringing me out here and reminding me to reconnect with myself. Look"—I point—"I have the bike with the baby seat parked right there, and Juni and I are going to go back to my place, where I have the funnest stuff planned for us. What do you think, June-June?" I reach for the baby, who dives at me, grinning. "Want to come to Tabby's house?"

"Housh!" she announces.

"What do you think, Ben?" Natalie casts a covetous eye at the hamper and canoe.

He hesitates. "I don't know . . ."

"Housh!" Juniper insists.

"Say yes and thank you," I say.

Ben smiles. "Yes and thank you."

"Have fun, you two lovebirds. You've earned it." I whisk Juniper toward the bike. "Don't forget your life vests!" I call and they laugh; it's the constant counselor cry when camp is in session. Natalie is already slipping off her shoes and pushing the canoe in the water.

Juni and I trundle down the path to the cabins without incident as she keeps up a cheerful if unintelligible commentary on the way, every now and then punctuating it with a word I recognize, like "birb" or "twee."

At the cabin, I unload her and set her on the floor in the kitchen, showing her how to open the cabinets and pull out the pots and lids her toddler heart desires. Then I go to work.

An hour later, as the pasta water starts boiling, footsteps crunch on the gravel leading to my door. Calmly, I scoop up Juniper and settle her on my hip, knowing it will keep me from getting punched. I throw open the front door as Ben, freshly soaked from a foundering canoe, is lifting his hand to knock, an equally drenched Natalie beside him. A dry but ticked-looking Sawyer, reeking of rose bubble bath, stands behind them.

It's exactly who I expect to see, exactly when I expect to see them. And still, my heart flips at the sight of Sawyer so close for the first time in almost a decade. The crinkle lines around his eyes have deepened, and he has a faint five o'clock shadow he'd never been able to grow before. Like everything else in camp, Sawyer has gotten a glow up.

"You guys are right on time." I give them my sunniest TV host smile.

"You did this." Sawyer points at me.

"I did," I admit without an ounce of guilt. "It's exactly what you deserve for making me think Sawyer wasn't around."

The three of them exchange glances. No one tries to argue the point.

"Now who wants to explain to me what the"—I glance down at Juniper—"*heck* you guys were thinking?"

"Heck!" Juniper says.

Natalie sighs, and I step aside to let them in. "I should have known you were up to something when you agreed to the fire ceremony so easily."

They shuffle past me, and I shut the door. "Okay, guys. Start talking."

CHAPTER TWELVE
TEN YEARS AGO

There were only so many personality types in the world, and every one of them found their way to Camp Oak Crest in the summer. There were a few things you could count on: at least a quarter of your cabin kids would be introverts. At least one of them would cry every night the first week no matter what you did. At least one of them would be a massive gossip. At least one of them would be so bossy it ended in mutiny by the fourth day.

Unfortunately, the other thing you could count on was at least one hijacker emerging each summer, one on the boys' side, one on the girls' side. As a counselor, I always crossed my fingers that whoever the hijacker was, she wasn't in my cabin. And I lucked out every year.

The hijacker was always a kid who was going to grow up to be either the boss of a major crime syndicate or a rock star. They were the kid everyone else in the cabin looked to for approval, and they rarely used their powers for good. They liked to set the temperature of their group, and their attitude would determine whether everyone decided to go along with an activity, or whether it would be declared . . . shudder . . . *babyish*.

It didn't seem to have anything to do with their mood, either. It was just, periodically, they needed to flex and remind the counselor who really set the tone in the cabin.

Sawyer's second year, he did *not* luck out. He had a hijacker named Max. Interestingly, hijackers weren't necessarily the biggest talkers in their group. One of their skills was inherently knowing exactly when to talk and when to shut up. But Max, he was one of the rare talkative hijackers. And Max's favorite subject for his fellow eleven-year-old boys was why girls sucked.

It wasn't like Sawyer didn't try to rein him in: he did. But Max—like all hijackers—couldn't be contained. And since our cabins were regularly scheduled to do things together, my girls had to listen to Max's opinions about them and their entire gender.

"Girls suck at sports," he'd inform everyone, calmly and coolly, like he was stating a fact. We'd lose every match with them. "Girls are too emotional," he'd say if they expressed any reaction at all to anything. So they'd dial it back around Max. "Boys are better at wilderness stuff," he'd say, right before their group out-hiked us or beat us at tying knots.

Sawyer tried. But Max got into Sawyer's head as much as everyone else's.

The last straw came when Sawyer's cabin— under Max's "leadership"—or mind control, depending on your opinion of Max's motives—pranked our cabin, and we ended up having to do an all-camp intervention to deal with the fallout.

Generally, counselors were in on the pranks cabins pulled on each other. To the kids, it always made us cooler, but in reality, we were there to keep things from going too far off the rails. But Max the Hijacker decided to pull a prank without Sawyer's knowledge and conducted an underwear raid on our cabin while we were on the lake. But Max, even at eleven, was diabolical. They'd done it so sneakily, our cabin didn't even know things were missing until the next morning when a few of the girls were embarrassed they couldn't find their training bras.

It wasn't until the third girl mentioned hers being missing that I had begun to suspect we had a problem. And it wasn't until I herded the girls to the dining hall that we all figured out the problem at once: their bras and underwear were flying from the flagpole.

Oh, ha ha ha, one might think. What a classic summer camp joke.

And one might be right if it weren't for two things. First, this was a much bigger deal in the fifth-grade cabin than it would have been in the eighth-grade cabin. Eighth-grade girls would squeal in fake outrage and secretly be glad they'd been singled out. Eighth-grade girls in their own way were as dumb as Max's band of idiots.

But for eleven-year-old girls who were having to grapple with the existence of boobs for the first time? They largely resented the existence of them. Boobs were unwelcome intruders, and every girl knew it was a life sentence. At that age, bras were an annoyance, and half of them tried to hide the fact they even needed to wear one. This was usually their most modest year, where half of them were hitting puberty and half were not, and all of them hated it, no matter which side of the process they were on.

Just having the bras up there was bad enough, but Max—diabolical Max—had taken it so many steps further. Every bunk had a trunk at the end, labeled with the camper's name. They'd made a point of remembering which pair of underwear belonged to each girl, then, in marker smuggled out of multiple craft sessions, wrote the owner's name and the "girliest" thing they disliked about her on the butt of the panties.

"Sarah A runs like a girl." "Lucy F cries like a little girl." "Hailey W hits like—"

Well. You get it.

D.i.a.b.o.l.i.c.a.l.

My girls were devastated, and it was entirely possible I would have taken apart Sawyer bone by bone if I hadn't seen his face when his cabin walked up. My campers were either crying, clamoring in outrage, or standing in wrecked silence as other cabins joined us. His boys elbowed each other and smirked, waiting for the accolades from the other cabins for pulling an epic prank.

Sawyer's face went from curiosity to confusion to fury as he processed what he was seeing and rounded on his boys. "You're going back to the cabin this second. Right. Freaking. Now."

A few of them lost their smiles at that point, but not smirky Max. Sawyer pointed his boys in the direction of their cabin but jogged over to us before he followed after them. "Sisters, I'm sorry my boys did that to you. I hope you trust us counselors to set them right. We'll fix this. You deserve better. Please trust me."

Then he took off after his boys in an angry walk.

Their humbling was a thing of beauty I doubted those boys would ever forget. I knew my girls never would. Because they hadn't just poked a hornet's nest of upset fifth-grade girls; they'd stirred up every girl younger and older, and nearly every single boy too.

The oldest cabin of boys went straight to work getting the underwear down from the flagpole, and for the first time, I liked the eighth graders.

The rest of the dining hall was buzzing—did I mention angry hornets?—with indignation on our cabins' behalf, and all the other girl cabins stopped by our table to commiserate with our girls. But it was the visit from the eighth-grade girls that cheered my girls the most.

"Girls," their ringleader, a future CEO named Brooklyn, said, "We got you. We're going to set them right. Don't even worry about it."

And had any of Sawyer's boys seen the look in her eye, they'd have all called home and begged for extraction.

Everyone's afternoon activities were canceled, Max's cabin as a consequence, everyone else's by choice.

Director Warren always told us counselors that discipline wasn't about punishment; it was about changing behavior, and boy, did *that* lesson ever sink in. That afternoon, instead of sand volleyball and ceramics, Boys Cabin 11 was marched into the dining hall and met with a presentation on feminism—from the eighth-grade boys. I heard about it afterward, and I would have given *anything* to be there. Director Warren had given the counselors free rein with computer resources, and apparently, the burliest boy in the eighth-grade bunch, a bruiser named Nico who'd been playing tackle football for three years already, lectured them on menstruation, period stigma, and why the least they could do was not be jerks.

The seventh-grade boys did a Powerpoint on kickbutt women athletes, and the sixth-grade boys did a skit entitled "How Not to Be the Worst." Apparently, it involved things like not mocking characteristics about people they can't change— like their gender. And only paying compliments on things people could control, like their style, or their sense of humor, but not their looks.

The reason I or any of my cabin didn't get to see this ourselves was because all the females in camp huddled for Mission: Payback.

My cabin got the pleasure of rigging the boys' cabin, drowning them in "girliness." They sprinkled glitter on all their sheets, doused their pillows with perfume one of the other counselors donated to the cause, and put red dye into all their toothpaste tubes so it would foam pink when they went to brush that night.

And even that wasn't the end of it. After dinner, Sawyer stood at the front of the dining hall. "Ladies and gentlemen, Boys Cabin 11 would like to do a very special presentation with the permission of Girls Cabin 11."

I knew what was coming, but I hadn't told the girls. I looked at them all sitting on either side of our usual dinner table. "What do you think, ladies? Are you willing to give them a chance?"

The whole day had been healing for them, the indignation of the other boys making them feel understood, the hovering and sympathy of all the other girls soothing them. My girls all nodded. "We accept," said my future PTA president, Mia.

Sawyer's boys all filed to the front of the room, Max refusing to make eye contact with anyone. The first boy stepped forward. "Mia, will you please stand?"

Mia stood.

"Mia, I said you run like a girl. What I really meant is you play hard, run as fast as you can, and do your best, and that's cool."

"Thanks, Braden," she said, and sat down.

Each boy stepped forward and did the same thing with each girl they had harassed, until it got to the second to last boy, Eli, who asked my shyest camper, Tess, to stand. But she shrank against the table and tried to make herself smaller.

Two eighth-grade girls came over to confer with her, and after a short, whispered conversation, they stood, Tess in the middle, flanked by the girls on either side of her, each with an arm around her shoulder.

Eli cleared his throat. "Tess, I said you cry like a little girl. What I meant is you express your emotions really well, and that's healthy."

Tess was very quiet, but we still heard her soft "Thank you, Eli."

The only person we hadn't heard from was Max. He'd kept his eyes down the whole time, and I wondered if that meant he wasn't on board with any of this, but when Sawyer prompted him, he stepped forward and cleared his throat. "Our cabin apologizes to you. It was mostly my idea, and I'm sorry. We learned important stuff about gir—uh, women, today."

"Like?" Sawyer prompted him.

Max looked lost. "Like . . . oh." His face

brightened. "A woman invented Kevlar, which is pretty cool. And also, I'm sorry you guys have periods. That sounds like the worst."

This got a cheer from all the girls, and Max's cheeks turned red as he stepped back in line.

Sawyer cleared his throat. "You forgot something, Max."

"Oh, yeah," Max said, stepping forward again. "Our cabin would like to take over all of your cabin's cleaning duties for the rest of the week."

That won another cheer from our cabin. "We accept," Mia said, smiling.

My girls were pretty happy when they went to bed that night, but truly, the icing on the cake was the next morning when Boys Cabin 11 filed into breakfast glinting of glitter and smelling like vanilla from their pillows.

Sawyer found me in the line for bacon. "Glitter, Tab. Seriously?" he said, a piece sparkling high on his cheekbone. "It's never going to go away. I'm going to be finding glitter until December."

I only smiled. "I told you last year, Sawyer. Payback is my specialty."

CHAPTER THIRTEEN
PRESENT

"You are one cold, calculating woman," rosy-smelling Sawyer says. He's sitting on the sofa, waiting for Ben and Natalie. I'd snuck a dry change of clothes for both of them to my cottage earlier, and they're changing in my room.

"A cold woman wouldn't have made sure they have a change of clothes or have dinner ready for everyone." I keep my voice even as I salt the water and add the pasta. I'd have preferred to make it fresh but at least the Alfredo sauce will be from scratch. I slice the butter into the warmed pan and let it melt. I'm glad for a reason to keep busy, or I might spend all my time staring at Sawyer's face, cataloging all the changes. The stronger line of his jaw. The new scar near his hairline. How had he gotten it?

Why did I care?

I shouldn't. But I do. I want to know the story the last nine years has written on his face.

"Fine. But you're still calculating," he grumbles, and when he sounds nasal, I glance over to find Juniper honking his nose.

"I'm not sure what you guys were up to, but I can't believe you thought you'd get away with it. Did you forget who won the Prank Wars three out of three years here?" I would have won my fourth and final year too, but I hadn't come back for the next summer because of the man Juniper currently has wrapped inside her chubby fingers.

"I told you both this wouldn't work." Natalie emerges from the bedroom in dry clothes, toweling her hair. "You guys are such idiots."

"We probably should have guessed," Ben mumbles to Sawyer. "How'd you pull this off?" he asks me.

"Nat, why don't you open the bottle of wine you left for me and pour a glass for everyone? I'll tell you the story while I work on the sauce."

She fetches it from the fridge and takes down four wineglasses.

"Yesterday, I decided to explore the new trail behind the cabins, and guess who was sitting on his deck when I reached the end?"

"But I said not to use that one," Natalie protests weakly.

"I told you it wouldn't work. She was always a rule breaker," Ben says.

"I prefer 'innovator.' And of course I was going to check it out," I tell her. "It would have worked better if you hadn't said anything about it at all. You're a therapist. Shouldn't you know that?"

"Probably." She sighs.

"I had to ask myself, 'Why are these three dummies going through so much trouble to keep

Sawyer hidden when the plan is obviously to trot him out at some point?' Right?" I fold in grated parmesan while I wait, but no one contradicts me. "We'll get to that, I'm sure. But we all know the rule for prank wars."

"Strike first, strike hard, no mercy," Ben says.

"By the way, I figured out where these two stole that from," Natalie says. "It's from the old Karate Kid movies, but I figured it out when Ben dragged me through the series reboot."

"You loved it," he retorts.

"I loved it," she agrees, "but all the seasons could have wrapped in three episodes if they all had a little counseling. Maybe a lot for that Johnny guy."

"She says that about every show," Ben says.

"Because it's true." She ruffles his hair.

"Anyway," I say, "wherever it came from, the rule stands. So once I knew you were up to something, I figured it was important to remind you of the rules. While you guys were all snoozing this morning, I snuck over and poured the bubbles in Sawyer's hot tub. I had to gamble he wouldn't use it before tonight, then I put the rest of the plan in motion."

I describe almost every detail, until I get to drilling a couple of holes in their canoe, which would cause it to leak so slowly, they wouldn't notice until they were too far from shore to do anything about it.

"The Great Sinking, Year Three," Ben said. "That was the year we realized one of the canoes had a leak and sent you and Nat out in it."

"Did we ever pay you back for that?" Nat delivers a light smack to his chest, then reaches over and rubs it absent-mindedly.

"Tabby Cat just did," Ben says.

"Then *I* shouldn't have been sunk too," she says, almost pouting.

"There's another canoe on order for you, by the way," I say. "It'll be here before your campers are. And when I snuck into the office to order it on your office computer today, I logged into your email and sent a message to Sawyer asking him to warm up the hot tub for you around six."

"I knew as soon as the bubbles started pouring over the sides it was you," he says. "The Great Foam Disaster of Year Two."

The liquid in the dishwasher year. "Yeah, it's funny now that I've paid you back for it."

Sawyer and Ben exchange a look, and Sawyer shakes his head. "She's scary."

"I warned you idiots," Natalie says, scooping up Juniper. "I told them it was a bad idea, but somehow they convinced me this was the best way to do it."

"Do what?" I ask. None of them answer. I fish a strand of fettucine from the pot and nibble the end of it to check for doneness, watching them as I chew.

Ben stares at the floor and Natalie busies herself pretending to pick something out of Juniper's hair.

Sawyer pushes himself up from the sofa and leans against the counter behind me, forcing me to turn and face him.

"Well, Tabitha, it's like this." He crosses his arms over his chest like he's settling in and making himself comfortable. "I want a do-over."

I frown at him. "A do-over?"

"Yeah, Tab. I want a chance to show you I've grown up, and I want us to fix our friendship."

I almost laugh. This is ridiculous. We haven't spoken in *nine years,* and he wants to be friends like we never stopped? But I say nothing because the look on his face is very clear:

Sawyer Reed means it.

Ben clears his throat. "Hey, we're realizing, uh, about the sunset and . . . the trail, and with the baby, while it's dark, um, so we should—"

"Are we the rudest if we ask to take dinner to go?" Natalie asks. "I hate to peace out on you, but Ben's right. Better get Juniper home."

I pack their dinners, glad for the fuss of leave taking so I can process Sawyer's words, not sure how to respond.

Natalie leaves me with a tight hug. "I was going to tell you tonight that he's here," she whispers. "I wanted to make sure you'd be okay with talking to him before you saw him."

"It's okay," I whisper back. "I trust you."

Once the Mendozas hustle out, I'm not sure what to say to Sawyer, but I came into this evening with the upper hand, and I'm not ready to give it up. I pull out a chair on my side of the table where Sawyer has plated servings of fettucine for each of us.

"What's this about?" I ask him. "I mean, 'Let's be friends' sounds nice, but you didn't show up here after not speaking for a decade to tell me we should pretend like no time has passed."

"Nine years." He twirls noodles around his fork, a thoughtful look on his face. "How about if we eat this dinner, play catch up, then walk down to the dock, and I'll tell you why I mean it?"

I stare at him, trying to figure out how we're supposed to "catch up" on nine years over a twenty-minute dinner. But whatever it is he wants, he isn't ready to spit it out yet, and Sawyer had always been stubborn about doing things on his own time, and that doesn't seem to have changed. I shrug and pick up my fork. "Sure, let's do that. What have you been up to since you dumped me?"

He chokes on his wine. "Maybe we ease into that. Let's play Five Questions."

It's another camp game we'd played with the new counselors every year. We'd make the first fire of the season, and everyone took turns in the hot seat while the rest of the group got to ask them five questions to get to know them better.

"Sounds great," I say. "I already asked my first one: fill in the last ten years."

"Nine. Well, I'm a developer now. I mostly try to protect or develop urban green spaces, buying up declining properties and revitalizing them."

"Like the camp?"

"Kind of. It's not urban, obviously."

"If it's not urban, why buy it?"

"You," he says. "Ben. Natalie. My younger self. Memories." He rubs his palms against his thighs, a nervous gesture he'd had back then too. "I have a pretty good sense of place. I have to; my company depends on it. I know when a property will thrive or fail. I can see what it wants to be when I look at it."

The soft buzz at the edges of my brain warns me my anxiety is gathering itself. "Oak Crest only wants to be what it is."

He looks at me like I'm sporting extra eyeballs. "I know."

"Are you going to develop the area more?"

"No. The new lake cabins and my house are it."

My mind quiets a bit, but the confusion still swirls even if the anxiety has ebbed. "Then . . ."

"One of the old counselors tagged me in a photo dump on Facebook last year. I went to untag myself, but then I got caught up in all the pictures. It made me wonder how Oak Crest was doing, so I looked it up, and the website said it was for sale. So I bought it."

I blink at him. "Just like that?"

He lifts and drops a shoulder. "I knew if I didn't, another developer would, only he'd turn it into a subdivision or something depressing. I had this gut reaction, like, nope, can't let it happen. It didn't make a lot of sense at the time, but I went with it."

"Does it make any more sense now?"

"Yeah."

I wait for more, but he stays quiet. "That's it? 'Yeah,' with no explanation?"

"You know what camp is like. Would you let it go if you had the choice?"

Okay, that got me. "You bought it because you wanted to save it?"

"Partially. It did cross my mind you might have a reason to talk to me again."

I didn't love the idea of a guy with deep pockets manipulating a woman with flashy purchases. I loathed the idea if it was Sawyer and me. "What if you knew up front I wasn't going to speak to you again no matter what. Would you still have bought it?"

"Yes."

No hesitation. Good. "Will Natalie and Ben have a job tomorrow if I say I don't want to rebuild our friendship and I walk away right now?"

"Tab, even at my worst, have you ever known me to be a guy who would treat my best friends like that?" His voice is tight.

I let my fork clatter to my plate, giving him time to rethink his words. Has he forgotten why we haven't spoken in forever?

He clears his throat. "Uh, right. That was stupid. Their jobs are safe. They're part-owners, anyway, if it makes you feel better."

"Marginally." I pick up my fork and twirl some noodles.

"I'll restate that. I bought it *mostly* to save it. The possibility of apologizing to you face to face was only a perk, not a reason for buying the camp. I also knew Ben was miserable in DC, so I asked if he and Natalie wanted to run it. A lawyer and a therapist with years of experience here? It couldn't be more perfect. They jumped at it."

"They're happy," I say. And since he's been open, I add, "I'm glad you bought it. There's something comforting about knowing Oak Crest will continue."

"Did it hurt to admit that?" he teases.

"Don't ruin the moment."

"Yes, ma'am." He eats more Alfredo. "This is amazing, by the way."

"Thanks." I'm still mulling his answers. It makes sense based on the Sawyer I knew. But there are blanks I've always wanted filled in. "I've kept tabs on you over the years."

He pauses and quirks an eyebrow at me. "How? Nat and Ben said you don't even like to hear my name. They were pretty sure my plan to surprise

140

you this week would end in murder. I think they escaped so they don't have to testify against you in court. Tell them I said cremation and spread my ashes on the lake."

I nod, considering this. "What if my plan is to butcher and bury you? I've got skills."

"As long as it's on the grounds, I can live with it."

"No, you can't. You'll be dead."

He gives a single, soft laugh. "Then bury me somewhere with a lake view or Oak Crest is getting a new ghost."

I smile, remembering the countless conversations we'd had like this, our give-and-take usually leaving everyone else confused. "I'm not going to murder you."

"Probably for the best, even though most people would understand."

"True. If it was a jury of women, I'd walk free if I told them—" I break off and take another bite. I want to change the subject. "To answer your earlier question about keeping up with you, I check your Instagram sometimes. Enough to get a sense of what you've been up to. But I have questions. Probably nosy ones."

He sucks air through his teeth. "Unfortunately, you're way over the five-question limit."

"True," I say, standing and reaching for his half-full plate. "It was nice pranking you. Have a good walk home."

"But I'll answer them." He tugs the plate back.

I sit and smirk. "Next question: how come you acted like you couldn't even afford the camp store snacks when you were always a baby tycoon?"

This was the thing I hated discovering the most when I could bring myself to snoop on him months after camp. Because this was the one thing he'd out-and-out lied about. I'd found his sister's Instagram through her comments on one of his posts, and while Sawyer kept his posts low-key and impersonal, hers were a goldmine. Almost literally. Pictures of their family in their huge house. Pictures of them on a sailboat. Pictures of them in front of European landmarks.

Every picture of Sawyer had hurt for a long, long time. But his sister's had hurt worse because they told the story of a boy very different from the one I'd known. The question had slowly taken root. Was this why he'd never considered us being together after camp?

He shifts. "I was never poor. Just broke."

"Same thing."

"Not at all. Poor is a thing you can't get out of. Broke is a cash flow issue that resolves eventually." He shifts in his seat again.

"Sawyer." I point my fork at him. "You are literally being shifty right now."

He stills. "I'm not trying to be cute or do a marketing job on my past. Yes, I come from money. A lot of it. I went to private school all the way through college."

"Wait. You went to UMass." He'd worn a University of Massachusetts T-shirt around camp sometimes.

A hint of color heats his cheeks. "It was less obnoxious than the truth."

"Which is?"

"MIT?" he says. I gape at him. "Double major in engineering and business."

"MIT. A genius tycoon." It isn't sinking in. "Why were you out here every summer eating ramen on the weekends and saving your paychecks like you were never going to see another one?"

"Pride. I wanted to earn my own way. I wasn't dumb enough to turn down paid college, but I earned all my living expenses in the summer. I picked camp counseling because room and board is free, and there's nowhere to spend your money here, so it was easy to save. Then I lucked out and loved the job."

"So you were, what, Richie Rich the whole time?"

He shoots me an annoyed look. "That's exactly why I never told anyone."

"I've never seen MIT on your Instagram."

"It's on my LinkedIn," he says. "I don't hide it now."

He's got me there. I've never been on LinkedIn,

and his Facebook is locked down, so all my snooping has been on IG. "Is development the family business?" It would explain how he's been able to grow his business so fast. "Is Camp Oak Crest now a Reed Family holding?"

"No. I inherited a trust fund from my grandmother when I turned twenty-six and used it as startup capital."

"Kind of a random age."

"She read an article about how human brains fully mature at twenty-five. She figured if she made our trust funds available at twenty-six, we wouldn't make any idiotic impulse purchases when we got the money."

"Did it work?"

"For me, yeah. I have two sisters and six cousins, and they've all done okay with it. We're not talking millions here, but I'd been flipping houses for three years by then, and combined, it was enough seed money to move into commercial property and make something happen."

"How much are we talking?" It's unforgivably nosy, and I don't care.

"Do you have any idea how judgy you sound right now?"

"How much?"

He sighs. "We each got a half-million dollars."

My fork clanks again. "My grandma got me six pairs of socks for my twenty-sixth birthday. But they were warm."

"You're being the worst right now, Tab."

He's not wrong. But it had become so obvious the more I'd learned about the real Sawyer that there had never been a chance he would fall for me. Me with my state college education and my working-class parents and my small-town roots.

One picture on his sister's feed in particular had pancaked me, a post from her wedding on the first New Year's Day after Sawyer and I broke up. New Year's Eve was the worst holiday to spend alone, but I'd sat in my room, rejecting Grace's efforts to get me to go out with her and some friends.

Apparently, the oldest Reed sister had gotten married the day before. The shot was at her wedding, a formal evening affair inside a posh hotel in Spain. The bride and groom stood at the top of the grand foyer staircase, their attendants flanking them, Sawyer with the groomsmen, the other sister with the bridesmaids. The guests below were in tuxes and evening gowns, holding up champagne to toast them, and I'd stared at it for hours, realizing how big the gulf was between Sawyer and me.

I'd thought my prom was fancy, with the moms getting together to serve us a sit-down dinner in someone's backyard decked out in twinkle lights; the girls in discount dresses from JC Penney; the boys in rented tuxes or their dads' too-big suits. We'd felt sophisticated, dancing in the transformed

Creekville Community Center. That looked like kids playing dress up in cheap costumes compared to the elegance of this wedding.

"Tabitha?"

"Sorry." I focus on Sawyer again. "Your Bruce Wayne inheritance threw me. It's like finding out your college boyfriend had a superhero alter ego."

"I don't fight crime. Just city zoning boards and municipal tax commissions."

I eat a few more bites, studying him in open fascination. Regardless of my dislike for him, he is objectively dead sexy. He lets the silence lie between us and puts up with it. "Are you creeped out I keep staring at you?"

"No," he says. "I've been able to watch you whenever I want over the last five years, so fair is fair."

It's my turn to blush. Five years ago, I started the YouTube cooking channel that led to my network show. He's openly admitting he's been tracking me closely for a long time.

"What you've built, it's incredible," he says. "You did that all on your own with a cell phone and an internet connection. Impressive as hell."

My blush deepens. "I'm pretty proud of it."

"You should be. I knew when you had to run the whole kitchen the summer Marge quit you were going to do amazing things. And you have." He pauses, like he wants to add something. "I

146

was sorry you didn't come back the next year."

I shift in my seat. Now we're getting to the real stuff, the stuff we've been dancing around. "That summer worked out for the best." I'd gotten a job as a dishwasher in Roanoke's only fine dining restaurant and worked my way up to line cook by August. The executive chef ended up writing me a recommendation for culinary school.

"I'm glad to hear it did for you." He glances at his empty plate. "Are you still hungry? If not, let's take that walk down to the dock."

He helps me clean up the dinner mess, and then we head out to the dock.

It's an out-of-body experience walking with him to the dock. At least it's the new one. There's no way to avoid the memories of sitting on the old one, talking for hours. Or to ignore that if this were anyone but Sawyer, an invitation from a hot guy to take an evening walk to a dock would hold the promise of potential. Romance. Connection. But it *is* Sawyer, and there's no chance I'll forget it.

Long talks weren't the only thing that happened on the old dock, and there is no way to forget that kind of pain.

CHAPTER FOURTEEN
NINE YEARS AGO

I stared down at the sunrise picnic I'd prepared for Sawyer. It was the last day of camp. The campers had gone home two days before, and the counselors had spent the last two days prepping the camp to close, packing away sports equipment and canoes, hauling the lifeguard chair back to the storage shed, cleaning out the kitchen, and stripping all the bunks.

The whole place would be a hive of activity again as the other counselors woke, but in this last rosy pink hour before the leave taking started, Sawyer and I would have the camp to ourselves, the only ones crazy enough to get up this early on the one morning we could sleep in a bit.

I watched as the sky lightened, wondering where he was. He was never late, but it was almost fifteen minutes past when he said we'd meet, and the stuffed French toast I'd gotten up in the dark to make him was getting cold.

Last night had changed everything. We'd sat on Moon Rock overlooking the lake, and I'd never felt a moment so perfect, the kind of right you feel in your bones and the roots of your hair, and even inside of your soul.

I'd looked over at him, and the words that had been simmering inside me since the middle of summer bubbled up. Words that made no sense when he went to school ten hours away. Words that my mother had warned me never to say until I'd graduated and begun my career. Words that set themselves free anyway.

"Sawyer? I love you."

He'd glanced over at me, drawing a slightly ragged breath. His eyes had darkened, his head had dipped toward mine, and he gave me a kiss that whispered *I love you too* to the quietest parts of my soul.

This final day would be a turning point for us; instead of checking in casually over the next nine months, we'd leave in a relationship, find ways to spend our breaks together, and wait impatiently for next summer.

But when I heard the scuff of shoes on the dock, I turned to see Ben, not Sawyer. My stomach clenched. Something wasn't right about the tight set of his shoulders, or the way he wouldn't meet my eyes.

"Ben? Did something happen?" I asked. "Where's Sawyer? What's wrong?"

"Nothing. Everything's fine." He stopped and swallowed. "Tab, Sawyer left. He got a ride an hour ago."

"What? Why?" We'd both planned to take the final airport run on the Rust Bucket to squeeze every minute out of our last morning together.

"He said he needed to head back early."

"Ben." He still wasn't meeting my eyes, and I got the first inkling that Sawyer had meant our kiss last night very differently than I'd taken it. "Talk to me. What did he tell you? Did he say if this is about last night?"

"No. Kind of." He ran his hands through his hair, his eyes meeting mine but sliding away. "Yes. He's worried he gave you the wrong idea. He totally loved hanging out with you, Tab—"

"Don't." My voice was flat.

Ben stopped talking. He couldn't have looked more miserable if he was tied to an anthill with third degree sunburn.

"I can't believe he sent you out here to do this."

"I can't either," he said.

"What did I do wrong?" I asked, confused and suddenly tired. Tired like part of me sensed how badly this was going to hurt when it sank in.

"He said . . ." Ben waved his hand as if I could fill in the blank.

"Tell me."

"I am going to kick his ass," he mumbled. Then louder, "He said camp is camp, and real life is out there. And it's time to go back to real life."

Bruno Mars wouldn't throw himself on a grenade if it hurt even one millionth as much as Sawyer's words did. I absorbed them like invisible body blows, each one hitting a vulnerable organ. "I feel sick."

"Tab, I'm so sorry."

"I feel sick." Then I spun and vomited into the lake, bringing up the bile that had begun churning when I realized Sawyer had already left.

"Oh, Tabby, no." Ben hurried over to rub circles on my back until the heaving stopped. "What can I do?"

I took deep breaths, my hands braced on my knees. "Nothing."

"I hate this. Tell me what to do."

I calmed my breathing and straightened, feeling the acid in the back of my throat and a warning sting in my eyes and nose that meant tears were coming. "Just be a better guy than him, Ben." I gathered up the edges of the blanket I'd laid out, hauling the whole thing into a bundle, not caring about the food tumbling off plates and making a mess inside. I thrust it at Ben. "And burn this to ashes."

Then I walked away to pack and leave Oak Crest for the last time.

CHAPTER FIFTEEN
PRESENT

Sawyer and I reach the end of the new dock, but there's enough light from the quarter moon to see the silvery shape of the old dock across the water. Enough to remind me why I'm not falling for whatever Sawyer is selling.

He slips off his shoes and sits at the end, letting his feet dangle in the water. "Join me?"

I want to pace while I listen, get out some of the tightly wound energy building inside of me, but I follow his lead and sit beside him without a word.

"All right," he says. "A do-over and why I mean it."

"This should be good," I say.

"Maybe not this first part." He sighs. "Honestly, it took me a while to regret that last morning at camp." I tense. He's right: not a great start. "But once I woke up to what an idiot I'd been, I've regretted it every day since. The more time goes by, the more I regret it."

"Glad to hear it." I am. It's grimly satisfying, like when one of the mean girls from high school has an ugly kid.

"Then you'll love the next part, because the

reason we're here right now, you and I, is so I can say I'm sorry."

Slowly, the tension seeps from my shoulders. It's the one thing he hasn't outright said, and until he hinted at it being a reason for buying Oak Crest, I hadn't realized how much I'd wanted to hear those words all these years, even when I'd insisted I didn't care.

"Two years after our last summer here together, I started dating a girl," Sawyer continues. "I really liked her. I was almost twenty-three, and I figured it was post-college and the right age for me to fall in love for the first time."

That stings. Maybe everyone wants to believe their first love is mutual. But it's also very Sawyer to put a timeline on love, to decide it was "time," as if any of us has any control over that. It makes me think of his backup plan to marry if we're single at thirty. That's only a few months away for each of us.

Is he . . . ? No. I doubt every sentence we've ever exchanged is burned into his brain like they are into mine. He won't remember that throw-away bargain if I bring it up, even if it proves his pattern of arbitrary deadlines. Those work for college graduations. Not life events.

He makes a lazy circle in the lake with his foot. "Spoiler alert: that relationship didn't work out. And when it ended, it took me a while to get over. It made me realize what a jackass I'd been to you, sending Ben out that morning while I ran away. I knew it was wrong at the time, and I tried to apologize for it. But it took me a while to realize how wrong."

There was a time when I would have given anything to hear those words. I sit with that as he falls into silence. That's . . . big. I don't know how to take it all in.

"I've had a couple more relationships since then," he continues, "but both of them lost steam. It's a better way to end. It's less messy that way, you know?"

"Than chucking an emotional hand grenade and running away? Yeah, I know."

"You're definitely still mad." His voice is resigned.

I lean back on my hands and consider that. "No," I say at last. "I don't think I am. My old self might still be mad at your old self, but the Tabitha on this dock now is not mad at the Sawyer on this dock now. Current me isn't even mad at old you. You were a kid."

"An extremely, super dumb kid?" He quotes my fire ceremony words.

"You heard that?"

"Natalie told me. She was trying to convince me this was an extremely, super dumb idea."

"So why do it now? Or do it this way? Are you chasing the high of summer camp?" I make the joke because the tension between us has built with each tricky topic we're tackling.

He faces me directly, the moonlight glinting in his eyes. "Basically. You laugh, but it's true. When I found out this place was for sale, I came to see it. I don't know how to explain it, but the second I turned onto the camp road, the last decade disappeared, and I was eighteen-year-old Sawyer, heading into an adventure I had no idea if I could handle."

It's an eerie echo of my own feelings when Natalie had driven me in.

"I walked around, looking at the old bones of the place, and I couldn't separate myself from the past anymore. None of us can, can we? That's what Natalie says. It shapes us no matter what. And Camp Oak Crest is a big part of who I've become. I started figuring out who I was and what I wanted. Found my best friends here. Including you."

These words soothe me, a balm on old hurts. That's how I had felt then too.

"Maybe you make best friends wherever you go," he continues, "but I don't. It's rare. The more I thought about it, the more I wanted it to be like it was. The four of us again. No more trading custody of Ben and Natalie."

"Sawyer . . ." I don't know how I want to finish my thought. Two full days in Oak Crest have shown me that I've grown more than I thought

I had since that last summer. But I don't know what that looks like going forward.

"You don't have to say anything. But I have two requests. First, see the moon?"

I nod. "Can't miss it."

"It's a third-quarter moon. Do you remember what that symbolizes from camp astronomy nights?"

I run through the list in memory and smile when I find the answer. "Forgiveness?"

"Yeah. I want to say again I'm sorry for the way I treated you back then. If I had it to do all over again, I'd do it differently."

Maybe the moon is working its forgiving magic, but I find myself drawn to the spell of his words. "What would you change?"

"I'd have come out here myself that morning. I'd have made sure you knew how awesome I think you are. I would have figured out how to leave as friends."

I let the words settle over me, staring out over the water. "That would have been better."

He shifts, drawing his feet out of the water and turning his whole body toward me. "Everything in me says I took the wrong fork in the road back then. This is where you and I were always meant to be. Friends. Good with each other, Natalie, Ben, and this place. I know I can't rewrite the past. But I hope you can accept my apology." His eyes are soft and earnest as they meet mine.

Weeks of pain, months of feeling less than, years of figuring out how to be good enough. But I did figure it out. So I tell him honestly what I'd realized on the old dock yesterday afternoon. "I forgive you, Sawyer."

He looks away, and his whole body relaxes. At least a minute passes before he says, "Thank you."

He's done me a favor, honestly, because I feel lighter inside. We sit in more silence, and it's comfortable, like that last summer.

Eventually, he stirs and turns toward me. "Can I push my luck?"

"Stretch . . ."

He smiles at the old camp name. "Hear me out. You can always say no."

"No."

"I meant after I say my idea."

I give a fake annoyed sniff. "Fine."

"I knew I was going to be lucky just to get a chance to apologize. But I'm serious about the friendship too. You've always been one of the coolest people I know. I took it for granted, but I wouldn't do that again. Will you give me a chance to earn back our friendship?"

I do love the idea of not putting Ben and Natalie in the middle. It would be nice to show up for their important stuff and know Sawyer and I can have civil conversations. But friendship gets harder the older I get. Less time, less in common with people. I'm not sure what he's asking for.

"What kind of friends are you hoping we'll be?" I'll never make assumptions about what he wants again; he has to spell it out.

"We'll be the kind of friends where we can hang out together at Oak Crest during the off-season, and you'll never have to stress about coming here. We'll be hiking-and-hanging friends. All of us sitting by the campfire friends. Watch horror movies with Ben and Natalie friends."

I don't know. He's painting a pretty picture, but it's not how adult friendships work. "It takes time to build a friendship like that. Time we don't have. But I promise we don't have to take turns with Natalie and Ben anymore. That's a pretty big win."

"I have a plan," he says.

"A plan," I repeat. "To be friends? That is so . . . you."

"I don't leave important things up to chance," he says. "We're both here for a week. Remember how long a week felt during camp? Lots of strangers became best friends by the end of those weeks, so if you're up for it, we've got a decent shot."

A bubble of laughter wells up in spite of myself. "I appreciate the enthusiasm, but you're paying me a lot of money to make this gala happen, remember? And Natalie, despite her calm therapist vibe, will probably burn down your house if you try to replace her as my best friend."

"I'm not trying to replace her," he says. "I'll tell her so myself. I just want us to have time to find our own vibe as friends, so we're not doomed to awkward small talk over juice boxes at Juniper's next birthday."

"I appreciate what you're saying, but this week is crazy. I've got so much prep to do for the gala, and—"

"Confession."

The word stops me short. "You have *more* to confess?"

"I never intended for you to run the kitchen this week. Lisa is extremely good. She ran the food services for the local county schools until she went to culinary school and became a chef. She's going to do an amazing job, and you can help her or not. Whatever you want. But I'm hoping you'll give me three dates over the next three days."

"Dates?" I get an anxious, panicky feeling in my chest.

"Friend dates. *Hangs,*" he says, "three hangs to reconnect. Rebuild. At the end of the week, if you feel like we should stay small-talk-over-juice-box friends, I'll accept it."

I'm almost tempted. Almost. The idea of the four of us being as close as we were, it's appealing. But it's wishful thinking, and not the kind of thing that gets fixed in a week. Also, he'd be basically paying me $25,000 to just chill. No way.

I climb to my feet and smile down at him. "I have an early start tomorrow. Let's call tonight a win and work our way up from juice boxes." I'm about to leave when I add, "Thanks for doing this, Sawyer. It feels good to clear the air. Pop into the kitchen anytime this week. I can talk and work at the same time." Then I do start up the dock.

"Tabitha Winters?" His low, warm voice calls after me when I'm halfway back to the shore.

I stop and turn. "Yes?"

He stands and slides his hands into his pockets. "I double-dog dare you."

"What?" I repeat. He did *not* just—

"I double-dog dare you to give me this week. At the end of our third hang, we end up back here, on this dock. If you're not convinced, then I say a polite hello to you over a future juice box."

I laugh. I can't help it. "I can't believe I'm even considering this. You're literally trying to buy my friendship."

"Earn it," he corrects, hope in his eyes. "Is that a yes?"

I stare across the lake, thinking. I've been an adult in every area of my life except this one for years. It's time, I realize. I'm grown up enough to be an adult about this part too.

"Tabitha?" He's moved closer now, and he touches my elbow. It's light. He's not trying to keep me there or take hold of me. It's like he can't help it. And I know. I know from the second I can sense each individual ridge of the whorls on his fingertip brushing against the soft skin above my elbow. I know even before the goose bumps break out despite the warm night air.

I drop my hands and turn to him with a smile because I'm almost laughing at myself. This is ridiculous. "Okay, Sawyer."

One corner of his mouth turns up. "Yes?"

"It's a double-dog dare. Of course it's a yes."

CHAPTER SIXTEEN

I get up early again the next morning and go to my tiny front deck to do yoga stretches and greet the sun. And think. And think. Then I think some more. About how strange it is to feel okay toward Sawyer. But also how normal it is. I need to debrief with Natalie.

I dress and let myself into the camp kitchen again. Lisa is already there, prepping to feed the small army of counselors. "I hear you're a ringer, and you don't need me in here all week."

She pauses in whisking a huge bowl of eggs. "I enjoyed you?" It's unconvincing.

"No, you didn't. I stressed you out, and you didn't need me to teach any of the stuff I was teaching you."

She gives me the best imitation of a deer in the headlights I've ever seen.

"It's fine, Lisa. You did a great job of playing along. You'll do fine at Camp Oak Crest."

"You're not mad?"

I grab an apple from a nearby fruit bowl and lean against a counter as I crunch into it. "Have you seen Sawyer Reed?"

"No, not since yester—"

I cut her off with a headshake. "I mean have you seen him *ever.* Like, looked at his face. His very nice face."

Her lips twitch. "I have."

"Imagine you spent a whole summer making out with Sawyer Reed. And you break up at the end of the summer. And you don't talk for ten years. Nine," I correct myself. "Then he shows up and says he's arranged an extremely complicated plan to get you here and wants to spend the next few days with you. All day. You following me?"

She sets the bowl aside, whisk forgotten, and fans herself, and I don't think she even realizes it.

I point to her fan hand. "Exactly. Would you be mad?"

She stops fanning. "I guess I wouldn't be."

I nod and take another bite of apple, point made. We drift into our first comfortable silence as she whisks again.

"Mind if I steal rations to make the Mendozas breakfast?" I ask when I'm done with the apple.

"Not at all."

I take what I need and walk up to Ben and Natalie's house.

"Knock knock," I call, opening the door. Natalie's sitting in a rocking chair, Juniper on her lap, playing with the lapels of Natalie's fuzzy bathrobe.

"Hey," she says, smiling at me. It's a slightly nervous smile. "What are you doing here?"

I set my bag of goodies on the counter and plop down on the sofa across from her. "You went along with Dumb and Dumber's plan because Sawyer told you he wanted to apologize?"

She sighs. "I know you've needed closure all these years. The plan was to use our fire ceremony Monday night to help you work through any memories this place was bringing up for you. Like exposure therapy for anxiety patients. Let you process, throw it all away in the fire, then see how you felt about seeing Sawyer face to face. I was going to come over last night and talk to you about it."

She leans forward, her face serious. "But you have to believe me, I was never going to spring him on you if you weren't open to it. And I definitely had no idea he wanted a do-over." She covers Juniper's ears and calls Sawyer a rude name.

"Dumesh," Juniper repeats.

"Good job," I tell her. "That's delightful."

"Dumesh, dumesh, dumesh."

Natalie glares at me. "Junebug, let's not say that word."

Juniper bounces on her mom's lap. "DUMESH DUMESH DUMESH."

Natalie groans and reaches for a well-loved stuffie. "Mommy is the dumesh," she says, handing Juniper the toy.

"Nat, don't worry about it. I know you're always looking out for me."

"I am. One hundred percent. So . . . on that

note, how are you feeling? Things go okay last night?"

I consider my answer. "I need to cook while I think. You in the mood for breakfast?"

"If it's served in anything besides a sinking canoe, then yes."

"You deserved it," I retort, already going through her fridge.

"Fair."

"Last night was okay. Even good?"

"Tell me about that."

I crack some eggs. "Running around here yesterday setting you guys up was carefree. Happy. Felt like a teenager again. Sitting on the dock and having a serious conversation with Sawyer was familiar too. But is it clouding my judgment?" I beat the eggs, channeling nervous energy. "This place totally messes with your head."

"In a good way?" Natalie asks.

"I don't know. It feels good right *now,* but so did our last summer until it didn't. But it doesn't matter because Sawyer double-dog dared me."

"Uh oh. To do what?"

"Hang out. Whatever you call a date when it's only friends. If I can honestly say I don't want us to all be BFFs at Oak Crest forever after that, he'll disappear completely."

"There is so much that idiot did *not* tell me when he hatched this stupid plan."

I grin. "That's because he's *not* an idiot. I'm

165

sure he knew you'd feel obligated to tell me what he was up to. But it's okay. Maybe we're not all going to do yearly s'mores activities together, but it would be good if I could release all my Sawyer baggage and close that chapter with a better ending."

"And get into a real relationship. With someone else!" she adds when I glare at her.

"I've been in real relationships." I date a lot. It's not my fault none of them last long. I have a hard schedule with taping and cookbook research and . . . and . . . "I dated Evan for almost two years."

"And why did you break up?"

Because he was the British heir to a hedge fund fortune, and when I couldn't come up with any more excuses why I couldn't meet his posh London family, I panicked and dumped him. "Doesn't matter," I say airily, like there's any chance Natalie will miss that I'm deflecting. "This is about trying to be friends."

"Good plan." Her voice is mild.

"I need a favor. Turns out Sawyer's watched all my YouTube stuff. I need to do a deep dive on his socials besides Instagram to put us on a more even playing field."

"Ben needs the main desk, but you can use the nurse's office computer."

While I cook, we chat more about how the first day with counselors will go, the impending arrival of their upscale guests tomorrow, the plans for the opening gala, and how Juniper is the world's most perfect baby.

Ben walks in as I plate the first omelet and sounds relieved I'm not there for more revenge.

An hour later, he's settled behind the front desk returning emails and phone calls, and I hole up in the nurse's office to start my crash course in Sawyer. I know his Instagram well—I caught up on it when Natalie told me they were buying the camp—so I start with LinkedIn.

I've barely finished reading through his list of professional accomplishments—his many, many accomplishments—when there's a loud crash followed by the clatter of chair parts bouncing. It's quiet for a second before Ben curses enough to earn a hundred camp demerits.

He appears in the doorway, holding the seat of his desk chair in one hand, one of its rolling wheels in the other. "I'm guessing you loosened all these?"

"Yep. Thank you to the camp gods for letting me be here when it fell apart."

He scowls. "You're not going to put it back together, are you?"

"Nope."

This meets with a growl and a short silence. Then, "Does this make us even?"

"Yep."

"Fine." He disappears back to the main office.

Camp Oak Crest is turning out to be as fun as I remembered.

Two hours later, I've read through every relevant trade magazine article about Sawyer that I could google, savoring the quotes, the words from his own mouth about what he's doing. His passion and intensity come through clearly. He's not the slightly shy and sometimes awkward boy he was as a counselor. But I knew that before we even finished our fettucine.

I have to end my research sooner than I want to, but only to get ready for our first ~~date~~ hang: canoeing.

He knocks a half hour later, and I'm ready, a swimsuit beneath my cotton tank dress, water-friendly sandals on my feet, sunscreened and ponytailed for the adventure.

"Hey," he says when I open the door. He's dressed in gray trunks, a soft-looking blue T-shirt, and Tevas exactly like the ones he used to wear. He'd dressed like that every day of summer camp, but something about it hits me differently now. His chest is broader and deeper, and his cheeks have lost their last bit of baby softness. I want to reach up and run my fingers along his jawline to see if it's as chiseled as it looks, but I refrain.

"You look great," he says, "except for . . ." He reaches out and brushes at my nose with his thumb. "Missed some sunscreen there." But he smooths it across my cheek, and heat follows his touch before he wipes the rest against his shorts. "Got it."

Whoa. *No. Stop it.* It's the kind of thing I would do for Natalie or Juniper.

"Ready to get on the water?"

I nod. "Let's go."

A canoe waits for us by the new dock, and when we reach it, I spot the gear in the bottom. "Fishing, huh?"

"Yeah. I'm thinking a friendly competition. Whoever catches the smallest fish has to cook the winner dinner."

"Sounds perfect. Hope you have good catfish recipes, because I'm going to catch a giant one for you to cook."

"Big talk, Winters. Get in the boat." He offers his hand to help, and his palm is lightly calloused when I take it. He also rests his hand on my back, waist-high, like I need the extra support to navigate the bow, which is currently only in about two inches of water. I narrow my eyes, but he's not meeting them. I let go as soon as both feet are in the canoe and settle on my seat so he can push us out. He does, giving us a smooth launch before hopping in, and we slip into an easy rhythm as we paddle.

"There's a good spot not too far from the center of the lake," he says.

"You come here often enough to have a fishing hole?" I have to call my questions over my shoulder, but that's okay. I'm not ready to sit eyeball to eyeball with him yet.

"I sort of lucked into this one, to be honest. I only make it out here about once a month and some holidays. I'll probably come less in the summer when it's crawling with kids."

"Are you in Chicago the rest of the time?"

He laughs. "I don't know if I'm in any one place most of the time. I have projects all over. St. Louis. Detroit. Farther east. I've got six major projects under development right now, and about that many smaller ones, so I have to pick and choose where I am."

We talk baseball—he's a Boston Red Sox fan—until we reach his spot and put our paddles down. I turn, resettling myself on the small bench seat.

He slides the poles from beneath the seats, only this requires him to close a hand around my bare ankle to get to them.

He's *flirting* with me! What the—

"When we played Five Questions the other night, I didn't get to ask any of mine. You up for it?" he asks as he hands me a pole.

"Trapped in the middle of a lake and obligated to answer any five questions you ask." I rummage in the tackle box for a lure, which I can do without mauling him. "Gee, Sawyer, you sure know how to show a girl a good time."

"Hangs at a summer camp do revolve around a theme."

"Outdoor activities and camp games?"

"Nailed it. But a reminder before you jump in and try to swim back, this is a double-dog dare."

I lay the fishing pole across my lap and study him. He's up to something, and I'm going to crack him. "I don't want to get away from you."

"That's a relief." There's a sincerity in his words.

"Have you thought I hated you this whole time?"

"Natalie's made it pretty clear you'd rather not occupy the same spaces as me. I don't blame you." He gives a soft laugh. "Man, being around you makes me feel like a dumb twenty-year-old kid again."

"I don't hate you. I was pretty mad for a year or so. But I didn't hate you." I consider that. "Well, except the first summer when I didn't come back for camp, and I was working in a kitchen sixty hours a week during the hottest summer in Virginia's history. I hated you a few times that summer."

"I wish you would have come back," he says. "That last summer wasn't the same."

I shrug. "It would have been pretty uncomfortable if we were both here. Trust me, you had a better summer with me not around."

"But not better food. We never had better meals than the summer you ran the kitchen."

"That's why I'm really here, isn't it," I say, careful to keep my tone teasing. "You're trying to reclaim the glory days of Oak Crest, and you know you need my cooking to do it."

His eyes crinkle at the corners. "Busted."

I study him frankly. The fit of his shirt, the light gold of his skin, the fall of his hair. It's all working for him. His smile fades as he watches me back, slowly clocking my eyes, my mouth, my mouth, my—he is really staring at my mouth a lot.

I can dish it back. Why not? He's forgiven, but it would have been nice to hear, *I never should have dumped you* instead of *I should have dumped you myself instead of by proxy*. Will it hurt anything to show him what he missed out on?

If we were going to see each other regularly? Yes. But we're not. I've had plenty of friends meet, fall in vacation love, and say goodbye to their fling without a backward glance on either side at the end of a week. What if I really gave myself over to play this week? To youthful abandon like it's the last year of my twenties and not the last year of my eighties?

Will it affect our ability to be awkward juice box friends? No. It will only *enhance* the awkwardness. I'd practically be doing us a favor.

We're talking one juice box event a year, max, that we're likely to cross paths. I'm seeing only upsides here.

I think about it for another moment as Sawyer recasts his line. His shirt rides up about an inch above his waistline as he draws back to cast. It's a tight, toned inch, and I enjoy it until he straightens to talk to me again and his shirt falls.

I curve my lips into the slightest of smiles. An invitation. A challenge. This is the level of dating I've mastered since college. The higher my star rose, the more men wanted to date me. I've gone out with some of the healthiest egos in New York, and I've learned all their smoothest moves. *This* is my comfort level. It's almost instinctive, the urge to flirt as a form of control. I set the pace. I decide what happens and when. Or if anything happens at all.

Sawyer catches my smile and goes still for a couple of seconds. Then, with a slow blink, he leans slightly toward me, watching my mouth the whole time. What has he learned to do with his quick and generous mouth in the last nine years? I'm on a beautiful lake with a gorgeous man, who wants to be friends. Why not be friends with benefits?

I could rewrite that summer but walk away with my heart intact. Best idea I've had in ages.

When his face is inches from mine, my eyes flutter closed. I wait for the familiar brush of his lips, the skitter of electricity I've never felt with the same intensity with anyone since.

But instead of his lips, I feel the softest puff of his breath, as he says, "No way."

My eyes fly open to find his staring right into mine. "Excuse me?"

"No. Way."

"Are you . . . laughing at me?"

"I am definitely laughing at you. I'm earning your friendship, and I'm not giving you any chances to wiggle out of it by claiming I changed the terms. We were good as friends. Great as friends."

"What makes you think I was going to kiss you?"

"Like I could forget your 'kiss me' face."

I grip my paddle. "You must have because that wasn't it."

"Don't be embarrassed, Tab. Makes sense we might slip into old habits as we get comfortable with each other again."

I watch him for a second, giving him my pleasant smile I use when we're doing a transition into a commercial break. He was flirting with me. You don't get to twenty-nine and miss signs like that. What is he up to? "You're getting too much sun, I think. Misreading signals."

"You're saying that wasn't your 'kiss me' face?" There's a mild challenge in his tone.

"That's what I'm saying."

He looks relieved. "Oh good. It just wouldn't be fair to you if I kissed you." He wedges his pole and starts tying a lure like there's nothing more to talk about.

"What do you mean, 'it wouldn't be fair'?"

"Because, Chef Tabitha"—his gaze flicks up to mine—"I'd kiss you so thoroughly that you wouldn't remember ever tasting anything else in your life but me." He goes back to tying his lure. "Can't ruin your career like that."

Oh my.

Heat unfurls low in my abdomen, and I swallow hard. But he's acting like this is all no big deal, and I'm not about to let him see he's gotten to me, so I nod slowly, like I'm considering his words. Faster than he can blink, I scoop up an enormous spray of water with my paddle, the bulk of it splatting right in his face and making him gasp.

"You need to cool down, friend." I have the paddle settled innocently in my lap by the time he finishes sputtering. "You're right, Sawyer. Being friends is way more fun. Welcome back to Camp Oak Crest, Stretch. Game on."

CHAPTER SEVENTEEN

"I don't know how you did it, but you cheated." I cross my arms and glare at Sawyer, who holds the largest speckled trout I've ever seen anyone pull from the lake.

"Don't be a sore loser." He pats the fish's head.

"You ever known me to be a gracious winner?"

He smirks. "No. No, I haven't."

"Tell me how you cheated."

"Better idea: admit defeat and tell me how you're going to cook this fish. I want to imagine it."

We've been on the lake for two hours, and that's about an hour longer than I like to fish, but Sawyer had made the time go fast with his jokes. He'd even answered direct questions about his family and college and work, stuff he dodged in the old days.

I sigh. "Fine. You win. But I don't know how I'm going to cook the fish yet. Where am I doing this?"

He raises his eyebrows. "How do you feel about my house?"

I hoped he would say that. I want to see what kind of space he chose for himself. "Sounds good. I'll have to do an incredibly thorough amount of rummaging to figure out what I have to work with."

"Why does it sound like your rummaging will go beyond my kitchen?"

I lift and drop my shoulders. "Who knows what culinary inspiration might be hiding in your sock drawer? Or medicine cabinet? I'm inspired by all kinds of things."

He only laughs. "Rummage anywhere you want. I don't keep secrets." I open my mouth, but he corrects himself before I get a word out. "Besides the thing about being Ben and Natalie's silent partner and planning an *Ocean's Eleven* level caper to lure you back here to the scene of my adolescent love crimes."

"Maybe don't say love crimes when you're trying to get a woman back to your house in the woods. And maybe not 'lure,' either."

He closes his eyes for a few seconds. "If I call some old girlfriends on the phone and put them on speaker for them to testify that I'm generally pretty smooth, will you believe them?"

I tsk. "Tough sell since I knew you when you were twenty."

He gives me a hangdog look before he straightens, a glint in his eye. "How about our first kiss? The one that counted. That was pretty smooth."

I drop my eyes to his mouth. "It wasn't bad. If only there were a way to refresh my memory . . ."

He smirks and stows his winning fish in a small cooler. "We better put you to work before you start trouble, *friend*."

I laugh as he grabs his paddle and steers us to the private dock. When he ties off the canoe and reaches down to pull me onto the dock with him, I'm curious enough to see inside his place that I resist the impulse to pull him into the lake.

His "place," it turns out, is a gorgeous contemporary home with distinct Scandinavian influences, full of clean lines and light streaming through his modern lakeview windows. Intentional pops of color surprise me. I would have figured Sawyer for a more traditional, rustic guy, but I've only known him in a summer camp setting. He's managed to integrate his own style with the natural landscape, and I like what I see. It's telling me more about him than all the conversations we'd ever had in our counselor days.

"This is beautiful." Clean, disciplined, and peaceful because of it.

"Thanks. I stayed at a house like this in Norway, and I'd never been in a place that felt more like me. I tried to recreate it here."

"Is this your primary place? Home base or whatever between all your trips?"

"No. This was the place I promised I'd build myself when I hit certain business milestones." He gives a small grimace. "That sounded more pretentious than I meant it to."

"No, I get it."

"Did you do anything like that? Any big splurges when you hit it big?"

"Not really." The money had been needed elsewhere.

"Not even a trip or anything?"

I have no regrets about where the money went, but the explanation is heavy for the day we're having. I consider glossing over it, but as I look around his deeply personal space, I *want* to tell him the truth.

"My dad got sick a couple of years ago. Lymphoma. He's self-employed, and his insurance wouldn't cover a drug trial his doctor wanted to enroll him in. So I did."

His eyebrows draw together. "I'm sorry, Tab. Is he . . . ?"

I wave away the worry in his voice. "He's fine. Full remission for almost a year now. The trial worked. Best present I ever bought myself."

"Now I feel shallow for loving this house."

"Don't. If it makes you feel any better, when I renegotiate my next contract with the network, I'm going to get a big enough increase to buy myself a racehorse. An expensive one."

"You want a pony?" There's a laugh in his tone.

"Sure. You can't grow up in rural Virginia without wanting a pony of your own. Feel better about your practical house now?"

"Yeah, actually."

"I aim to please." I wander over to study the framed photograph over the fireplace.

"That's the house in Norway."

I can see it, how the place in the photo served as a starting point for this one. "Have you been back?"

"No, but I'd like to." For a second, I imagine it, wandering in the crisp Nordic air beside Sawyer, listening as he points out everything he loves about the house.

But that's exactly what I don't want to do: stray into times and spaces that extend past Saturday and the gala. Sawyer and I have only existed in here and now. When I was young and immature, it wasn't enough. But I've had enough life experience since then to recognize that some magic exists only in a certain time and place, and there's a wisdom in embracing it fully for where and when it is.

Now to figure out that embrace . . .

I turn toward the open doorway. "Want to show me to the kitchen? I have a cheater fish to cook."

"Sticks and stones," he says.

"I wasn't trying to hurt your feelings, just stating facts."

"I wasn't talking about that rhyme. I was listing all the things you could have used and still not caught a bigger fish than I did."

"Ooooh," I say, darting for one of the indigo throw pillows on his pale gray sofa. I snatch it

180

and start after him, but he's already ducking through the doorway, laughing. I chase him through a sunny dining room, too intent on getting him back to absorb the details, but in the next room, I stop short, the chase forgotten.

We have entered the kitchen. Calling it a home kitchen is like saying Notre Dame is a church. This gleaming space is the cathedral of home kitchens, gleaming copper pans hanging from a rack over—what else—an enormous Viking range.

The hand wielding the pillow falls to my side, and I turn in big-eyed silence, devouring every detail.

"You like it?" he asks. His eyes are on me, intent.

I only nod and keep turning. I can't wait to explore his built-ins and investigate his pantry. It's probably organized with brilliant Scandinavian efficiency. "Yeah, I like it."

I drop the pillow and trail my fingers over the blue enamel knobs of the Viking. *Oh, my precious*. My cheeks heat even though I wasn't dumb enough to say it out loud.

"I'll put Speckles in here until you need him." He opens a birch panel to reveal a fridge I will fantasize about tonight. I know it. "Let me know what else you need but explore wherever. If I don't have something here, I can ask Lisa to send Kylie or Jared over with it."

"Point me to your pantry and be warned I can and will make myself at home in any kitchen."

"Good. I want you to. Pantry is over there." He points to a door. "Is it going to make you uncomfortable if I hang out here while you cook?"

"No. Do you still suck in the kitchen?" He'd always floundered when his cabin had dinner shift.

"Not as much," he says, smiling. "You want a sous chef?"

I hesitate. "I don't know. Do I?"

Instead of answering, he goes to a wooden bowl on the windowsill above the sink and pulls out a tomato. He's already scored points by not keeping it in the fridge. If Rachael Ray is known for her deep love of EVOO, my viewers know me for my constant pleas to store their produce correctly.

Next, he pulls a Wusthof chef's knife from a knife block that is a work of art in itself, grabs a bamboo chopping board, and sets the tomato on it. His movements are relaxed. I note how easily he finds everything, how he holds the tomato with his fingers tucked under like a trained chef would and begins to slice, his knife so sharp it slides through without any mushing.

I'm going to swoon.

"How about if I make a salad while you do your thing?" he asks. "That way I'm out of your hair."

A laugh lurks below those words. He has clearly acquired superior kitchen skills in the last decade. Not superior to mine but better than he has any right to be without training.

"Got any other cool tricks I should know about?" I ask.

He meets my eyes—his in an unmistakably heavy-lidded sexy smolder—and gives me his half smile. "A few." Then he goes back to slicing.

He—

What—

I . . .

I turn and bump into a cabinet and throw a quick glance back to see if he noticed. He's concentrating on his tomato, but when I turn around again, I swear I hear a single, soft laugh.

I add it to the list of things I owe him payback for, a plan taking shape in my mind.

He's got game now, it's true. But so do I.

An hour later, I serve him a fish that once inspired a minor sultan of Oman to propose marriage, but I'd passed. He'd sent me a divine Balenciaga bag the next week as a sign of his gratitude. I'm not even a handbag girl, but no lie, that bag made me understand the obsession.

"It smells amazing, which is not a thing I usually say about fish," he says.

He's set the table at the breakfast bar in the kitchen, and I'm glad. I don't want to be in a formal dining room with him. I want it cozy, even if this kitchen is twice the size of my generous kitchen in Brooklyn.

I've plated our dinners already, his salad fresh and bright beside the fish and pilaf I made.

"I wouldn't normally serve tomatoes out of season," he says. "But I wanted to impress you with my knife skills."

"You did," I promise. "And when you didn't store them in the fridge, and had a properly sharpened knife, and even knew tomatoes aren't in season yet."

I pick up my fork and knife, keeping my eyes on my plate so he won't know how badly I want to see his reaction to the fish. "People don't understand how much of a difference those details make. I preach that stuff on my show all the time."

"Where do you think I learned all that? I told you, I watch your show. We've cooked together a ton of times. You just didn't know it."

"Seriously?"

"I prop my iPad on the counter, stream the show, and make stuff with you step-by-step. I have to pause it a lot, especially if it's a technique I don't know, but I've got most of them down now."

I sit back, completely speechless.

His eyebrows go up. "Creepy?"

No. Definitely not creepy. I shake my head.

He takes his first bite of fish, chews twice, pauses, lets out a soft sigh, and keeps eating.

What does that mean? I'm out of practice in

reading him. He has to like it. It's good fish. I can tell before I even taste it.

I take a bite to make sure.

"Incredible," he says as I verify that fact with my own tastebuds, and I relax.

I need for there to be words between us, light words, distracting words. It feels dangerous to sit in silence with this man. I feel a verge, and casual conversation will keep me from its edge.

"Tell me more about Norway," I say.

"One of the most beautiful places I've ever been," he begins. The rest of the meal passes easily as we share notes on travel.

He refuses to let me help with any of the remaining cleanup when we're done. "I've got it. I'll walk you home."

We're quiet on the trail. He doesn't speak again until we stop in front of my cottage.

"I had a great time today."

I smile up at him. "I did too. I like making new, uncomplicated memories here. Friend."

"Yeah." He reaches out and tucks my hair behind my ear then lets his hand fall away. "I agree."

I haven't been this nervous about a goodnight on the doorstep in years. I want him to kiss me. But also, I don't. I don't want the game to be over yet. Either way, I can't stop staring at his mouth.

He notices and smiles, leaning down. But he only slides his arms around me in a hug. It's not a comforting hug. It's not a "had a great time" hug. It's a hug that says "stay tuned for more" as he pulls me against him and makes his hands active participants, molding me to him from hip to chest. I feel every one of his next three breaths before he lets me go, and that's when I quietly release the breath I've been holding since he touched me.

"Goodnight," he says quietly and waits to see me in.

"Keeping me safe in the high-crime 'hood of Oak Crest?"

"No. Just stealing every extra second with you I can, friend."

"Nicely done, Sawyer Reed," I say softly, and he gives me a small smile. "Good night, friend." I slip inside and lean against the door.

No, definitely not ready for this game to be over yet.

Chapter Eighteen

It's early when I wake up, and I decide to head for the lodge even though Natalie has also made it clear Lisa has the kitchen fully under control and bringing me in had always been a cover story.

"We wanted you here. It wouldn't have felt right without you," she'd explained during our long breakfast yesterday. When I insisted again on waiving my fee, she'd swept aside my objections. "Nope. Sawyer is cutting that check whether you like it or not."

"Great. Tell him to make it out to the Oak Crest Foundation." That's the charity making it possible for underprivileged kids to have a sleep-away camp experience.

"I told him you'd say that. Work it out amongst yourselves."

I slip into my kitchen kit anyway. I like being in the kitchen, and I like Lisa, so I'll spend my morning helping out until it's time to get changed for whatever "arts and crafts" Sawyer has planned this afternoon. That's all I know to expect.

At three o'clock sharp, he knocks, and I answer to find him in black plaid shorts and a gray T-shirt that looks so soft, my fingers itch to touch it. I'd suffered from that impulse a few times in the canoe too. He has to stop with these soft T-shirts, or . . . well, he needs to stop.

I fold my hands beneath my armpits and lean against the doorframe, trying to appear super casual in my white cotton shorts and flowy orange tank top. "Crafts are a trap," I say. I'm notoriously bad at them.

"Does it make you feel better if I picked something neither of us can mess up?"

I straighten. "Yeah, actually."

"Let's go." He turns then stops and turns back around. "If I say we're doing this at my house again because it's the only quiet place to work around here, do you promise not to think I'm seducing you?"

I roll my eyes. "You've made it clear that's not the plan."

"It's just with the VIP guests checking in today, the rest of these cabins are going to be booked, and there's not a corner or a closet where you won't trip over a counselor around camp."

"It's okay. I believe you." I badger him for details on the walk over. "Are we making lanyards?"

"Classic, but no."

"How about a dream catcher?"

"Nope."

By the time we step into his clearing I've guessed leather stamping, finger crochet, tie-dye underpants, and voodoo dolls. Turns out to be none of those either.

We climb the stairs to his deck, and I burst out laughing. He's set up a folding table like the ones in the lodge for crafts, but this one is more beat up. A few bins full of string in every color imaginable sit on it.

"Friendship bracelets?"

"Felt like the right move." He grins at me, and I love that his smile lines are carved deeper now around his mouth.

"Points for theme, but bad news: I can definitely mess these up."

"We can figure this out." He leads me to the table and slides onto the bench beside me.

While he opens the bins, I study the tabletop. It's scuffed and worn with years of old paint and glitter cemented to its surface, bumps of dried glue, stray crayon everywhere. "This is beat up enough to be one of our original camp tables."

"It is, actually." He sounds like he's working so hard to be casual. He doesn't meet my eyes as he pries loose the last bin lid.

"Why hold onto it?"

"Seems like a smart thing to keep in the garage. Never know when you're going to need an extra table."

I eye the string colors he selected. "How dare you, sir?"

He holds red, white, and navy blue, his face

way too innocent. "What? I thought these were classics that never go out of style?"

Red Sox colors. I snatch them from his hands and throw them off the deck.

"Fine. Those aren't the colors I wanted anyway." He picks through the bin again and comes up with teal, yellow, and white. I squint, trying to figure out how he's trolling me this time. "The colors from your *'Dinner Reborn'* logo."

My heart goes a tiny bit gooey. Not only does he watch my show, he's paid enough attention to remember the logo? I clear my throat. "What are your college colors?" I pick out gray, black, and red when he tells me. "Okay, show me how to screw this up."

"I've seen you spatchcock a turkey. You got this."

I do not "got" this.

Twenty minutes later, I glare up at him from a hopeless chunk of knots. "Maybe this is a metaphor for our friendship." I peer at his. He has a half-inch section of neatly alternating teal, yellow, and white lines. "Is this because you're an engineer? Is this why you can do precision knots?"

The tips of his ears redden. "Not exactly."

I wrap my hand around his fingers so he can't tie anymore. "Sawyer Stretch Reed, tell me what you're not telling me."

He looks down at our hands and turns his so

our fingers tangle. "I made my niece teach me how to do them, and I practiced. I can help you if you want."

I brush my thumb along his. "I do want."

His eyes meet mine. For a second, it falls so quiet it's like every living thing in earshot holds its breath. Then his eyes slide away, and he turns on the bench, drawing one leg over it to straddle it. "Turn around," he says. "I need to sit behind you to help."

Let it never be said I don't sacrifice for art. I whirl on the bench so he can wrap himself around me for this tutorial. He moves the string taped to the table and resecures it on the bench in front of us.

"Do this." His legs bracket mine, and he reaches around me to pick up the loose strings. His voice rumbles in my ear, sending goose bumps down my arms. He places a different color thread between each of my fingers and lets a teal string hang loose. "Watch." I keep my eyes on his hands, weaving in and out of the strings wound around mine. I've always loved his hands. His long fingers, his slightly rough palms.

He finishes a row of teal. "Got it?"

"Better hang out while I try." I take a yellow string and don't even try to copy what he did, messing it up so he'll have to stay and tutor me longer.

He offers corrections every now and then,

which I take, then promptly mess up the next time. After the fourth knot, his low laugh gives me more goose bumps. "How are you so bad at this?"

"Show me again."

He does another row, and when he turns it over to me, I mess up.

After the second knot, he rests his chin on my shoulder. "Tab."

"Yeah?" I barely have breath after the light rasp of his chin against my bare skin.

"Are you doing this on purpose?"

"Depends. Are you going back to your seat if I do this right?"

He goes motionless. He doesn't say anything for a long moment. Have I pushed the game too far?

"I better stay here as a supervisor."

Relief ripples through me. "I bet I could do a much better job if you did."

"I'll sit right here like one of those trainers in the corner of a boxing ring, keeping you loose so you can do your best work." He settles into a gentle neck rub, and I nearly swallow my tongue. "Is there a problem?" he asks when I haven't moved after a few seconds. His tone is knowing.

Oh, Sawyer Reed. You forget who you're dealing with. "No, it's just, I was thinking." I make my next knot in the bracelet with no problem. I turn my head as if to see him better while I talk, scooching back slightly as I make the adjustment. His knees press against mine in a warning. I bite back a smile. My move puts our mouths close together. "You're right about the kissing."

He's quiet for a second. "I am?"

"Yeah. We should definitely not do the friends with benefits thing. Take it off the table. Eliminate the mystery, you know? Then there's no wondering if each moment is *the* moment I'll find out what you've learned in the last ten years."

He swings himself around to settle in front of me on the bench. "So like, for instance, if I leaned over right now"—and he does, moving slowly as he speaks, his eyes on my lips—"to kiss you, you would definitely say no?"

His lips hover a couple of inches from mine.

Sneaky, sneaky, Sawyer. I close the gap until there's barely room for a breath between us. "Right," I whisper. Then I straighten and go to work on my knots. "Hope you like this *friendship* bracelet."

"I'm sure I'll love it." He moves back to his original spot to work on his. The air vibrates between us, and I'm not sure who I've punished, exactly.

"Tell me what it's like to be super famous," he says.

I snort. "I'm famous enough to sell cookbooks,

which is exactly the right kind of famous. I can move around New York without people recognizing me too often, and that's how I like it."

"Do you like it there?"

"Love it. It's hard not to."

"Tell me about it."

So I do, telling him about my favorites, from bookstores to lesser known parks, and hidden gems of cafés to the ethnic markets in Little Ethiopia and Chinatown where I go for inspiration.

"You ever think about leaving?" he asks after a while.

"I'm happy there. My career is there. I couldn't make it work anywhere else, and I don't want to." I lay my cards on the table, so he doesn't get the wrong idea from our game.

"I like it too," he says. "More than I thought I would. I guess Chicago prepped me for it."

"Have you been there much?"

"Every month." I glance over at him in surprise. "I'm developing a project in Secaucus. I stay in the city though. I'll have to try the places you mentioned."

Well, that's a large bomb to drop and then keep tying knots as if nothing happened. "You're in New York *every month?*"

"I am."

I pause in my bracelet making, trying to process that.

"Come here. I want to show you something." He stands and walks to the corner of the table, the one farthest from me, and waits for me to join him. When I do, he points down to some faded Sharpie letters in the corner. "Can you read that?"

TW + SR.

No hearts. No "4-ever." Just plain black Sharpie, and even though I don't know Sawyer's hand-writing, I suspect I'm looking at it.

"I couldn't believe it when I found it during renovations."

"That's why you kept this table?"

He pulls a Sharpie from his back pocket. "I've been waiting to update this. Now feels right." He bends down and adds something beneath the initials. "There."

I lean forward to see it better. Now it reads, *TW + SR For Real.*

He goes to his spot on the bench and pulls tape from the table with a soft *snckkk*. He comes back with his finished bracelet and picks up my wrist to fasten the teal and yellow bracelet around it. "Friends, right?"

I look down at the neat rows he'd learned to tie to impress me. "Yes. Friends."

His finger feathers over the bracelet, grazing my skin, but I feel it *everywhere*. "I'm glad to hear you say that. Thought you might be getting . . . sidetracked."

The rat. His soft touches are torturous. "Not at all. I'm fully here for this. What's next?"

He releases my wrist. "Wait right here. I'll be back." He disappears into the house and reappears with a grocery bag filled with two-liter Diet Cokes. He fishes around in the bag and produces two rolls of Mentos.

"You're kidding," I say.

"Would I kid about soda rockets? Let's take this to the yard."

We spend the next hour trying to generate increasingly fizzy explosions and laughing, and I think about how much fun any kid would have playing in this forest-enclosed yard.

Shoot, it's fun for me. I can't remember the last time I laughed this much, especially when Sawyer makes a major miscalculation and ends up with a face full of Diet Coke.

He tops it all off by leading me to the opposite side of his house and the open garage, revealing two ATVs. "I borrowed them from the camp. There's some pretty cool trails around here. You down?"

"I'm down," I confirm, beelining for the bright green one.

For the next two hours, we race and explore, checking out the side of Lake Lupine opposite camp, a part I've never explored before. It's as lake-y and woodsy as our side, but I love driving through it with Sawyer, frequently stopping to admire a bird or a plant or whatever catches our attention.

Mostly that's Sawyer. He's got all my attention, and everything else—the giant lake, big forest, and basically Mother Nature—get whatever scraps of attention I have left.

This reminds me so much of old summers. The jokes, the easy vibe, the sense of adventure and possibility of what we'll find in the next glade or hollow. But nothing reminds me of that time more than my uncertainty about Sawyer. The same questions that ran through my mind then run through it now: *Does he like me? Like, like me or* like *me? Does he just want to be friends for real? It seems like there's more there, but how much* more*? I want it to be maybe "fun summer make out" more, not the angsty kind of more. So what if he* likes *me? Do I hit him with a water balloon and escape? Do I want to escape?*

We finally drive the ATVs back to the main office. We cut the engines and Sawyer smiles at me. "Walk you home?"

"Sure." I remove my helmet and leave it on the seat, and we head toward the guest house trail. He doesn't try to take my hand or even start a conversation. He's always been like that, instinctively understanding how to respect my space. And now, like then, it's a comfortable silence as we walk the half mile through the woods. When it ends at the clearing for the family cabins, he stays on the trail as I step out from the trees.

"Have I made my case for friendship yet?" he asks.

I give a careless shrug. "I don't know, *buddy*. I was promised three dat—hangs—before I decide. Need to gather more data."

"Fully supported. I was thinking a picnic. Tomorrow. The old dock. Sunrise."

The scene of the crime. The one that screwed us up all these years. Same place. Same time. Same activity.

What. Is. He. Up. To?!

CHAPTER NINETEEN

I wake up the next morning to a thunderclap followed by a knock on the cottage door.

Sawyer.

I hop out of bed and throw on my robe, reaching the door as he knocks again. But when I open it, Natalie stands there in a dripping poncho, smiling, and I pull her in out of the rain.

"Hey. I didn't wake you up, did I?"

Fully aware my fresh bedhead looks like Juniper styled my hair with an eggbeater, I point to my curls. "Nope. This is a choice."

"Bold."

"What's up? Something wrong?"

"No, everything is good. But your sister called the office last night asking for you. She said you're in big trouble and call her back right away, but also, it's not an emergency. And Sawyer said to tell you he'll figure out a different activity."

I smile. "Thanks for telling me. Sorry you had to come all the way down here to deliver that. You could have sent Kylie or Jared with it."

"Sure, but when I told them to hit you up for all the details on your sexy times with Sawyer, they expressed concern."

"Dork. There are no sexy times to report. Why would you even think that?"

"Make some up and thrill me."

I point to the small table. "You sit there and be quiet while I make coffee. I will not make up any sexy times, but I do have stuff to tell you."

She pulls off her poncho and holds up an unopened one she's brought for me before setting them both on the coat hooks by the door. I describe the first two dates to her, and as always, she's the best audience ever. Gasps, questions, exclamations, a hand clap when I tell her about the flirting over bracelets.

"I can't wait for Juniper to be your flower girl next year."

"Um, jumping the gun there." Her joke sends a prickle of sensation through my stomach, chest, and palms, but I can't interpret it. It's a sudden surge of something, but I can't tell if it's adrenaline or nausea.

"Just manifesting what I want. Thanks for the coffee. It's Ben's turn to watch Juniper today, so I need to go run the office. Pop in whenever you want to call your sister back." She washes out her mug then leaves.

I finish my coffee and change quickly so I can go find out what Grace needs. I bike up to the office, frowning at the sky turning the lake gray. I'm sure Sawyer has a—well, a backup plan for the rain, but I'm always less anxious when I know what it is.

Natalie is helping a couple at the office counter

when I walk in, so I wave and duck into the nurse's office. I have Wi-Fi calling here so I don't need the landline.

Grace picks up on the first ring. "Tabitha Leigh Winters, are you at Oak Crest?"

I wince. "Why are you speaking to me in capital letters?"

"Why didn't you tell us you're in town?"

"Us? Where are you?" She lives in Charleston.

"Creekville," she says. "I'm helping Noah pack, and we drive back on Sunday."

"That's this weekend?" I knew Noah had already accepted a teaching job in a school district out there, but I hadn't realized he had finished here.

"Yep. Wednesday was the students' last day, and today it's his, but we got most of his school stuff packed up already. So anyway, when are you coming here?"

"I'm not," I say. "I'm at Oak Crest for work, so that's why I didn't tell Mom and Dad. I knew it would be too busy for me to get away."

"Tab, come on. We see each other once a year. Let's break the record and see each other *twice*. I'm sure Nat will let you borrow the Rust Bucket to drive over."

"It's a non-rusty newer van now."

"Sounds terrible. Borrow it and come see us. At least for a couple of hours."

"If I'd known you were going to be here too, I would have totally planned for it, but—"

"Tabitha, it's Memorial Day weekend. You have to come see Grammy and Grandad."

It's a dirty card to play. They're buried in Creekville Memorial Park, and we used to visit their graves every Memorial Day to pay our respects when we were kids.

"Grace . . ."

"They're so sad."

"Ugh. Hold on." I poke my head out of the nurse's office, and sure enough, through the main office window, I can see dimples in the lake as the rain pelts it. I debate for a minute, but truthfully, I could use some downtime to process yesterday's hang with Sawyer. I go back to the phone. "I hate to reward you for being a little manipulator, but you win. I can make it out for a few hours."

"Good," she says. "Text me when you get to the store."

We hang up, and I'm trying to figure out the least damp way to let Sawyer know about my plans, but he's standing in the office when I walk out.

"Hey," he says. "Fancy meeting you here."

I blink at him. "Did I conjure you?"

"Uh, no?"

"I was literally coming to look for you."

"You found me. What's up?"

I crook my head at the nurse's office, and he follows me in.

"I had to come here once when I got a bloody

202

nose during Capture the Flag," he says. He looks at the single bed and desk. The space is even smaller than a standard exam room. He frowns at the bed. "You don't think Warren and Debbie—"

I clap my hands over my ears and glare at him.

He lies down on the cot. It's narrower than a twin bed and he has to bend his knees to fit. "It's definitely gross to think about them in here. We should test it and see if it's even possible. For science."

His dark eyes glint at me, and my jaw drops the tiniest bit. I think he's joking, but all I'd have to do is take the two steps to reach him, and neither of us would be laughing. We'd be—

Natalie pops her head in the door. "You didn't shut this all the way and we can hear you," she hisses. Sawyer makes a face like, *Oops,* and I bite my lip to keep from laughing. "Also, we've totally tested it, and it definitely works." Then she disappears, leaving us gaping after her.

"That was information I could have lived without." He jumps to his feet so quickly that I do laugh. His mouth twists. "Yeah, yeah, it's funny because you aren't the one who laid on it."

"And I can't thank you enough for making sure I never do." Thunder rumbles. "Since we have a rain delay, I'm going to go into Creekville. My sister called because she heard I was at camp. She's in town to move her boyfriend out to

Charleston, and I'm going to hang with her for a bit."

He gives an easy shrug. "I had a pretty good Plan B lined up, but that sounds more fun. I've always wanted to see Creekville."

I freeze. This is awkward. "Oh, I didn't mean . . ."

The tops of his ears go pink. "That you wanted me to come," he finishes.

My stomach drops in an I-did-a-bad-thing way. "It's not that I don't want you to."

His forehead furrows. "So you do want me to come?"

"Um, well, not that either. It's just . . . we're going to go visit my grandparents' graves and the only slightly more exciting place we'll go is the hardware store. You're not missing much."

He doesn't say anything, only watches me for a few seconds.

"Can I get a raincheck?" Another low rumble of thunder sounds, and I point to the ceiling. "Like a literal one? Just until tomorrow. We could do our third hang tomorrow, right?"

"I can't," he says. "I have to help make sure we've got everything ready for the—"

"Gala," I finish, embarrassed I forgot the whole reason I'd come here. Even though I hadn't needed to do much work beyond designing the menu, my "star power" will still be a big perk for the VIPs, according to Natalie. "Right, of course.

Don't know why I said that. What if we make the gala our third date?"

He smiles, but I can tell it's taking effort. I've hurt his feelings by not bringing him with me to Creekville, but . . . that's home. And Sawyer is Camp Oak Crest.

"Good plan," he says. "Guess I'll go check with Ben to see what he needs help with."

"Right, and I'll see you tomorrow."

He steps out of the office, not meeting my eyes. "Enjoy Creekville."

"Cemetery should be a blast."

He winces. "Wow, I'm a jerk."

I grin. "No, I am. It's not sad to go there. They died when I was young, so I've had plenty of time to get used to it. Our family likes going."

He comes back in and reaches out to cup my jaw, his thumb running lightly over my lips. My breath turns shallow. "Is there such a thing as a Tabitha onion?" He doesn't take his eyes off my mouth.

"No," I say, and the movement presses my lips against his thumb, like a kiss.

He lets his hand drop and meets my eyes. "There should be. Layers and layers."

Then he walks out, shutting the door firmly behind him.

CHAPTER TWENTY

I park Natalie's Yukon behind Handy Hardware, the store my dad has owned my whole life. Grace had to take over running it last year while he was sick, but once he was in remission and his strength came back, she had gotten her own life back on track. Not only had Boeing rehired her, she'd gotten a promotion.

I'm happy for her. We'd had some misunderstandings last year, mainly because I didn't want anyone to know I was paying my dad's bills. It would have stressed my parents out too much. Paying those bills was equivalent to buying a new Tesla every month. Staying on top of those payments meant grinding even harder at work, pushing myself to exhaustion to promote my cookbook, taking every endorsement opportunity that came my way.

My funds had gotten excruciatingly low a few times, but now, slowly, my savings is rebuilding. And I'd do it all again in a heartbeat. But this time, I'd tell Grace, so we didn't lose another year to tense conversations and hurt feelings because she'd thought she was doing all the helping on her own.

I walk around to the front of the store, admiring the assistant manager's window display. She's done a Memorial Day barbecue-themed scene, and it makes me want to buy a Traeger just to have as much fun as she's making the mannequins look like they're having.

Paige, the window genius herself, is behind the register when I walk in. She looks better than the last time I saw her at Christmas where she could have been the poster child for overworked single mothers. She's put on badly needed weight. Her hair shines and her skin glows.

"Hey, Tabitha. What a surprise! I had no idea you were in town."

"Technically I'm not. I'm at Camp Oak Crest doing an event, but my plans were canceled because of the rain, so here I am."

"You mean you canceled your plans there and came to see us because you love us more," my dad said, emerging from the landscaping aisle.

"That's exactly what I meant," I say as he folds me into a bear hug. "Where's Grace?"

"She's coming." He gives Paige a sympathetic smile. "Said to tell you Evie is unpacking everything as fast as Noah can pack it."

Paige gives a resigned sigh. "She's going to miss her uncle."

"Are *you* okay with him leaving?" I ask.

Paige is Noah's younger sister, and unless I suck at reading people—and I don't—she'll be Grace's sister-in-law sooner than later. If Noah doesn't propose by Christmas, I'll buy everyone in my family an actual Tesla. Even six-year-old Evie, who will no doubt figure out how to drive one faster than her adoptive grandparents—my mom and dad—who offered themselves for the job at Christmas, probably tired of waiting for Grace and me to produce grandbabies for them. They're all-in kind of people, so Paige and Evie now live in the apartment above the garage for the cost of utilities, an arrangement they all love.

That was also when Paige had put together the most thoughtful present for Noah, even better than the puppy I gave my mom so she'd back off of me and Grace. Paige had presented him with a compelling case for why he should follow Grace four hundred miles south to Charleston. But now that his departure is here, maybe she has regrets.

But she's nodding. "I'm going to miss him, but I'm excited for them. And Evie and I have proven to ourselves we can totally do this. I finished two classes this semester in business management, and I'll get my associate's degree next Christmas. And I learned a ton."

"It's true," my dad says, his arm around my shoulder but beaming at Paige like he often beams at Grace and me. "She tries everything she learns here, and sales have never been better."

"There have been a few misses," Paige confesses. "But even those teach me something."

I smile up at my dad. "Do you know how lucky you are to have her?"

He gives me a squeeze. "We sure do. Now tell me how the camp is looking."

We talk until Grace shows up a few minutes later, dressed in joggers and a T-shirt, with a sweaty face that says she's been doing some heavy lifting.

"Hey," she says, giving me a hug. "Still drizzling, so let's get the cemetery tools and wait for a break in the rain over at Bixby's. But seriously, Tab, please don't bug her for her chocolate croissant recipe again."

We grab the mini-broom, rags, and brass polish we'll need for the cemetery and walk over to Bixby's Café. From there we'll walk on to the cemetery. No point in driving when all these places are separated by less than ten minutes on foot.

"Good to see you, Winters girls," Taylor Bixby says when we walk in. "What can I get you? And no."

"She means no, you can't have her recipe," Grace tells me.

"I know. Almond torte and please?"

"Still no," Taylor says, smiling.

"I'm always going to try," I tell her.

"Acknowledged. Never going to happen."

"Acknowledged."

We've just gotten our orders when the door opens and Lily Greene walks in, looking as vigorous as ever with her perfectly set white hair and Lilly Pulitzer dress. She spots us right away. "Is Memorial Day the new Christmas?" she asks. "How delightful to have you both in town. I assume you'll be heading to the cemetery soon. Have you bought flowers yet?"

"Not yet, Miss Lily," Grace tells her. "What do you recommend?"

"I recommend you not buy flowers, that's what. I've got an overabundance of lilies-of-the-valley, and if you don't mind walking over to the cemetery with me, I'd be pleased to share them with you. I think your Ruth will love them."

"Grammy loved lilies," I say. "We'd be happy to walk over with you."

She orders her tea and joins our table, her gaze on the rain outside. "It ought to clear shortly. These things don't last long this close to summer. Now tell me for real, my dears. What brings you both back to Creekville today?"

Grace catches her up on getting Noah moved to Charleston, but of course, Miss Lily already knows all about it. She'd nudged them along a couple of times. She does that sometimes if she doesn't believe things are moving at the correct pace. You rarely ever feel her doing it, but many a Creekville resident has suddenly found themselves exactly where Miss Lily thought they should be. And when. And with who. Er, whom. She'd been my dad's English teacher, so I'd better get that right.

"And you, dear?" Miss Lily asks, her guileless blue eyes fluttering to me.

"You know Camp Oak Crest?"

"Of course. You worked there in college."

"Right." I try to not look discomfited by her extraordinary recall and catch her up on the grand reopening.

"And you're their star attraction for this gala," she says. "It's generous for you to come back so often to help us out."

"It is," Grace agrees. I smile at her, having done her a similar favor over Christmas. That, and nudging her to give Noah a shot. I have no idea she means to return the favor until she leans toward Miss Lily with a conspiratorial smile. "Also, her first love turned out to be the silent partner in this reopening, and he orchestrated this whole thing so he could get her back to the camp and rekindle something."

My jaw drops as Miss Lily's eyes sparkle. "Do tell."

I glare at Grace. "Natalie told you."

She doesn't deny it. "You heard Miss Lily. Do tell."

"There's not much to tell." I begin the delicate process of sidestepping their questions. "It's not a rekindling thing." At least, it *better* not be, but who knew after his sunrise dock picnic suggestion? "We're rebuilding a friendship so our mutual friends aren't always caught in the middle."

"Was he truly your first love?" Miss Lily asks.

"Yes," Grace confirms.

"And how is the rebuilding going?"

"Fine," I say.

"But there's nothing more?" Miss Lily presses.

"How could there be more?" I shift in my seat, not liking the full weight of her attention. "I haven't spoken to him in nine years."

"Until this week," Grace corrects me.

"And it's going well?" Miss Lily asks.

"Yes, given everything," I say.

She nods. "You'll have plenty of time to plan a spring wedding for next year. I'd be delighted to host a dinner for you. Or a brunch if you prefer." She turns to Grace as I try to figure out how this conversation got so far off the rails. "Grace, dear, a bridal shower would be loveliest of all. I'm sure your mother will want to throw it, but will you assure her I'd be delighted to offer up my home?"

"Excuse me." I've wandered into a parallel universe where people are having conversations about my life that make no sense. "I'm not getting married."

She is, Grace mouths.

"Stop that." I give her a stern look.

"Where is he, by the way?" Miss Lily asks, glancing around as if it's only now occurred to her that we're missing my fiancé.

"At the camp."

"He didn't want to come home with you for a

visit?" She frowns, like she might be changing her position on this wedding that is absolutely not a thing.

"He did," I admit, not willing to throw him under the bus when he can't defend himself. "I didn't invite him."

"Tabitha," Grace says on a groan.

"Is there something wrong with him, some reason you wouldn't want to bring him to meet your family?" Miss Lily asks.

"No, of course not."

"I don't see anything 'of course' about it." Her gaze is narrowing. This has never been good news.

"There's nothing wrong with him. He's smart, funny, successful, handsome. You'd love him."

Grace responds to this by throwing her hands out as if to say, *Well? Where is he?*

"We are only *friends*." I try to articulate the feeling that kept me from bringing Sawyer along. "It's been great spending time with him. *At* Oak Crest. The last few days have given me *closure*."

Miss Lily frowns slightly at "closure."

"Can you give him my number?" Taylor calls from behind the counter. "I'll marry him."

Miss Lily looks from the pretty café owner to me. "I'd venture to guess Taylor has not by any means been his first offer in the last several years."

"Probably not," I agree.

"I've seen him. Definitely not," Grace says.

Miss Lily takes a drink from her teacup, her eyes steady on me as she returns it to the saucer. "You didn't bring him with you because you're afraid."

"I . . . what? No."

"You are," she says, not at all ruffled that I've contradicted her. "What frightens you more: discovering the two of you exist outside of your summer camp memories? Or discovering you don't?"

Grace's eyes grow big, and her lips form a silent O before she mouths, *Mic. Drop.*

Miss Lily pats my hand. "I'm sorry, dear. I would normally help you figure that out over the course of a month or so, but since you're only here for the afternoon, we've got to do the AP version. I'll stop tormenting you, but I leave you to consider that question. You're afraid to put something to the test. You should ask yourself why." She glances toward the window. "The rain has stopped. Shall we head to the cemetery?"

Grace and I rise and follow her outside, listening to her gentle rambles as we walk. She's telling us about the graves she'll visit, and her memories of the three local men killed during World War II. I've always loved Miss Lily's stories, but I'm barely able to follow from one to the next as her question chases itself through my mind.

I'm not afraid to put anything to the test. I proved that by coming to Camp Oak Crest. I'd laid my ghosts to rest before I knew Sawyer was there.

But even as we sweep and clean our grandparents' shared grave, even as we set Miss Lily's flowers in the attached vase, even as Grace and I part ways at the store, even as I drive the hour back to Oak Crest, I hear Miss Lily's question in my mind:

What frightens you more?

CHAPTER TWENTY-ONE

I rise early and throw on my kitchen togs. I have lots of thinking to do, and there's nowhere better for me to do it than with a knife in my hand.

Lisa's in the kitchen already, of course.

But so is my mom. And it's only then do I realize I never talked to her yesterday.

I'd planned to stop by the house on way out of town, but I was so distracted by Miss Lily's question that I'd driven on autopilot all the way back to Oak Crest.

I'm a crap human. There is no way around this fact.

"Mom. I'm so sorry."

She gives me a bright smile, but she's a bad faker. Grace is the same way. You can read their faces like a clock. "Hey, honey. I thought since I missed you yesterday, I'd come here and see you."

I walk over and hug her, resting my head on her shoulder. "Mom, I really am sorry." There's literally no way to explain how I accidentally blew her off that won't make her feel worse. *I was so distracted by my college crush that I forgot to come see you.*

"I had a feeling I'd find you if I hung around the kitchen long enough," she murmurs into my shoulder.

"I'm helping Lisa prep for the gala dinner tonight. Want to help?" My mom and I don't work well together in the kitchen—she forgets I do this professionally, and I forget she was my first kitchen instructor—but I owe her at least this much.

"Would love to."

I grab her a clean apron from the supply closet and introduce her to Lisa as my mom.

"I connected the dots," Lisa says.

"You ready to do this?"

"I'm ready," Lisa says.

I planned the weekly camp menus, and this gala dinner is meant to be elegant while referencing the food Camp Oak Crest will serve the kiddos. I chose a theme of "Campfire Deconstructed," polished versions of summer camp classics.

The trusty foil dinner of ground beef, green beans, and corn will become a filet mignon—portobello mushroom for our vegetarians—with rosemary fondant potatoes, sweet corn tamale cakes, and nut-roasted green beans. Similarly, instead of s'mores, we're doing a decadent chocolate cheesecake on a graham cracker crust topped with chocolate ganache and finished with house-made marshmallows we'll toast with the mini-torches usually reserved for crème brûlée.

It's a good menu with enough novelty for the meal to feel special without being so innovative that the guests won't enjoy it. The big money donors filling up the other seven cabins later this week paid two thousand per person for this dinner, so their enjoyment is paramount.

There's plenty of prep to do, and while Lisa doesn't *need* my help, I need to be here, keeping busy.

"Let's make crusts, Mom. We need enough for eight cheesecakes." Enough to feed our guests plus all the counselors later. We take our boxes of graham crackers and large Ziploc bags to a corner out of Lisa's way and set about crushing them. It's cathartic. Pounding and smooshing things in the kitchen usually is. They have to be ground fine, so I go over the crumbs with a rolling pin for good measure.

After we each demolish two boxes of crackers, my mom breaks the silence. "Why didn't you come see me yesterday?"

"I . . ." I haven't thought of an answer that isn't hurtful. So that's what I say. "I'm sorry. I didn't mean to hurt you."

"How did you think I was going to feel when you never stopped by the house?"

This feels intentional to her, and I understand it. "I forgot, Mom. I know that sounds bad, but I was distracted, and I got in my head and zoned out and drove here. I know that's thoughtless, but I hope it's better than thinking I blew you off on purpose."

"That you didn't even remember to come see me?" She pounds even harder at her crackers. "It's not better."

"I'm sorry."

We work in excruciating silence. I deserve every uncomfortable second of it.

"I think you did it on purpose," she says. Her voice is calm and quiet.

"Mom, I swear I—"

"Hear me out, Tabitha. Sometimes you can do things accidentally on purpose."

I don't respond because I have no idea what she means. I've only ever used that phrase as a joke, like when I would accidentally-on-purpose do things to bug Grace.

"There's a word for it," she says. "I forget it exactly, but maybe trauma response?"

"Mom, no. My life hasn't been nearly interesting enough for me to claim any trauma."

She shakes her head. "I don't know if trauma means what we think it means. Like war or bad accidents or anything violent. It can mean . . ."

I glance at her when she trails off, but she's wearing her concentration expression, like she's working through what she wants to say.

"It can mean you've had an overbearing mother with unreasonable expectations of you because she's trying to live through you vicariously. And maybe as she's pushing you to go further, she makes you feel like you're never good enough.

And so maybe you hardly ever come home anymore—"

"Because I'm busy, Mom, that's all." I hate hearing her sound so sad.

"Or because you know it's a place where you'll always feel like you're lacking. Maybe yesterday, when you were in town, you told yourself you would stop by, but some deeper part of you, the part that tries to keep you safe, it drew you out on the road and past our neighborhood, and you got back to your happy place."

I've completely stopped pounding crackers. "Have you been talking to Natalie? That smells like therapy."

She smiles and looks almost proud of herself. "No, but I've been seeing a counselor. Turns out your dad being sick was trauma for me too. And I've been *your* trauma."

"No, Mom, you haven't."

"I have. But I had a chance to figure a lot of this out with Grace last Christmas. I've thought about it ever since. It wasn't hard to figure out how it applied to you and me since it was the same thing."

At some point, the kitchen got quiet, and I realize it's only the two of us left. Lisa must have tactfully slipped out and taken her helpers with her. I feel bad. The last thing she needs is my family drama disrupting her gala preparations, but this conversation with my mom is important.

"Grace mentioned you'd talked some things through."

She stops smashing crackers. "I know you have lots to do. I really am here to help, and I don't want to hijack this whole day with family drama. Here's what I'll say, and then we better go get Lisa and get back to work: I love you. I'm sorry I've been judgmental about your career choices. That was about my stuff, not yours. I'm proud of you."

She goes back to crushing. I watch her, surprised, my hands full of crackers. Surprised . . . and overwhelmed. I've needed these words for a long time. My whole life. I had no idea I would get them today, and I almost can't take them in.

She smiles. "It's a lot. You don't need to say anything. I love you. We can talk about this another time. Now that Dad's better, maybe I can even come see you for a few days in New York?"

She's suggested coming to visit in the past, but I've always put her off with excuses about a busy taping schedule or promotional obligations. But this time, I nod. "I'd like that."

"Okay. Good. Tell Lisa she's safe to return."

I find her sitting at a dining table, reviewing the schedule for the day. "Sorry about that. We're done. Come on in."

My mom and I get back to work. And that's it. She doesn't push the issue, and she hangs out for a couple more hours helping before she needs to get back home to handle one of her real estate clients.

When she leaves, I give her a hug. A big one. The biggest one I've given her in years. And I've already set aside a weekend next month for her to come visit.

I walk her out to her car and wave as she drives off.

Well. This has certainly been a week for emotional bombshells.

Back in the kitchen, the whole time I work, I replay the last three days with Sawyer in my mind. From the minute he appeared on the porch with Ben and Natalie to his caress in the nurse's office, I turn over every look, every word, every touch.

The intensity in even our simplest interactions makes my pulse race. Or pound? I don't know. Why can't I tell the difference? Shouldn't I know this?

I channel my anxiety into cracking and beating the eggs. The cheesecakes will need to start baking soon to give them time to cool, then chill, and once I have them all in the oven, I can move on to prepping the corn cakes, which will also need to chill before baking.

At five-thirty, Lisa orders me home to get ready. I'll oversee the dinner service, but instead of my usual comfy kitchen clothes beneath my smock, I'll wear a dress, so I look decent when

222

Ben brings me out to introduce me to the dinner guests.

At six o'clock, I rush back to the kitchen, and the mad dash begins. I love this part of every dinner service, the moment where I feel the energy kick up a notch in preparation for the incoming diners. I want to do an especially good job tonight and treat Ben and Natalie to the most delicious meal of their lives so they can see how far I've come since the days when I'd cooked camp dinners in the old kitchen.

And Sawyer. It matters to me what he thinks. More than it should for someone I hadn't seen in nine years. And who I'm rebuilding a chat-over-juice-box friendship with.

It matters more than it should that I haven't seen him since yesterday morning in the nurse's office. That I keep finding excuses to work by the window in case I catch a glimpse of him outside. That I'm bummed when a crew of counselors comes in to decorate the lodge interior, and he's not there giving them orders.

The muted voices coming through the swinging kitchen doors grow louder as more guests arrive, and at seven o'clock, Ben's voice sounds on the PA system, welcoming everyone to this dinner with a menu designed and overseen by Camp Oak Crest graduate and celebrity chef . . . me.

I grin at Lisa as I slide the first plated sweet corn tamale cake onto a tray. "Let's go." She grins back, and we're off, buzzing and darting around the kitchen for the next hour as we send out appetizers then dinners. The counselors doubling as servers bring back a stream of compliments as they flit in and out, and finally, as the energy in the kitchen simmers down, Natalie pops in.

"I know you're sending out dessert soon. We'd like to bring you out with it. Ten minutes enough time?"

"Plenty."

"Ben will call your name, and we'll have you come through the doors followed by the platters of cheesecake."

"Got it." The servers are filling the rolling carts with sheets of plated desserts, so I duck into the broom closet, shuck off my chef smock, and trade my kitchen Crocs for red heels. I'm gladder than ever that I packed them even though I'd dithered in New York over whether they were too much for a night like this. But I love an excuse to go glam, and since I had to keep the rest of my outfit simple beneath the smock, the four-inch strappy sandals are a gorgeous counterpoint.

I walk to the head of the queuing servers and listen to the door until I hear, "We'd love to bring out one of Camp Oak Crest's most illustrious alums, Chef Tabitha Winters!"

I step through the doors to the applause of the seventy-five guests, smiling and waving as I make my way to the front of the mess hall. It's

224

been transformed into a high-end venue with tulle swaths, twinkle lights, and wildflowers, and I join Ben at the mic.

"Let her know how much you've enjoyed your first meal at Camp Oak Crest so far!" Ben orders into the mic, and the applause swells again.

"Thank you, guys," I say, doing the "settle down" gesture after several seconds. "Our counselors are bringing you our reimagined s'mores cheesecake with a chocolate ganache and house-made marshmallows. Part of the reason I know how to pull off a dinner like this is because of the opportunities I got as a camper, then counselor, here at Camp Oak Crest. Your kids will thrive here under the care and leadership of Ben and Natalie Mendoza, and we thank you for the generous donations that will allow even more kids to experience the magic these two incredible people are making here. Please enjoy your desserts!"

I step away from the mic to accept a hug from Natalie, who escorts me to a seat next to her at the head table, where I end up with Sawyer on my other side.

"Hey," he says, as I settle into my seat. "Dinner was incredible, but not half as amazing as you look."

"Thanks." The compliment makes my cheeks feel as warm as they did when I was standing over the gas range searing the steaks. I feel like I want to jump out of my skin, but I force myself through quiet calming breaths as a counselor sets a slice of dessert in front of each of us. I'm not about to confess this will be my third piece today, but dang, I make a good cheesecake. I'm not skipping this. "Everything been okay out here?"

"Great," he says. "We've even had several people increase their donation after spending the day doing camp activities."

Ben is speaking again. "And now to bring up our partner who has made a dream come true for Natalie and me, I'd like to present the developer of this project and many other sustainable green space projects around the country, Sawyer Reed!"

Sawyer gives a soft but distinctly annoyed curse. "He was supposed to leave me out of it," he grumbles, but he pastes on a smile and stands. He tries to acknowledge everyone with a wave, but Ben's gesturing for him to come up.

As Sawyer makes his way over, Ben continues, "Sawyer has worked tirelessly over the last six months to secure enough donations to fund one hundred kids over the course of the summer, kids whose lives will be changed forever, like all of ours were."

"He raised all that on his own," Natalie whispers, her eyes shining as she watches Sawyer walk up.

I choke a tiny bit on my cheesecake as I do the math. It means he raised over a quarter of a million dollars while overseeing a dozen other major projects.

Sawyer takes his place at the mic and smiles at the applause, even though it's tight around the edges. He never did love the spotlight. "Thank you to all of you for helping us meet our goal. I was a lucky kid and had a lot of advantages growing up, but I learned more from my summers at Camp Oak Crest than at any other time in my life. About friendship, loyalty, hard work, and honor."

"And love," Natalie whispers. "But we don't want to remind parents of the possibility of summer romances."

I hush her with a pinch and turn my attention back to Sawyer.

"Every year I was here, I watched campers leave this experience changed for the better with skills and connections they still use ten and twelve years later. I wish every kid who wants the experience could have a shot at it, and I'm thrilled a hundred more of them will get it this year. We hope to build a pipeline from camper to counselor so every Oak Crest graduate who wants to can come back to work and become a part of the next generation of campers' growth."

He pauses, and I get the feeling he's managing his emotions. Then he fixes his eyes on me, and Natalie digs her fingers into my thigh. "Anyway, I experienced the greatest summer of my life here, and I believe that's what's in store for your kids. Thank you."

"Oh, Tab," Natalie says over more audience applause. "How can you not—"

I pinch her again. "Stop. I need to think." Ben catches Sawyer's sleeve and they have an off-mic conversation, each smiling slightly.

Sawyer meant every word he said tonight. And he's meant every word he's said in the last three days. As that sinks in, so does reality. No matter how much we talk about Oak Crest preparing us for real life, it *isn't* real life. I know what I need to do.

"I have to check on Lisa," I tell Natalie, rising as Sawyer makes his way back to us. "I'll talk to you later." I head for the kitchen, pausing long enough to scrawl a quick note before walking out the back door. And then I keep going.

CHAPTER TWENTY-TWO

Until the sunrise breakfast suggestion, Sawyer's request for a do-over had seemed like a joke, or as fleeting as the summers here had been. I'd thought it would be a fun way to flirt and make him even sorrier for dumping me that summer before we'd go back to our own separate real lives. I'd have an apology and closure, and that chapter would be done forever.

Every woman who matters to me is caught up in the romantic ideal of a rekindled first love, but the idea of seeing Sawyer in New York, of taking him to my favorite places . . .

It's hard to imagine. One time, during a commercial break when I'd been doing a cooking segment on the *Today* show, I'd glanced at the live audience outside and seen a kid I knew from middle school at the front of the crowd. She was grown now, obviously, but it had taken me a full thirty seconds to process why I recognized her. She was so out of context that my brain sorted through a dozen possibilities of how I knew her before it landed on the right one. Even then, it wouldn't compute. I felt like I was living in a sci-fi movie where I was simultaneously experiencing the past and the present.

It felt weird then. It feels worse now.

I sit on the end of the old dock and wait, listening for Sawyer.

I left the gala over an hour ago, and I'm beginning to wonder if Sawyer hasn't gotten my note to meet here or if he did but isn't coming, when footsteps sound behind me. I turn as Sawyer makes his way to me.

"Hi," he says. "I feel overdressed."

He's wearing his suit from dinner minus the jacket. I'd gone home and changed to shorts and a sweatshirt, and I tuck my knees beneath it now as a cool breeze blows off the lake.

"Thanks for coming."

"Sure." He holds himself still in the way that hints at waiting, a coiled pause as if he's unsure which direction he should go, forward to me, or back to shore.

I hug my knees, praying the words I need are waiting for me. "Coming back here was both better and worse than I expected it to be. It brought me right back to my time here as a kid, and that was mostly good. So much of my camp experience was the kind of thing the best movies are made of. But it also showed me that my last summer here—the last day of my last summer here—hurt me more than I realized."

He toes his shoes off, removes his socks, rolls up his cuffs, and sits beside me, letting his feet dangle off the dock where they don't quite touch the lake.

"I was hoping against hope I was coming out to hear you say something different than what you're about to say."

"How do you know what I'm going to say?" It's a stupid question. A stalling tactic. He's reading me correctly.

"Because you didn't bring me to Creekville."

I glance over at him. "It was just a quick trip."

"To your hometown. And you didn't want me there." He sighs. "I can't be mad at you for how you feel. But we've had different experiences on these last two days. Maybe even a different experience in our last camp summer."

"Are you trying to say you were more into me back then?" Because I will shut that BS *down*.

He leans back on his hands and looks out at the water. "It is what it is."

"I hate that expression. What does it even mean? And what does it have to do with that summer? Do you have any idea how I felt on that last morning, sitting here and hearing Ben tell me you ran away? I cracked open my heart and poured it out for you, and your response was to bug out early and send Ben to break up with me."

"I was scared." He says it quietly, but he meets my eyes. "All that night after Moon Rock, I wrestled with this big feeling. I didn't know what it was. I didn't know what I was supposed to do with it. It had me so freaked out, I ran away."

"I feel so flattered." My nails dig into my palms

231

as I hold myself together even tighter. This is the fight we never got to have, but I still don't know how to have it, because he's right: I can't be mad about the way he felt. Or feels.

"I'm not explaining this well. That feeling, it wasn't fear. But I reacted to it with fear. By the time I figured it out, it was too late to go back and apologize," he says. "Remember how I said I decided I was ready to fall in love after college, but it didn't work out?"

I raise my eyebrows. Like I was going to forget that particular emotional papercut.

"What I didn't say is that it's because the longer I dated her, the more I realized that wasn't possible. Because I had already fallen in love. With you. Two years before."

That steals my breath. I know the feeling. I haven't consciously compared other relationships to ours, but I was always chasing an emotional high I hadn't found since that summer. Since those giddy days of being consumed by thoughts of Sawyer, waking and sleeping.

I stand, too restless to sit with the information. "Why didn't you say anything?"

He climbs to his feet too. "Two years after you'd made it clear you never wanted to talk to me again?"

I give a single nod, like, *Okay. Fair enough.*

"I also knew we had completely different lives happening in totally different places," he says. "I

232

told myself that for a few more years. And then Oak Crest came up for sale, and the ghost of Tabitha Winters would not go away."

He reaches over and touches my elbow, tugging lightly at the fabric of the sweatshirt. "Tab. For me, from the second we decided to buy it, it was about finding a way back to you. I loved you then. I love you now. I thought all it would take was this place and a little time to convince you of that. But it didn't."

"You have no idea how much these words would have meant to me then." The ones he'd left me with instead had filled sleepless nights, eaten away at my insides, chewed up my self-confidence, and hollowed me out for a long time.

"But not now?" he asks.

I try to sort through the riot inside me. So many conflicting emotions and thoughts. It's chaos, and I can't even know most of its pieces. This was the last conversation I expected to have when I came back to Oak Crest. And despite off-the-charts chemistry between us the last couple days, that hadn't prepared me for this conversation either.

This beautiful man is standing here and telling me he loves me. He's asking me if that means anything to me. He deserves an answer. That's what I know for sure.

I take a deep breath. "It matters now too. It tells me that I can trust my instincts, and that was the worst thing about that summer. I left feeling like I couldn't. I'd thought we shared the same feelings, and more than just hurting when I found out you didn't, I doubted myself. That I knew what was real.

"So I threw myself into finishing my degree and applying to culinary school, then I threw myself into my career, and I didn't give relationships much of a shot. I dated, but every time it started to get real, I panicked. What if I was wrong again?"

Sawyer sighs. "I'm so sorry."

"I know. I do."

"I wish I could go back in time and punch my own face," he says, winning a small laugh from me.

I'm exhausted. All this reconciling and sharing feelings with him, my mom, him again. I stand and pull him to his feet. "I'm glad you tricked me back here." I smile up at him, and a tight knot I've carried for nine years unwinds inside me. It's a warm and wondrous feeling. It's forgiveness.

"I didn't know how much I needed this talk. I think you get exactly how much you hurt me, which you could only understand if you'd also felt the same thing. And understanding that . . ." I keep my eyes fixed on the knot of his tie. "It means my instincts were good. The only time I thought I loved someone and that he loved me back, I was right. It was real."

"It was real," he answers, barely more than a whisper. He pulls me toward him, and I lean my head against his chest, listening to the steady beat of his heart while he holds me. "I need to confess something," he says after a minute. "The more time I've spent here, the more I've wondered if there's a way to fix the past. After these past few days, I'm sure. It can be real again."

I freeze and listen to three more heartbeats. Then I step back. He's slow to let me go, his hands trailing down my arms as I slip away. "You said friendship, Sawyer."

"Because you were so mad that first night. I could read you well enough to change my plan."

"What change? What plan?" I feel suddenly cool even though the air is warm.

"We made a deal, Tab. Do you remember? We're both single, and we're turning thirty. Those were the terms."

"The marriage pact?" I laugh. "The terms of a deal we made when we were dumb kids who thought forty was old."

"I'm not kidding," he says quietly.

I sway like the dock tilted, but Sawyer stands as solid as ever. *What is happening?*

He steps so close I have to look up to meet his eyes. He rests his hand against my cheek, his thumb brushing against my cheekbone softer than the light lake breeze. "Tab. We sealed it with a kiss. I brought you here to collect."

CHAPTER TWENTY-THREE

Run. Stay. Push Sawyer in the lake and see if it clears his head. These are my options.

"Is it that crazy?" he asks when I've stared at him in dumbfounded silence for at least ten seconds.

"A hundred percent," I say without hesitation, stepping back so his hand drifts down, away from my face.

He smiles. "Even after two amazing days together? We click. We connect like we never broke up. Something about us works like it doesn't with anyone else. At least for me. You don't feel it?"

I do, but I'm not handing him that ammunition. "I still know you well enough to sense you were going to ask for something more, and here we are." I should have found a way to cut him off sooner, to save him from the ask so I could save myself from having to give this rejection. "I'm so relieved we've patched up things enough to share Ben and Natalie again. Let's leave it there."

He tilts his head and studies me. "You're running."

I blink at him and point to my feet. "I'm right here."

He shakes his head. "The look in your eyes is

exactly how I felt that morning I snuck out early. I regretted it. If I promise you that staying will save us from wasting another nine years, will you believe me?"

I can feel myself want to, and it makes me angry. I spent too long putting him in the past to weaken because his attention salves my twenty-year-old self's pride. It makes me snappish. "I can't believe you thought you could lure me back here and spring that stupid backup plan on me."

"It's not stupid."

"It's *so* stupid. You know what *I* looked like that morning nine years ago? I was standing at the end of this dock puking. *Puking,* Sawyer. So much vomit." I feel a rising sense of hysteria at the absurdity of this. My anxiety is spiraling. I don't care. "I bet I fed this whole lake full of fish on that vomit. Yes, that's gross," I almost yell when he winces. My fingers bunch and twist my sweatshirt hem. "That's how bad I felt. And I bet those fish had babies, and those had babies, and there are great-great-great-great-grandfish of those vomit-fed trout that day, swimming around with puke DNA from that one time when I was totally abandoned by you on this exact stupid dock!"

"Whoa, whoa, Tab, hey, it's okay." He reaches out and grasps my upper arms, gently but firmly rubbing them like I'm cold. "I hear you. It's okay."

I'm shaking, I realize. I hate this. And I hate that his rhythmic strokes are actually calming me.

"Breathe," he says. "In slow, out slow."

I glare at him, but my breaths sync with the arm rubs. "I'm fine," I say several seconds later.

"You sure?" He's still rubbing my arms, his hands warm through the fabric of my sweatshirt.

I nod and step back. "And I don't think there are any puke fish in the lake."

He eyes me cautiously. "You good?"

I meet his eyes, specifically because he couldn't do it that last morning. "I'm not marrying you. I'm not even going to date you. You're right to guess that not taking you to Creekville was a clue. I wasn't consciously thinking about it at the time. But I'm figuring it out now, why the idea felt wrong to me."

I wave my hand toward the camp, toward the warm lights glowing from the lodge windows in the distance. "We've never existed outside of this bubble, Sawyer. Not even when we were messaging during that year between our last two summers. Those were an extension of this. But neither of our real lives outside of here have ever had anything to do with who we are together at Oak Crest. You didn't even want to tell us the truth about your background or school."

"That was a mistake."

"I'm not judging it. I'm offering it as proof we carved out a place in time, and we made it what we wanted it to be. And we are so *blessed.* I'll believe that forever. Very few people ever get to do it. I can't believe we got to come and relive it, even for a few days. I bet that almost never happens. Thank you for that."

"It worked because it's more than magic. It's more like fate, Tabitha. It knocked once and I ran away. We shouldn't do that again."

I love his voice. The low warmth of it. Even now when he is saying crazy things, I want to curl up in his words. I squeeze my eyes shut for a second. I have to focus. "The camp road is the border for this magic. If we go past it together, it bursts. I agree this week has been a gift. We were both due some closure, but . . ."

"Tab." He runs a finger through his hair. "I'm not dumb enough to think we're going to figure this out in a single week. I know we've got a lot to learn about each other, but I've always known who you are at your core. You've always known that about me too. I was more myself here than I was anywhere else, even though I didn't share all the facts of my life. I showed up as myself, and you saw me. You *saw* me," he repeats.

His fingers lightly circle my wrist, and I don't pull away. "I just want to convince you to give me a chance. However long it takes. Until Saturday. Or December. Or retirement."

"You and I together, that's only here. It only works here." This feels so true to me. It's the only thing that makes sense of the near-panic I felt at bringing him home.

"You don't know that," he says. "We can't know until we try. As sure you as you feel we're a here-only thing, that's how sure I feel this was always just the starting point."

I look at him, really look at him, holding his gaze. His eyes are sincere. He believes every word he's saying.

What if he's right? What if this feeling, this warning inside me, is wrong? Just my anxiety trying to run from a risk?

"Tabitha," he says, barely louder than a breath. He sets his hands on my shoulders, and I feel the current run between us again. "Let me show you."

He leans forward. It's a controlled, careful movement, offering plenty of time for me to move away, but I don't. His eyes flicker to my mouth, and not even dynamite could move me now.

The first touch of his lips on mine is gentle, and he draws back a couple of inches, scanning my face, testing to make sure this is okay.

I answer by reaching up and sliding my hand around his neck, pressing him forward again, and this time when his lips meet mine, he has no questions. This kiss is inevitable.

I'd thought I was a pretty good kisser when I was twenty. I'd thought Sawyer was a good kisser when he was twenty.

We are both much better now.

His kiss is sure, the pressure firm as he tightens his grip and leans closer. I open for him, inviting him in, and the silk slide of his tongue is so familiar I want to weep, but also so sure now, so confident in taking, that I ache in a way I never had back then. The kiss goes forever, until I can't take this leaning anymore, until I begin to resent every molecule of air in the space between us.

He pulls me closer, his hands sliding up to cradle my head, warm against my scalp, sending more fire burning through me. He's kissing me like he can never drink deeply enough, and I feel wanted, needed in a way no one has ever made me feel. Why isn't it like this with anyone else?

I pull him even closer, a deep, satisfied growl rumbling up from his chest as he lifts me, my feet no longer touching the ground. This is so good. It's never this good? I want to wrap every bit of myself around him, and I almost do—

Until I remember.

I pull back from him, and he lets me, his hands falling to my waist to support me as I lean slightly away, struggling to find my breath.

"Tabitha."

"Sawyer." He flinches as he hears the apology in my voice.

He rests his forehead against mine. "It's never like this with anyone else."

I can barely hear him above the sound of my

heart. "I know. But it's only like this because of this place and these circumstances."

He lifts his head and softly brushes his thumb over my lips. "Do you really believe that?"

"I do." His thumb stops moving, and I take his hand in both of mine, hoping I can warm them and in some way make up for the words I say next. "You were my first love, Sawyer. Maybe no one ever gets over that. People have their first love when they're young, when they're not yet who they're going to be. In a way, my twenty-year-old self, that Tabitha, she's captured perfectly in amber, and she's never going to change. She's never going to not love that Sawyer."

His eyes move back and forth over my face, confused. "That's not a small thing, Tab."

"I know. It's a great thing. It *was* a great thing. But your instincts told you then that it wasn't going to be a thing past camp. You knew. I get it now too. If I had taken you to Creekville today, showed you my dad's shop, gotten you my favorite pastry, walked you through town showing you where I came from, you'd start to see."

"See what? Why I'm so into you? What made you so you?"

"Sawyer, no." I draw back, putting space between us. "You'd see that the magic fades." I can feel as surely as I know what a dish needs to make it right that if we try to take this outside of

242

Oak Crest, I will fall for Sawyer even more. But we won't work.

We live eight hundred miles apart. We have demanding careers. I'm never going to fit with his upper-class family, and he can't fathom mine or my small-town upbringing. But I'll still fall for him, and we *will* fall apart. When that happens, I'll lose a bigger piece of myself than I did the first time.

Yes, we have history. Yes, we have chemistry. And yes. There's magic.

But magic always exacts a price. And this is too high.

"Tomorrow morning, I fly back to New York. Real life begins."

"And I'm not part of it."

"Sawyer—"

He shakes his head. "No, don't. You're scared, Tabitha. But I never want you to feel like I don't respect what you want. I wish this week would have ended differently, but I'm glad you played along."

"I'm serious, Sawyer. It's the best gift anyone has ever given me."

He nods, accepting the thanks. "I'll walk you back to your cabin. One last quiet forest stroll for old times' sake?"

"I'd love that."

We stay quiet on the trail to the cottage. I don't know what he's thinking, but all I can focus on is the prickling of my lips from his kisses and wishing I could be selfish enough to ask for one more.

At the cottage, he stops on the next to last step while I unlock the door. I turn to face him, searching for a parting thought. "Sawyer—"

"Tab." Another headshake as he goes down the stairs. He stops at the bottom. "One last thing. If first loves end and don't survive outside of bubbles, why are Ben and Natalie married with a kid?"

I open my mouth, but I have no answer.

"Yeah. All right. See you around."

And then he walks away.

CHAPTER TWENTY-FOUR

"You sure this is what you want to do?" Natalie asks as I fold my black dress neatly in half and make it the last layer on my suitcase.

"I've got to get back," I said. "I've got work."

"Don't you have a three-month filming hiatus?"

I look up from zipping my bag. "Yes, Miss Pays-Too-Close-of-Attention. But I have to use this time to work on my next cookbook so I'm not trying to cram it in around my filming schedule. And I need to figure out what I want to cook next season and start locking down pre-production stuff."

"And also run away from Sawyer. That's a bonus, right?"

I sigh. "I'm not running away."

"No? You know I'm literally a relationship expert, right? I see someone who is attuned to Sawyer, who is *very* attuned to you. I see chemistry and comfort, and a whole lot of curiosity on your face. You know who else had and has that? Ben and I."

"Natalie. Come on." I turn from my suitcase and rummage through my handbag to make sure my ID and wallet are there. "I'm not going to try to make a relationship work with my summertime crush from when I was twenty."

"But do you say 'I love you' to a crush?"

I stop and meet her eyes. "Coming back here and talking to him was good. It was healthy, and we're at a point where we can both join you and Ben for important occasions. It would have been worth it for that. But that's it."

She watches me closely.

"What?" I say, when the scrutiny makes me feel twitchy.

"I don't believe you. Other people might, but I don't. And if I don't, I know you don't."

"You don't believe I'm going to pack up and go back to my life in New York? Watch me."

"I don't believe you're over him. I would think if the last nine years taught you anything, it's that you don't heal what you don't confront. It'll keep getting in your way."

"But I *did* confront it. I told him how it made me feel. We got a chance to reconnect in a more positive way." My stomach flips remembering the kiss last night on the dock.

Natalie snorts.

"What happens in Vegas stays in Vegas for a reason. Ditto Camp Oak Crest," I say.

"Right, except the last time something happened with you two at Oak Crest, it followed you for years. I'm telling you, that's what's going to happen now."

"It's not. I got closure."

"How does Sawyer feel about it?"

246

I ignore her in favor of doing a final sweep of the bedroom to make sure I haven't left anything behind.

"Tabitha?" Her voice is calm but insistent.

"Why do I think you already know the answer?" I call back to her.

"Because I do. Come talk to me about it."

I walk back out of the bedroom. "Nat, come on. You can't talk someone into being in a relationship."

"Of course not," she says. "Not if both people aren't feeling it. But you *are*."

"You're not supposed to tell me how I feel, therapist."

"I'm not *your* therapist, so I can call you on stuff if I want. I'm calling you on it right now. You're seriously ready to walk away from Sawyer, go back to New York, and throw yourself into your work, and you don't see any problem with that?"

"I do not." I give the final T extra force, the sharp snap of a fresh bell pepper.

"Really," she drawls. "You don't think every date you try to go on will fall short to the what-if of you and Sawyer like they have for nine years?"

I grab my suitcase, sling my purse over my arm, and head for the door. "Maybe at first, but it will be fine. How committed are you to keeping me here and changing my mind? Are you going to drive me to the airport, or do I need to bribe a counselor?"

"Ugh. I'll take you. But mark this down as the day your best friend tried her hardest to change your mind."

"Noted. Let's go." I swing open the door to discover Sawyer there, about to knock, his eyebrows raised in surprise at my sudden appearance. "Hey."

"Hey." His eyes drop to my suitcase. "Ben asked me if I'd take your luggage up to the car on the ATV so I'd have an excuse to ask if you've got five minutes."

"She does." Natalie closes the door behind me and bumps me onto the porch.

I roll my eyes. "Not even as subtle as Ben's Truth or Dare."

He gives me a tired smile, but he still looks so good. He's in gray shorts and a teal polo, his sunglasses tucked into the neck, worn Vans on his feet. He takes a deep breath. "I know this week didn't end the way I hoped it would, but it's major progress that we can hang out now."

"True. I was running out of creative excuses for why I can't be at a Ben and Natalie thing when it's your turn. I'll be seeing you over many awkward juice boxes."

"Or we could get wild and plan to be real friends, period. Like we can comment on each other's Instagram, even."

I gasp. "Sir, such liberties."

"It's not like I suggested texting."

I shudder. "Do you know some people even like to speak on the phone? Like call other people and talk? My mom does this to me. I don't like it."

"Ben does it to me too," Sawyer says. "He's worn me down over time."

"Natalie too. Those two can't be trusted, upending societal norms and kicking it old school."

"Is that a yes to commenting on your Instagram?"

"I don't know," I say. "If I comment on yours, is it going to send you into an existential spiral where you try to squeeze the meaning out of every syllable?"

He answers with a polite smile.

"So that's just a me thing then," I say, which makes him laugh. "Sure, Instagram is fine."

"Now I'm dying to know. What would happen if I *did* text you?"

"Depends on the text. Is it, 'You up?' " That's current code for a booty call.

"Uh, no. I heard you loud and clear last night. It'd probably be something more like 'I whipped my egg whites, but they didn't do that thing like yours did.' You know. Meaty stuff."

"That's eggy stuff."

"Right. I don't know how I even feed myself."

I consider his question for real. "Maybe send a

text, and I'll see how it feels when the text comes in."

"Fair enough. But we're good, right?"

"We're good." We're good if I don't look at him too long and notice the way his hair falls into his eye just so. It's ridiculous for a businessman. He needs to get in for a cut. And we're good if I don't look at his hands and remember that neck rub. I love when a man has strong, confident hands.

"It was good to see you, Tab. I better get your luggage up to the office."

Natalie yanks the door open, shoves my suitcase out, and closes the door again.

"She's the worst," I say loudly.

Sawyer grabs it and brings it to the ATV. I watch as he fastens it, feeling like this goodbye is unfinished. When he grips the handlebars like he's about to sling his leg over it, I say, "Wait!" He stops and turns. "Should we hug?"

He considers it for a second, then gives a single shake of his head and a tight smile. "Give me about a year and I'll be ready for that." Then he's on the ATV, the motor roaring to life, and in seconds, he's disappeared into the trees.

CHAPTER TWENTY-FIVE
EIGHT YEARS AGO

I stared down at my shoes for the first day of work. They were serviceable black Doc Martens, the kind made to handle the scuffs, scrapes, and dropped food and pans of a busy commercial kitchen.

It was strange to see them and not the sneakers I usually pulled on to hit the ground running on my first day at Oak Crest. Today, like summers past, I was going to Roanoke. But instead of catching the camp shuttle from the airport, I'd be going to Martin's, an upscale restaurant whose head chef had hired me as a prep cook. It was a half step above dishwasher, but I was lucky to get it since my only formal kitchen experience had been taking over from Marge for six weeks at Oak Crest when she'd quit the previous summer.

Grace was home for the summer too, but I got the car since she could ride with my dad or walk to the hardware store. I'd parked a block down from the restaurant, not even wanting to park behind it as directed out of fear I'd accidentally take someone's unofficial space.

This was going to be a long hot summer spent in the bowels of the kitchen. A big part of me already missed Oak Crest and the rush of first-day excitement when each new session of fresh campers started, of the blessed breezes that sometimes blew off the lake, of late nights around campfires and lazy afternoons in the woods. Natalie. Ben.

But not Sawyer.

I hadn't seen him in ten months, since the night I'd gotten everything so very wrong, but it wasn't like I'd felt free of him. He'd DM-ed and texted for the first month or two of the semester, checking in on me, requesting to talk. Finally, an apology. *Sorry. I didn't mean it to go like this.* Eventually, when he'd heard nothing from me, the messages had dried up all together.

I was glad. It had taken until Christmas before my heart stopped lurching at every alert in case it was him. I didn't know if he even knew I wasn't coming back this summer, and I hoped when he realized I wasn't there, he would feel bad and know it was his fault.

I smoothed down my smock and walked to the restaurant. I hated that even now, on the first day of an unrelated job, he was at the front of my mind. When would it not be like this? When would he not be a constant part of my day? Ten months of my silence hadn't done the trick. Taking an extra class each semester to keep myself too busy to think or feel hadn't done the trick.

Being this close to Oak Crest was a risk in

terms of feeling his presence, thinking about what they—he—was up to. But I could get a better start here as an aspiring chef than I could at any of our Creekville establishments, and I could only hope work would keep me busy enough to distract me.

I pushed into the restaurant and found my way to the kitchen, where I presented myself to Chef Marc.

"Ten minutes early, Winters. That's good. Now get on the line. Hieu will show you what to do."

The day was as grueling as I could have hoped for. I worked six hours straight, washing produce, peeling root vegetables, chopping, chopping, chopping. My back ached, my hair reeked of onion, and I couldn't feel my feet anymore, but I'd had no time to think of anything else, and I walked to my car exhausted but feeling like the day was a success.

At least I did until I turned on my phone and found three texts waiting for me. One each from Ben and Natalie telling me they missed me. And then . . .

SAWYER: It doesn't feel right without you here.

I studied that for a long time before I started the car. I could respond. I could say, "Too bad you broke us."

Or I could let him suffer in my silence.

So I did that.

It took about three weeks before turning off Interstate 81 into Roanoke didn't make my stomach dip. Sawyer was in my thoughts every day, maybe even every hour, but the pull to keep driving on to Oak Crest had eventually eased.

On particularly stressful days in the kitchen—days where we had a big reservation or a VIP—I would curse his name in time to the thwacks of my chef's knife chopping up vegetables. But mostly, I knew this prep cook job was right for me. My thoughts started splitting evenly between Sawyer and how to tell my mom I would be going to culinary school after graduation instead of getting an MBA.

In July, I got a text that hitched my breath.

NATALIE: Tabby Cat! I miss you! We want to come see you!
TABITHA: Who is we?
NATALIE: Me and Ben. We're off Sunday. When can we come?
TABITHA: After 2. Slow until dinner prep at 4.

She sent me a thumbs up, and I stared down at our conversation. She'd know I was checking to make sure Sawyer wasn't coming. They were still friends. I knew that. I didn't expect her to drop him. But she'd figured out quickly that I didn't want to talk about him, or even hear about him casually.

Sunday, I made sure my hair was in a neat French braid, and I put on waterproof mascara and a light shade of long-lasting lipstick. The other cooks gave me funny looks, but I ignored them and went to work.

Normally, I spent the time between shifts reading or napping in my car, which I'd started parking behind the restaurant. But today, I hung up my smock and sat at an empty table in the front, waiting for my friends.

Natalie pushed through the door, Ben right on her heels, and scooped me into a gigantic hug. I hugged her right back, happy to get one of her squishes, but for a second, I thought I glimpsed the top of Sawyer's head over hers. It was the right color hair and the right height. I straightened, but he was gone.

Natalie followed my gaze. "He caught a ride to town with us, but he's going to do his own thing."

I nodded and let it drop, instead giving Ben an enthusiastic hello. We walked over to the ice cream shop and got cones, then continued to a shaded bench where we sat and talked, them catching me up on camp shenanigans and asking me about Martin's. Sawyer's name didn't come up at all, and it was obvious in its absence, but I was glad. I already thought about him too much;

I didn't want to have to talk about him too.

Too soon, Natalie and Ben had to head back to camp, and I had to go back to prep for dinner service. I got two more big warm hugs, and waved to them as they left me at the front door of the restaurant.

Was Sawyer waiting for them just out of sight? Would they tell him how I was doing? Would he even ask?

I trudged back to the kitchen and spent my few spare minutes sharpening my knife while I pondered the biggest question of all: when would I stop caring about those questions?

It was a good thing I couldn't have seen eight years down the road to the answer: never.

CHAPTER TWENTY-SIX
PRESENT

New York feels surreal once I'm back in town. I watch the neighborhoods pass from the train window as we leave Newark. I've lived here for five years, all of them in the same small apartment in Brooklyn. I'd planned to move to Manhattan if my cookbook sold well. It had, but then I was paying my dad's medical bills, so I didn't have the funds for an upgrade like I'd planned. What I *could* afford was to live without a roommate, so now I had the small two bedroom for myself, my old roommate's bedroom now serving as my office.

I open the door and let myself in, appreciating the quiet. My old roommate, Dan, had been fairly easy to live with, but he'd had a habit of rescuing the most ornery cats while also not being super diligent with their litterboxes. I miss the cats. I don't miss the smell.

I set my suitcase on my bed and unpack before I do anything else. Dan always insisted this was the sign of a serial killer, but if I don't do it now, it'll stay packed in my room for another month. I'm either hyper-organized or a disaster. I try to be hyper-organized.

I get ready for bed, order noodles from my favorite shop around the corner, curl up with Netflix, and decompress. Every time my thoughts drift to Sawyer, I jerk them back to my TV where I'm streaming a true crime about a girl who disappears in LA only to be discovered months later in the rooftop water tank of a sketchy hotel. Not much room for sentimental musings with that as my soundtrack.

I don't set an alarm for the morning. I'm an early riser anyway, but there's nowhere specific I have to be tomorrow either. We won't start taping *Dinner Reborn* until early September, which leaves me three months to use as I like. Except not really. I'll spend a lot of time working on my next cookbook, *Perfect Party Platters*, so I don't have to balance that while I'm shooting. I'll research recipes to make when we start taping. I'll spend time wandering the boroughs, trying new foods and markets, searching for culinary treasures.

But before I can do all of that, I need to make my Sawyer Recovery Plan. I didn't have one last time. I expected he would fade from memory over time. But he lingered like a ghost, always the shadow I compared other guys to, but his shadow had been enough for them to always fall short.

I have a major weapon in my pocket this time though: answers. I know why. I can write "The

End" on that story and move on. But mindfully. I have to make this plan with intention, so it works. Otherwise, Sawyer is likely to pop up in my thoughts at all the wrong times.

Ask me how I know.

Monday morning, I start by attending the Brooklyn Memorial Day parade. There is nothing like a parade—for any occasion—to make a huge city feel like a small town. Even though it's 10 AM and the air already hints at the heat and humidity to come, watching the veterans and Cub Scouts march by reminds me so much of the Christmas festivities in Creekville.

After the parade, I buy a bike because I liked using one at Oak Crest so much. Then I ride it to Lookout Hill in Prospect Park. The landscape there feels more like Oak Crest than any place I've found in the city, and I park my bike, find a bench, and unpack the notebook I brought with me, because of course I have a notebook to impose order on the chaos Sawyer tried to introduce in my life.

THE SAWYER RECOVERY PLAN

I write the title and stare at it for a long time. Ten minutes pass, and the paper is still otherwise blank. Then twenty. When my Apple watch buzzes to remind me to be active, I pull myself together and set my pen to paper. This is ridiculous. Sawyer isn't an unsolvable problem. I cross out the title and rewrite it, going over the letters again to make sure my brain understands what I expect it to do.

THE SAWYER RECOVERY PLAN
THE SAWYER RECOVERY PLAN

1. Every time I think of Sawyer, sing a distracting song. Pick an earworm.
2. Use a daily affirmation. **I am happy with my life as it is.**
3. Develop a new hobby. Macrame? Maybe make plant holders for Xmas?
4. Every tenth time I think about Sawyer, find a match on dating app.
5. Every twentieth time I think about Sawyer, go on a date with someone else.
6. If all this fails, see therapist. NOT NATALIE.

I sit back and study the list, pretty satisfied with it. This can't fail. And if it does, I'll try something more drastic. Sometimes Dan works as a palm reader. Maybe I'll take him up on his offer of services if worse comes to worst.

Right now, I'm optimistic. I'm underlining *Not Natalie* when I get a text and glance down at my phone.

I don't recognize the number, but when I open

it, it's from the very man I'm making a detailed plan to forget.

SAWYER: Get home okay?

Well, what do I do now? I'd forgotten about this variable when I was making my list. Sawyer not only has permission but pretty much an invitation to reach out. It feels weird and petty to revoke it now.

Do I count any messages from him as thinking of him? How does this factor into my recovery plan?

I study the list again, then decide on a solution: contacts from Sawyer don't count against me as long as I say my affirmation five times after each one. Yes, that's good.

TABITHA: Yes, safe and sound. You back in Chicago?
SAWYER: Not until tomorrow. It's a busy weekend to fly. Letting the crowds thin.

I send him a thumbs up emoji and start my affirmations. *I am happy with my life as it is.* It would be better if he were already in Chicago though. It's way too easy to picture him in Oak Crest, water sluicing off his body after a lake swim, or dip in the hot tub, or . . .

I sit up straighter. *I AM HAPPY WITH MY LIFE AS IT IS.*

This will work. This will be fine.

It's not fine.

Sawyer checks in every two to three days, always with something non-threatening. Messages with a picture of a street cart captioned, "Chicago hot dogs are better," then another one a few days later with a piece of thick Chicago-style pizza reading, "But New York has better slices. TELL NO ONE."

I say my affirmations every time. I still end up running an earworm on an endless loop. Unfortunately, it's the "Hamster Dance" song, a high-pitched series of notes that are sort of square-dance sounding? You'd think if anything could kill someone's lov—

Whoa. I mean, if anything could distract someone, it's a hamster square dance song on repeat.

Nope.

This list will take practice, that's all. I have to be consistent.

I am. I consistently think about Sawyer and wonder what he's up to.

When I'm sitting on Lookout Hill exactly one week later reviewing my list, I have to accept I've made zero progress. It's time to work farther down the list.

I google craft classes and find someone teaching

macrame at a near-ish community center. I register online. The class starts in two weeks, and I can't take two more weeks of this.

I've been doing Number Four (Every tenth time I think about Sawyer, find a match on a dating app). A few times a day, in fact, because the rules are the rules, even if I wildly underestimated how often I'd find myself thinking about him.

Now I have a backlog of more matches than I can ever get through, and some of them have been messaging me. But a week into this, if I'm going to be honest in following the list, I need to go out on at least . . . I check my Notes app to tally the Xs I've been using to keep myself honest.

Eighteen dates.

I swallow hard. Well, those should at least be useful distractions.

Several of these guys have already messaged me, so I open the messages and read through them. I dismiss eleven of them immediately for the following reasons:

- Three start their messages with: Sup. No punctuation, even.
- One starts with: Sup? Still not enough.
- One starts with: 'Sup? And that's an *almost* but nope.
- Three send me variations of: you're cute.
- One sends a nude: this has never worked. On me. On any woman.

- The final two have at least one grammar error in their messages.

I'm not even setting a high bar. All my remaining candidates have to do is say hello with a complete sentence and correct punctuation. That's literally it.

I narrow my options to set up a week of dates, ideally one a day. Since the app's algorithm does a lot of heavy lifting on the matching, the chance of finding one of these guys compatible is good. Probably even high. I narrow to my top three: a veterinarian, a news producer, and a real estate agent. Then I send their screenshots to Natalie with a text asking who I should pick.

> **NATALIE:** None. You know who you should be with. I'm not supporting this nonsense.

I glare at the phone and send a text to Grace.

> **TABITHA:** Which of these guys should I match with first?
> **GRACE:** None. Natalie says I can't support this nonsense.

Natalie is playing dirty.
I send her the picture of the veterinarian and

tell her I'm giving him a shot first. Then I do, answering his message which was a polite hello followed by a question about what kind of cooking I do since my profile says I'm a chef.

I tell him I do a cooking show that focuses on making dinners at home and ask him about his veterinary practice.

By the next morning, we've exchanged a few messages. His name is Brandt, and we have a lunch date scheduled at a vegan place he likes. I guess a vegan veterinarian makes sense. And I have no issue with eating vegan since I like anything fresh and well-made.

I get ready by putting on a yellow and navy summer romper, giving my curls a fresh spritz of styling spray, and sliding on cute sandals before walking three blocks to the café.

Brandt is waiting for me at a sidewalk table, and he stands to shake my hand when I walk up. He's cute. Not like a model. More like Hallmark handsome, the kind of cute that exists in real life.

"Nice to meet you, Tabitha."

"Same." I take a seat—which he doesn't hold out—and settle in. It's okay he didn't hold the seat out. A lot of guys don't learn etiquette. "Are you on a break from your office today?"

He shakes his head. "Just ran out for lunch, but I liked your profile, and I didn't want to miss an opportunity."

"Thanks," I say. "So, tell me about your practice."

"Well," he says, "I like animals. Obviously. And I have all kinds of patients. People think it's probably mostly dogs and cats because of being in the city, but I see birds, hamsters, snakes, bearded dragons, turtles—wait, here. Let me show you." He pulls up pictures on his phone and scrolls through them for me. A chihuahua, an African gray parrot, a ball python, a gecko, a pair of guinea pigs, one long-haired cat, one black cat, a German shepherd, a three-legged rat, and a potbelly pig later, I sit back, my eyebrows raised. "You're right, that's a lot more pet variety than I would expect in Brooklyn."

"And that's just my apartment."

I laugh, but he doesn't. In fact, his mouth tugs down. "Wait, those are *your* pets, not patients? They all belong to you?"

"Most of them *were* patients, but their owners surrendered them for whatever reason. Now they're mine."

I blink at him. "You run a rescue out of your house?"

"No. They're my pets. It's not like I do fundraising or anything. Which is why we'll need to split the bill." He follows this with a wink.

Okay.

I don't mind splitting the bill at all. That's not the problem. I like animals. But I have never envisioned myself as Mrs. Dr. Dolittle.

Our conversation doesn't take off because I'm stuck on his eleven pets. But mainly the pig. I badly want to be invited over to pet it. But I also don't want to live with it or any of its feathered, scaled, or furry roommates. I don't even want to make eye contact with the scaled ones.

After mediocre conversation over good salads, I dig cash from my wallet and leave it on the table, then stand with my hand extended. "It was nice to meet you, Brandt. I don't want to make you late for your next patient."

He shakes my hand with less enthusiasm than when we met, and I think he knows I won't return any future messages.

I walk home, the whole time thinking about potbelly pigs. I got my mom a dog for Christmas. Maybe I can convince her to adopt a potbelly pig for me to visit every year. But beyond that, I won't be petting any owned by a medium-cute veterinarian in Brooklyn.

Natalie texts me two days later.

NATALIE: Did you go out with the vet?
TABITHA: Yes. Would marry him but he owns 11 pets. In an apartment.
NATALIE: So his place smells like a pet store? Tragic.
TABITHA: I'll never know.
NATALIE: Know who has no pets? Sawyer.

I don't dignify that with a reply. But it does make me think about him, and even as I start humming "Hamster Dance," I realize I haven't heard from him in almost three days.

I haven't been the first to text, but I always answer. I'm almost itchy to ping him and see what he's up to, but I resist. I'd have to add a whole new step to my list, like going for a five-mile run every time I text first.

I have two more bad dates under my belt before I finally hear from him. The first was the real estate agent, who turned out to have lied about his height in his profile. He's an inch shorter than me. That's not a big deal, but the lying is. I can't do the work it takes to put us on a level playing field if he's starting from such an insecure place.

The second, a news producer, has to reschedule with me twice because of breaking news. I should have seen it coming, but when he has to cut our date short because he gets an urgent call about a mayoral scandal brewing, I tell him not to worry about it, but promptly erase his number when I get home. I admire being committed to your work; I don't have any interest in being dumped for it multiple times a week. I don't like him well enough to work that hard.

Then there's the whole issue of how none of them measure up to Sawyer. None of them are as funny. None of them are as easy to be around.

None of them make my breathing shallow just by smiling at me.

When Monday rolls around again, I make my pilgrimage, notebook in hand, to Lookout Hill where I claim my bench and study my list.

Am I "happy with my life as it is"? Because I've said that a whole lot in the last two weeks, and as busy as I've been, I can't say I'm happier than when I started this list. Also, I'm sick of the freaking "Hamster Dance." Death to all hamsters.

I take a deep breath. I don't mean that. I only mean death to all hamsters who sing that song.

I've got two plays left, according to my list. I'll start my macrame class on Thursday, but somehow, I don't think it's going to be the magic cure I'm looking for.

Which means it's time to start thinking about a therapist. I have one I like. Jane. She helped me when I was coping with my dad's illness, but I haven't seen her in almost a year, since he started getting better. But I text to see if she can fit me in anytime soon.

As I think about the conversation we're going to have, I can already imagine how I'll explain about my Sawyer fixation, the plan I've made, and . . . why it's failing. And I know there's one other text I need to send. I compose it then pace my apartment for an hour before I do.

TABITHA: Hey, Sawyer. Been thinking. Probably doesn't make sense for us to text. Still cool with seeing you at Ben/ Nat/Juniper stuff. Be well.

It's awkward and the sign-off is stupid, but I'm never going to truly get him off my mind if I'm always waiting for another text from him.

Sawyer never answers back.

It's for the best.

CHAPTER TWENTY-SEVEN
PRESENT

"You did what?"

Jane normally keeps her voice calm, inflecting only to show empathy or interest, never judgment. This doesn't sound like judgment, exactly, but it's not *not* judgment.

I study my cute pink pedicure displayed by my favorite sandals. "I drove past his jobsite."

"Which is where?"

"Um, Secaucus," I mumble.

"You got on a train to New Jersey, got off, and hired a rideshare to drive you past his construction site?"

"It sounds crazy when you say it like that." It's a weak joke, and her response is narrowed eyes.

"Is he at the construction site?"

"No. I don't think so."

"But you wanted to drive past it because . . ."

Every answer is mortifying. I don't want to dig into this. "Can you cure me without, you know, dwelling on this stuff?"

"Tabitha."

I pick at invisible lint on my jeans. "I thought it would make me feel closer to him."

"But you started coming to me again because

you're trying to get over him. So what would you call this kind of behavior?"

"Self-defeating," I say defeatedly.

"Or even self-sabotage."

I flop back on the sofa cushions. "What am I supposed to do, Jane? I'm in here to figure out how to get over Sawyer, but it's not working yet."

Jane considers this. "Do you know what therapy is meant to do?"

"Fix people when they're doing dumb things."

Jane leans forward and rests her elbows on her knees. "We can keep doing this for several weeks, Tabitha. Or months, if you like. I'm confident you'll eventually reach the conclusion you need to reach. But I'd like to suggest an alternative, something to move you along faster."

"Hypnotherapy?" Anything to speed up this miserable process. "EMDR? Ketamine?"

"Close," she says. "Natalie."

She and Natalie were classmates in their licensing program. Natalie referred me to her.

"Have you been talking to her?" I ask.

"Of course not. But based on what you've explained of your situation, I predict Natalie can tell you exactly what you need to hear, and you can skip thousands in therapy bills if you're willing to listen to her."

"Natalie is going to tell me to move to Oak Crest and make babies with Sawyer."

"Give Natalie more credit," she says. "She loves you. She's got your back. She wants the best for you. Trust that."

"What if I don't want to talk to Natalie because she's biased?"

"Then you make an appointment to see me next week, and in the meantime, you think about why you would resist talking to Natalie."

"I don't like you," I say.

She gives me a placid smile. "You don't have to. You just have to trust me." She relaxes against her chair.

I pull out my phone and dial Natalie's cell, hoping she's somewhere in camp with a signal.

"What are you doing?" Jane asks, her tone mild. Cell phones are not permitted in our session because I'm supposed to be "present."

"Taking your advice."

"Hey, Tab." Nat's voice is cheerful as she answers, and I switch her to speaker.

"Hey, Nat. We're on speaker in Jane's office."

"Hey, Jane!" she calls.

"Hey, Natalie."

"Why am I on speaker, Tabitha?"

"I came to see Jane because my recovery plan isn't working. I asked her to help me get over Sawyer so I can move forward with appropriate romantic relationships. She said I could spend thousands of dollars to get to the fix or I could ask you."

"Told you she was a good therapist," Natalie says.

"That is not my current feeling," I grit out, getting more annoyed. "My current feeling is frustration that I can't get over Sawyer, and I need to because I'm not giving up ten more years moping."

"Right. Because you're working on the wrong problem," Natalie says.

Jane hides a smile.

"Tell me what you mean," I order. "I'm tired of guessing."

"You're not supposed to get over Sawyer. He's a healthy relationship for you. What you should be working on is whatever is making you *resist* Sawyer. That's the problem. Not him."

I shoot a look at Jane. Jane taps her nose.

I scowl at her, then the phone. "I kind of hate you both."

"Okay," Natalie says, still cheerful. "But now it's out there. You have the answer, approved by two very good relationship experts. Whether you want to or not, you're going to think about it. And eventually you'll figure it out. I just hope it doesn't take you too long."

"Why? Is Sawyer seeing someone?" I hear the sharpness in my tone, and Jane hides her mouth behind her hand.

"No," says Natalie. "But I don't think he has it in him to wait on you for another nine years, and I don't want him to have to do that. I'd like you to pull yourself together. Soon. He'll be back here for the Fourth of July. Doesn't that sound like a nice deadline for figuring things out?"

"I don't want a deadline," I snap.

"And yet you work so well with them."

"I'm hanging up on you."

"Loooooove youuuuuuuu—"

I end the call and cut her off. She's probably sitting in the main office right now, laughing at me.

"Do you want to add anything?" I glare at Jane.

She clears her throat. "No, she covered it. She's an excellent clinician."

I blink at her a few times. "So you're saying—both of you—my problem isn't that I need to get over my ex, but that I need to stop running from him?"

She nods.

I mull this for a while. I'm not sure how long. I sit on her couch and stare into the distance and imagine what it would be like to believe Sawyer. To believe there's a way to make us work despite the obstacle of lives in different cities. And of past hurt. And the fact that at a crucial point in my life, I wasn't good enough for him. Do I want to be considered good enough now just because I've "proven" myself with my success?

But what if we did figure it out?

I think of us in the canoe, laughing as easily as

275

ever even though we hadn't seen each other in a decade. I think of the air crackling with tension when we did a simple craft. I remember the heat leaping between us when we kissed, no part of us having forgotten how good it could be, each of us bringing more life experience to those kisses to make them even better.

Hotter.

Sweeter.

When my mind wanders back to the present, Jane is sitting, still and calm, like she can wait all day. I sigh. "How do I stop running?"

She gives me the biggest grin I've seen from her yet. "*Now* you're asking the right question."

It's not as easy as just changing my mind, it turns out. Jane gives me several journal prompts along with strict orders not to judge anything I write. I spend days writing, sometimes curled up on my sofa, sometimes on Lookout Hill. Sometimes in my head when I'm strolling the farmer's market for that day's kitchen experiments.

The prompts force me to cover ground from "What sacrifices am I willing to make in a relationship?" to "Which relationships in my life do I respect?" But when I get to Jane's office the following week, the final prompt is unanswered.

"How did it go?" she asks. "Any breakthroughs with the journal?"

I open it to the page with the blank prompt.

"It went pretty well, I think. It was harder than I expected not to judge my own thoughts."

"I agree," she says. "That's a pretty common discovery. What surprised you most?"

"I can't answer this one." I turn the notebook toward her. *"What does being in love mean to you?"*

"You found a stuck point."

"Yes."

"Why do you think you're stuck there?"

I scowl at the empty lines. "We both know why."

"Do *we?* I have a guess. I'd like to hear yours."

I know the answer to this. I knew the second I started thinking about what I would write. But I can't say it out loud for the same reason I couldn't write it down; it makes it too real.

When I don't answer after a minute, Jane asks, "Does answering scare you?"

I meet her eyes. "Yes. And I hate it. I'm a functional adult. Even a successful one. Why is that so hard to answer?"

"Why do *you* think?" Jane asks.

"Can I think about it?"

She smiles. "Do you really need to?"

I lean over and rest my elbows on my knees and head in my hands, running them through my hair over and over, not caring that it's going to wreck it. I know why I don't want to write or say the answer. "I'm not ready." The idea of talking this through makes my chest feel tight and the room too hot.

"Okay. I accept that you believe this is true. But let me ask you this: will avoiding the answer make it less true?"

"Yes."

Jane suppresses a smile at my quick answer. "Let me rephrase: will answering it improve your life or make it worse?"

I keep my head down for a long time, pressing my fingertips along the lines and curves of my skull, over and over. Finally, I lean back against the sofa cushions. "I don't know."

"That's progress, Tabitha. You've determined that avoiding this question won't improve your life but answering it might."

"Or it might make it worse."

"Or it might make it better."

I grab a pillow and hug it to my chest, my eyes peeking over the top of it at her. "But also possibly worse."

She rests her chin on her hand and watches me, her eyes soft and compassionate. "Try answering."

I answer the question.

She nods encouragingly, and when I'm done, she says, "Good. I'm proud of you. Now, can you say all that *not* into the pillow?"

I lower it. "Being in love means they have everything you love about your best friend except you also want to make out with them and be with them all the time, maybe even forever, even if logistically, there's no way to make it work."

She taps her chin. "Hmmm. Who in your life have you adored as a friend but are also wildly attracted to?"

"You're not funny," I inform her.

She leans forward. "I can't help it. It's a treat for me as a therapist to watch you having this breakthrough."

"I haven't had it yet."

"Let's try this again. Finish this sentence: being in love feels like . . ."

I swallow. Hard. "Being in love feels like Sawyer."

She sits back, looking the way I feel when I polish off a pint of gelato.

"Great. Now what?"

"Now you go get him."

I was afraid she would say that.

CHAPTER TWENTY-EIGHT

It's odd being back in my old bedroom in my parents' house. This is where I stay every time I come home, but it still feels like visiting someone else's memory. This room belongs to a Tabitha from a different dimension, someone I was before my life forked and took other paths.

The walls are a pale yellow, the bedding a frilly white I can't believe I ever loved. The shelves hold my favorite paperbacks. Those are what ground me, reminding me there was a version of me who once slept and studied and dreamed here.

I set down my suitcase and go downstairs to find my mom in the kitchen. "Need help with anything?"

She smiles at me. "You barely got here. Relax. Do I need to remind you of who exactly taught you to cook? I can handle the food prep."

"I know, but it's a lot of food." Every year, Creekville has a huge picnic at Founder's Park. At least a thousand people show up, and it's a potluck, which means it's also a massive, unspoken competition, all the best cooks competing to bring the dish everyone else raves over. The only prize is knowing in your heart that you did good, but it's enough for these cooks.

"You can peel eggs if you like," she concedes.

"Sure. Where are they?"

"Fridge."

This is when I realize I've been hustled. The fridge holds several flats of eggs. *Commercial* flats, holding thirty each. I'm looking at eight of them. "Mom? What are you doing? An omelet bar for the entire state of Virginia?"

She pauses and considers this. "Not a bad idea. I'll think about it for next year. But no. Those are hardboiled. I'm doing a twist on deviled eggs, but mine are going to be called angel eggs because they'll taste heavenly."

"You're making almost five hundred deviled eggs?"

"*Angel* eggs. It's a big picnic, hon. Get cracking." Then she laughs at her mom jokes, which are always orders of magnitude worse than any dad joke.

I pull out a tray and set it at the breakfast bar, settle onto a stool, and get to work. I can peel an egg in about ten seconds, but that's still going to take almost . . . I stifle a sigh. At least forty minutes.

"How's Creekville doing?" I settle in and listen as she catches me up on the news and gossip. It holds her for about twenty minutes as she slices and scoops the yolks out of the shelled eggs.

"Anyway, I think Miss Lily tried to set up Taylor Bixby with her grandson, but as far as I know, Taylor hasn't dated anyone in . . ."

She trails off and looks at me. "Do you know?"

Taylor's about two years younger than me, so we weren't ever tight in school or anything. "I don't think I've heard about her dating anyone, but I don't keep up that closely with her. Her Instagram is mainly baked goods."

"Well, that's all the town news. Now why don't you tell me why you're really here?"

"Nothing like a small-town Fourth of July," I say. "It's been too long since I had one." I don't know why I haven't confessed that Sawyer brought me back to Creekville. My mom and I have been mending fences since Christmas, but I don't know how she'll react to the news of a man in my life. Plus, I don't know if it's even true. I've texted Sawyer twice since my breakthrough in Jane's office. The first time, I said I was wrong for cutting off texting, and I wanted us to still be friends because I missed hearing from him. His answer was . . .

Nothing.

I tried again two days ago, asking if he was doing anything fun for the Fourth. More nothing.

All of which may explain why I'd planned to be on the road to Camp Oak Crest by now, and instead I'm hiding in my mom's kitchen.

"Sorry," my mom says. "I meant for you to tell me the *actual* real reason you're here."

Grace and I come by our sarcasm honestly.

"Am I that obvious?"

She shrugs. "It wouldn't be if you ever came home for more than Christmas. So I figure something must be up. What is it?"

I peel a few more eggs before I decide I'll tell her. She's been less judgy when we talk on the phone. I have to give her a chance at some point. "Do you remember when I was a counselor at Oak Crest?"

"Of course."

"Do you remember when I had a big crush on one of the other counselors?" Grace and I had never talked to my mom much about boys since she would only give us a lecture on not getting too serious until we established our careers. And I'd already moved to college by then, so it wasn't like I would have even been home to tell her much. But Grace had teased me about it enough times in my mom's hearing that she probably had known something about it.

"Kind of," she says. "He was from Boston or something?"

"Right. I ran into him in May when I came out for the grand opening, and I'm thinking it wasn't a crush after all."

She stops mashing yolks. "You mean it's more than a crush?"

"I think so. I thought the whole reason I stayed out of relationships was because you always told us to focus on our careers first, and that *is* part of it."

Her forehead wrinkles. "Tabitha, honey, I owe you—"

"Nothing. You owe me nothing. It was good advice. But it was easy to follow because I got my heart broken when I was twenty, and I never got over it. Maybe at some level I knew I was trying to protect myself from being hurt again, but it's more than that. I think I never fell out of love with him."

"Wow," she says, scraping a container of plain Greek yogurt into the yolks. "That's big. You better tell me about him."

So I do. About how we'd finally connected in our third summer, how he'd dumped me at the end when I said I loved him, how we'd avoided each other ever since. How he'd sprung our old marriage pact on me, and how he'd tried to win me over. And how I'd shut him down.

"I came down here because Natalie says he's at his cabin for the Fourth," I conclude. "I thought I'd see if I could get him back, but I've texted him twice in the last week, and he hasn't answered either of them. I'm not sure he's going to be happy to find me on his doorstep. If this was a book or a movie and a guy was doing this, I'd tell the girl to watch for the flying red flags when the dude kept harassing her."

"I don't think two follow-up texts after you were the one to end texting is harassment." Her voice is thoughtful. "I understand what you're saying about how it can be a red flag, but this is apples to oranges."

"And showing up on his doorstep unannounced?"

She thinks about that one longer. "What if you text him to let him know what time you're stopping by, and he can either tell you not to come or choose not to be there when you are. Then I'd say you have to respect his boundary."

I cock my head and study her, my fingers busy with the next egg.

"What?" she asks, brushing her cheek against her shoulder. "I have something on my face?"

"No. You're just being cool about this. Don't you want to lecture me about focusing on my cookbook or something?"

"Tab, you're grown. You've done remarkable things professionally. You deserve a good man, and if he's it, then I say go for it."

I stop peeling. "This is so weird."

She gives me a small smile. "You're not the only one who goes to therapy. Besides, Coal and I talk things out on our morning walks, and I'm getting a little wiser."

Coal is her charcoal-colored poodle, and I smile back, glad she and the poodle are so happy. I pick up the next egg and she tsks at me.

"Put that down." She gives my hand a light whack with her wooden spoon as I reach for the egg tray. "Shouldn't you be getting on the road to Oak Crest?"

"But . . ." I gesture at the five remaining trays.

She rolls her eyes. "I had this planned before I knew you were even going to be in town. I can handle it. And by handle it, I mean draft your dad when he's done puttering in his garden with Evie. Go. Put on something cute and get your man." I wince. "Did I not say that right? This girl talk thing is new. I'll get it down. And I won't say anything embarrassing while he's here."

"Oh." My stomach clenches. I hadn't planned to bring Sawyer back here, but I don't want to hurt her feelings. "I'm not sure we'll come back. I'm imagining us talking things out at his place and hanging out with Natalie and Ben, like old times."

She blinks at me a few times. "You've been in love with this guy for almost ten years, but you're not ready to bring him home to meet us?"

"I will eventually." It sounds awkward to my own ears. "I don't want to overwhelm him."

"You don't want to overwhelm the guy who was trying to convince you in May that you should get married?"

"It sounds stupid when you say it like that."

She has enough self-discipline not to confirm how stupid it is. "We'll be happy to meet him whenever you want to bring him around. Now get." She shoos me toward my room. "And good luck!"

"Thanks, Mom," I call to her as I head back to

change. I'd thought I was wearing a cute shirt already, but obviously she thinks I need to step it up. I wish I had our on-set stylist here to tell me which of my outfits says, "Take me back" to the guy who indirectly proposed marriage six weeks ago but who I then rejected followed by a borderline ghosting. All I know for sure is it's apparently not the floral blouse I'm currently wearing.

Suddenly, nothing in my suitcase will work, so I call the hardware store, relieved when it's Paige who answers.

"Hey, it's Tabitha. I'm sure I'm way over-stepping, but I need to wear something cute to impress a guy, and I hate everything I brought."

"Go up to my place," she says. "It's not locked. My closet is your closet. You did kind of build it." Grace and I had helped my dad build the addition when we were teenagers.

"Really?" I ask. "That's okay?"

"Absolutely."

"Thank you! You're the best!"

Ten minutes later, I've got on a yellow smocked peasant blouse, fitted with a square neck. It immediately makes my jeans look better even though I hated them five minutes ago. I switch my shoes to floral Vans—wedge sandals aren't going to do well on the trail to Sawyer's house— and I've run out of any more reasons to procrastinate.

With a deep breath, I take out my phone and text Sawyer one more time.

TABITHA: Hey. I'm in town and I'd love to see you. Thinking I'd drop by around noon?

I tell my mom goodbye and get on the road, because whether he answers or not, I'm knocking on Sawyer's door. But a big wave of relief washes over me when he texts back twenty minutes later.

SAWYER: I'll be here.

It's not "I love you and I can't wait to see you." But it's also not "No."
I'll take it.

CHAPTER TWENTY-NINE

I step into Sawyer's clearing and pause, taking a calming breath. I planned what I would say on the whole drive over, but while I don't need big words, these are big thoughts and big feelings, and I'm not good at articulating those. The only other time I've tried, the guy dumped me the next morning.

The guy I'm about to say this all to again.

Am I crazy?

I half turn to leave and possibly burrow in Natalie's cabin, but I remember sitting on Jane's couch and saying, "Being in love feels like Sawyer."

I take one more deep breath and step into the clearing, working on controlling my breathing as I make my way around to Sawyer's front door.

He answers within seconds of my knock.

"Hey," he says, a smile I can't read on his face. It's not shy. It's also not natural. He's smiling like I'm a project manager he doesn't get along with.

"Hey. Thanks for letting me drop by."

"Sure." We stand there for a few seconds before he steps back. "You, uh, want to come in?"

"Sure." Kill me now. This awkwardness . . . I hate it.

He leads me to the living room. He waits until

I sit on the sofa before taking an armchair. The armchair is opposite me, a rough-hewn wooden coffee table between us. Okay, not the strongest start.

"What brings you to Oak Crest today?" he asks.

I have four different possible opening lines here, but they all fly out of my head. What comes out is "You."

I cringe, a flashback to Grace's cheerleading days and their *BE AGGRESSIVE, BE BE AGGRESSIVE!* making me want to cringe. I should not have started on a cringe.

Sawyer's eyebrows fly up, disappearing under the irresistible swoop of his bangs. I want to brush them back so badly. I fold my hands in my lap instead. "What about me?"

"You didn't answer my texts." *Yes, that's much better. Now go on offense.* It's a hard fight not to roll my eyes at myself.

"It's hard to know what you really want sometimes," he said. "Seemed safer not to in case I got a third one saying not to text after all."

It had hurt him when I'd told him not to reach out. It would have hurt me too. "I'm sorry about that," I say. "Can I tell you about where my head has been?" The answer is, *So far up my own—*

"If you want," he says.

It's better than no. I clear my throat and figure out where to start, trying to measure my words. "You surprised me when you showed up for the grand opening. I knew coming back here would involve me laying my ghosts to rest. I've tried to convince myself all these years I had done that but being back here proved I was kidding myself. So I *really* wasn't prepared to deal with you in real life."

"You hid that pretty well," he says, "pulling off pranks like a boss."

"I reached for old tools."

His expression is a question mark.

"That's what my therapist would say. When we're in times of emotional stress, we reach for old tools. Even if those tools aren't good for us anymore. I reached for pranks."

He gives a single slow nod. "I guess I did too."

"Anyway, if I wasn't prepared to see you in the flesh, I definitely wasn't ready for you to bring up the marriage pact. But you said something important when I was here last. If this place is a bubble, then why are Ben and Natalie married with a kid? Why have they built a life together, most of which they built away from here? If you can't meet your person when you're a dumb teenager, why are they so happy now?"

I swallow some anxiety—a *lot* of anxiety—and meet his eyes. "I've thought a lot about that this summer. Sometimes it feels like the only thing I've thought about."

His expression has softened from intent but polite listening to something else. Understanding?

No. Recognition. It gives me more courage.

"It's not just this summer. You've always been on my mind, even when I thought you weren't. Dates that always fell short because it wasn't as easy as it was with you. Relationships that didn't work because the same chemistry wasn't there." His eyes glint, and I look away, not sure I can continue if our eyes stay locked.

"I've thought about that all summer too, and when I put it all together, I came up with one answer."

"What's the answer?" His voice is low and silky now. This is not College Sawyer anymore. This is Grown Sawyer, and I literally gulp. Like a freaking cartoon. He watches the motion of my throat like it's the most fascinating thing he's seen.

"You were right. That's the answer. You were right when you lured me here in May and proposed giving this another shot. I should have taken advantage of that time. I should have gone into it with a more open mind, not like it was a game. And if you're willing, I'd like a do-over."

He leans forward, his eyes alight, an almost-smile flickering on one side of his mouth. "Explain."

It's easy to see how this calm, self-possessed Sawyer has the beginning of an empire to his credit when he's not yet thirty. I deal with big shot corporate execs all the time, and he has the vibe of a man who gets exactly what he wants.

"One day. Three dates. At the end of the day, we kiss. If you can say you don't feel anything, we walk away and never speak of it again because I'd be too mortified."

His half smile appears. "When?"

"Tomorrow."

"Where?"

"Right here. I've already talked to Natalie, and I have it all planned." I'd even shipped a few things in advance to make sure it would all work. My stomach fizzes as I think about Date Two, a couples yoga session involving lots of entwining and staring into each other's eyes. I planned *good* dates.

He studies the floor, then leans back in the armchair. "No deal."

Now my stomach drops, all fizziness gone. "I'm sorry, what?"

"No deal. I've had time to think about it too, and you were right. This won't work. We won't work." He says it so calmly. I imagine it's how he shoots down business deals that insult him. He has no expression on his face, and I have no idea what to do next.

Between my confession of feelings, my intricate date planning, and my practiced monologues, I had never pictured him saying no.

"No?" I have to check because it's not clicking.

"No."

I have no idea what to do. I glance around the room like there's an answer, my eyes landing on the deck outside. That's it. Escape. I start toward the front door, desperate to get out of here.

Sawyer stands, and I stop when I'm at the threshold of the living room. "I understand," I say, even though I don't. At all.

"Do you?" It's like he's reading my mind.

"Yeah. I get it. Sorry I barged in." Is this where he changes his mind? Where he decides his pride isn't worth it and begs me to stay?

"No problem. Thanks for taking the time to stop by." His tone is polite again, his body relaxed as he waits for me to let myself out, hands in the pockets of his shorts, like he's standing in line for a hot dog at a Central Park street cart.

"Sure. Of course. Least I could do. I'll see you around sometime."

"Next Mendoza baby, maybe." His smile is still casual.

"Sure." I know other words. I can't think of them, but I must know other words. I reach for the doorknob. *One last chance, Sawyer.* "Well, bye."

"Bye."

I let myself out and escape, heading for the trail back to camp as fast as I can without running in case Sawyer is watching me. But based on his laidback dismissal, I doubt he is.

I pick up to a jog when I hit the trail and keep it

up until the halfway point where I come to a dead stop.

Wait.

Wait, wait, wait.

I am so stupid. I couldn't have done a worse job of making Sawyer feel like I didn't listen to him at all.

Tabitha, Tabitha, Tabitha. YOU IDIOT.

I turn and run back toward Sawyer's even faster than I ran away, arriving on his porch, a panting, sweaty mess. But I knock anyway.

He opens and worry lines crinkle around his eyes as I manage to wheeze a "Hey" after my sprint.

"Hey. Uh, what are you . . ."

"I had the wrong information when I asked you about those three dates earlier. I meant to say they would be in Creekville, all day tomorrow, doing all of our town's ridiculous traditions, and stuffed to the gills with my family and everyone who could possibly tell you embarrassing stories about my childhood, from shopkeepers to my Sunday School teacher. They will be intrusive, nosy, and offer lots of unsolicited opinions."

He leans against the doorway, smiling.

"Does that sweeten the pot at all?" I ask.

He gives a quiet laugh. "Yeah. A lot. Sure, Tabitha. I'll go on three dates with you tomorrow in Creekville, then I'll kiss you until your lips go numb, and we can decide if we're getting married."

Now it's my turn for my mouth to fall slightly open. "I don't know if—"

"Great plan, Tab. Text me the address. See you tomorrow." And he closes the door while I gape like a lake trout.

CHAPTER THIRTY

At nine o'clock the next morning, Sawyer walks into Bixby's looking like the posterchild for Hilton Head hotties, a light pink linen button-down hanging open over a white cotton T-shirt worn tucked into black shorts. He's completed the outfit with slip-on Sperrys, and my heart pitter-patters. Some women might like a bad boy, but I've always had a weak spot for a well-dressed Southern gentleman, and Sawyer's East Coast beach aesthetic is the same vibe. I kinda want to fan my face, but instead I stand and wave him over to my table for two.

"Welcome to Bixby's." I reach up to give him a hug hello. He pulls me close and holds me against him for a few seconds.

"It's good to see you," he murmurs in my ear.

Oh, lordy. Yeah. I need to fan my face. When he lets go, I gesture around the café as we step back and take our seats. "It's been around for longer than I have, but Taylor's been running it for the last five years. I ordered for you, if that's okay."

"Baked goods and coffee is a great first date."

"This isn't even the date yet. This is pregaming with the best hollandaise egg sandwich you'll ever have. I've tried getting this and the chocolate croissant recipes from Taylor, but—"

297

"Never gonna happen," she calls from the register.

I point over my shoulder in her direction. "But that."

He smiles. "Tell me what it was like growing up in a small town."

Before I can answer, Miss Lily has come in while we were talking, and now she stops by our table. "Hey, Tabitha."

"Hey, Miss Lily. This is Sawyer Reed. Sawyer, this is Miss Lily. She's the heart and soul of this town."

Miss Lily blushes and gives a dismissive wave. "Oh, stop with that. I didn't know you were coming to town. Your mother must be delighted."

"She is," I confirm.

"Well, I saw Grace and Noah heading into your dad's store. They look happy as ever. And it's nice to see your dad looking healthy, too. I know it's a load off your mother's mind. She says the cookbook is doing well?"

"It is."

"Good, good. If you're not tied up this evening, come on over and watch fireworks. My grandsons are shooting them off, so it might be a lot of foolishness, but there will be cold adult beverages and good food."

"Thank you, Miss Lily. We'll keep it in mind."

She takes her usual seat with her canasta friends, and I turn to look at Sawyer, who's grinning at me. "That's pretty much what it's like living in a small town."

"It's like that in Martha's Vineyard. My grandparents had a place there. I remember how everyone kept tabs on each other every summer."

"Welcome to the mix. I promise you word of my new gentleman friend will reach the end of Main Street before we even finish breakfast. Now you tell me what it's like growing up in Boston."

He does, talking about his family, including the two sisters he's only mentioned in passing, his parents, their high expectations, their house, his private school, the constant fear he wouldn't be able to keep up at MIT.

We pause only when the egg sandwiches come so I can watch Sawyer's eyes widen at the first bite, and it's worth it.

"Careful or you'll swoon," I tease.

"For real, if it were legal to marry a sandwich—"

"I'd have already married this one. Sorry."

"Fair."

Whatever questions I have, he's happy to answer them, and when we finish breakfast and start walking toward the hardware store, I ask him why. "You weren't this open when we were counselors. What switch flipped?"

"When I was a counselor, everything I had was because of my parents. It was weird to talk about it like it was mine. My *parents* had a nice house. My *parents* paid for my nice schools. But my success now is my own. Even with my inheritance, I couldn't have built up my company like I have if I wasn't good at what I do. It feels okay to say that. What I have, I earned."

He says it without any arrogance, and it is *sexy.*

We stop in front of Handy's Hardware. "*This* is the first date," I say. "This is my dad's store. I worked here from the time I was a kid, and I thought you should get a taste of what I can do besides camp activities and cooking. I think it's something we might have in common."

"I'm already into it."

"You don't even know what it is yet."

He gives me a cute smile. "I love hardware stores. There's nothing we could be doing in there I won't like."

"Come on, then." I bring him in and introduce him to Paige, explaining her many connections to our family now. She flicks a glance at my outfit and winks. I'm wearing my own white jeans, but I borrowed another shirt from her, a red Swiss-dotted halter blouse with white buttons up the front and tie around the waist.

"Hi, Tabby," Evie says, smiling from beside her mom. My dad must have brought her over to hang out with Paige while she works, just like he used to bring us with him. I introduce Sawyer to her too, and she gives a solemn nod. "I know who you are. I'm teaching your workshop."

"Our workshop?" he repeats.

"Yes," she says. "Let's go."

She flies around the corner and beckons us to follow her to the back of the store. My dad is waiting for us in the "Builder Buddies" corner where he holds Saturday morning workshops several times a year to teach kids basic wood-working and construction.

"Hey, Dad," I say, and Sawyer straightens beside me. "This is Sawyer Reed."

"Hey, son," he says, holding out his hand for a shake. Sawyer takes it, and when they let go, my dad gives me the slightest nod. He likes a man with a firm handshake. First test passed. "Take your seats and we'll get started on today's project." He pats a wooden box beside him. "Your mother has requested another outdoor planter."

It looks like a simple design, but I know better. This is going to take careful lumber selection and mitered corners. This is the next test. Sure enough, he turns to Sawyer, and in an overly casual tone, asks, "What wood do you reckon we should use for this?"

"May I?" Sawyer gestures to the box, and my dad gestures like, *Please do*. Sawyer crouches to study it, running his finger over the joins. "Heart-wood if you have it."

My dad scoffs. "If I have it . . ." But his eyes twinkle because Sawyer is right: a heartwood will do best outdoors. "Go on and pick it then."

I lead Sawyer to the lumber section. "You're doing great. He's already impressed. I can tell."

"What about you?" He reaches for a piece of redwood, not looking at me, but I can tell he's tuned toward me as he waits for my answer.

"Hey," I say, taking the redwood plank from his hand. "You don't have to impress me, Sawyer. All the most important things about you, I already know. I saw you in action for three summers. You impressed me then. I'm filling in blanks, learning details about you. But the big stuff? I know."

His eyes darken and drift toward my lips. I sway toward him, and we might have jumped the gun and gone for the kiss if Evie hadn't appeared right then, clapping her hands.

"Come on, guys. Let's make it!"

I step back and hand back the plank. "Good choice."

"I love that you know that," he says.

My breath catches the tiniest bit at the word "love" hovering between us in any context, but I manage a low-key, "Same. You might be the first guy I've dated who did."

"I was hands-on when I flipped houses," he says. "Had to save where I could on labor. Learned to do a lot of carpentry."

We follow Evie and spend the next two hours hanging out with my dad and making the box. I let Sawyer take the lead to see what he knows, and it's a lot. My dad is impressed. But I don't need any direction either, handling the tools and cuts with the comfort of someone who grew up around them. At one point, my dad leaves to answer a question for a customer, and Sawyer leans over as I'm tucking a marking pencil behind my ear. "You are damn sexy."

I nearly hammer my thumb and shoot him a hard scowl. He grins at me like he knows his words are undoing me.

When the box is done, my dad gives it a thorough inspection. "All right, son." He sets down the box. "You can marry her."

"Dad!"

But he only shrugs. "I figure that's why you brought him here seeing as you've never brought another guy around. See you at the picnic." Then he leaves to find Evie, who has wandered off in the last hour.

"Sorry about that." I can't even meet Sawyer's eyes, so I busy myself by bending to tie my shoe but remember too late that I wore white sandals. I sort of dust my toes instead.

"Didn't bother me," Sawyer says, and I look up to see his face as relaxed as it's been since he walked into Bixby's.

"Okay, then." I stand and smooth my shirt. "Ready for date two?"

"The picnic?" he guesses.

"You say picnic, I say gauntlet. Po-tay-to,

po-tah-to. Which there will be a lot of, by the way. Mostly in competing salads."

"Ready," he says. "Bring on Creekville."

"Careful what you wish for," I mutter as I lead us out of the store.

CHAPTER THIRTY-ONE

The Creekville Fourth of July picnic is in full swing when we arrive, the usual cheerful chaos of a hundred mismatched quilts and groaning food tables filling Founder's Park.

Children run in between blankets, friends of all ages calling to each other and catching up. It's loud and bright, and once again, Sawyer is smiling.

"Looks fun," he says.

"I can't be responsible for anything anyone might say to you."

"Tabitha." He stops and waits until I stop too and turn to face him. "Stop worrying. I'm just learning about where you come from. It's different from the way I grew up, and I'm loving being an observer."

"Okay, I'll relax." I start us on the long process of picking through the blankets toward the food tables, someone on every third quilt stopping us to say hello. My first-grade teacher, an old neighbor, two moms of friends from high school, my boyfriend from my sophomore year. They all want to know how New York is, and who Sawyer is, and the blaring unasked question underneath it all—and not in a subtle way—is *Who is this man to you?*

"Is it always like this when you come back or

is this because you're famous?" he asks when we breach the blanket perimeter to reach the first table of food.

"I'm not famous."

"You were on the cover of one of the cooking magazines at my grocery checkout last week. Jerk move when I'm trying to get over you."

I smirk. "Trying as in the present tense?"

He gives me his half smile. "No. Not present tense."

Oooh, heart-swoops. Good thing I'd already made peace with my feelings for this man in Jane's office or I'd think I was having a cardiac event.

I mean, I am. But not the kind that'll kill me. Probably.

We go down the table, picking and choosing from the many, many dishes. I subtly point out all the cooks giving us side-eye to see if we're picking theirs. "They'll do it when we sit down to eat too, watching to see what we like and what we don't."

He gives a soft laugh. "That's a lot of pressure. Is this a you-thing or an everyone thing?"

"They'll do it to anyone. There'll be so much side-eye today it's a wonder they don't turn into halibut. But they'll be extra interested to see how I react because of my job."

"And how will you react?"

"Like I love everything I'm eating," I say with

a grin. "Except this pasta salad." Each dish is labeled with its title, allergens, and the cook's name. "That's Camille Lynch's, and she was mean in high school." I scoop some on my plate. "The trick is not to oversell it by looking outright disgusted. It's a slight pause and a blank expression before I discreetly push it to the side of my plate and try something else."

"Petty," he says.

I give him my "are you kidding me" face. "I paid you back for way less than this in the counselor days."

"True," he says. "I knew what you were when I picked you up."

And it makes me smile because he does know me. He's always known me pretty well, but he's definitely getting a deeper sense of me the longer we're in Creekville. I feel vulnerable, like I'm walking around in a hospital gown giving a prime view of my backside, but I know I need to be okay with this. I've just never gone through this process with anyone else before.

"Tab!"

"That's Grace," I say, turning at the sound of her calling my name. "My sister."

"Right. I met her once when you nearly scared me to death that one time for laughs."

"Oh, yeah." I grin up at him. "That was fun. Let's go over, and I'll introduce you again."

Grace and her boyfriend, Noah, Paige's brother,

are sitting with my parents, Paige, and Evie on a cluster of red, white, and blue quilts.

"Hey, guys," I say as we walk up. "This is Sawyer."

"Hey, Sawyer," they say in chorus, and I introduce him to Grace, Noah, and my mom.

She pats the empty space beside her. "I saved y'all a spot."

"This is the *real* Fourth of July grilling," I tell him under my breath.

Sawyer makes a small choking sound, like he swallowed a laugh.

As soon as we're on the blanket, my mom starts in on Sawyer, asking him more questions than a Congressional committee. He answers her with good grace, not overexplaining, but also not ducking anything. But when she veers into where his home office is, I jump in. These are choppy waters, stuff Sawyer and I haven't talked about how to navigate, and I don't want to ruin the afternoon by diving in now.

"Any idea who the winning essayist is, Mom?" That'll distract her. I explain to Sawyer, "The eighth graders all enter an essay contest about why America is the land of the free and the home of the brave. A committee of local veterans picks the winner and announces who during the lunch. The winner reads their winning essay, and they get a hundred dollars and a box of fireworks to shoot off."

"Free fireworks? Is it too late to enter?" he asks.

"Only by about fifteen years." I pat his arm. I wish I was bold enough to take his hand, or that he'd take mine. I wish I was more comfortable displaying my affection, but it's hard when I know every single person in our field of vision will be watching and dissecting our every move, from the café this morning to now. Especially now.

It's so easy when it's the two of us. But we haven't had much time to be "us" around other people, and no time since he turned up at Oak Crest in May. I don't understand the rules for existing as us outside of the bubble, and I'm okay with figuring them out, but other than a short moment in the lumber aisle, it hasn't seemed to cross Sawyer's mind.

My mom is super into the question of the winning essayist, and she breaks into my thoughts with her speculations. "I thought it would be an Allred. It's an Allred about every other year. Bob Allred is the patriarch and also the VFW post commander. Veterans of Foreign Wars," she explains.

"Ah," Sawyer says.

"But the thing is, I saw Jennifer Blount's youngest, Carter, wearing a button-down shirt."

"Ahhh," I say. Because this *does* make everything clear.

"What am I missing?" Sawyer asks.

"You should be able to spot an eighth grader by sight," I say. "Just look for the surliest teenagers. Tell me what you notice about their clothing."

He scans the crowd before turning back to us. "They're all in T-shirts."

My mom nods. "Carter wearing a collared shirt is a dead giveaway. It's him. I bet the only reason that kid even entered was to win the fireworks. He's a hellion. Good luck to us all if it's him. Watch your back come sundown."

Sawyer laughs until he realizes the rest of us aren't.

"It won't be good," I tell him. "Imagine that Max kid from our second year with a box of fireworks and not enough adult supervision."

"Got it."

My mom continues the grilling while Grace and I catch up and she tells me about her promotion at Boeing. We visit with everyone who stops by our quilts, but it never deters my mom from picking up where she left off with Sawyer.

Finally, I lean over and tell him in a voice too low for my mom to hear, "Don't worry. It's essay winner time and the torture will stop."

Sure enough, the mayor stands on the small dais in the middle of the park and turns the mic on. It gives a loud squeal and Evie claps her hands over her ears. The mayor gives a short-ish speech about the fine youth of Creekville and the good men and women of the local VFW hall, then clears her throat and takes a dramatic pause.

"And now, I am pleased to present to you the winner of this year's 'Home of the Free' essay contest, Carter Blount!"

My mom gives a self-satisfied smile as we applaud. And holy terror or not, Carter Blount wrote a good essay. Grace leans past me to tell Sawyer, "Watch her. She is super sappy about patriotic stuff. She's never made it through the national anthem without crying, even when it's just instrumental."

"Shut up," I tell her, but my voice is thick because Carter used the phrase "our forebears' dreams" and it's made me slightly weepy.

Grace winks at Sawyer and turns back to listen to Carter's monotone reading, and I don't dare look at Sawyer. It's one thing for him to eat my high school nemesis's pasta salad and meet pretty much every teacher I've ever had growing up, but I'll be damned if he gets to watch me fall to pieces when the high school orchestra plays a slightly off-key rendition of "Proud to Be an American" while the crowd sings along.

When the Fourth of July program is over, the first people begin to drift out of the park, off to prep their own family or neighborhood cele-brations. We stay, visiting with friends and neigh-bors, my mom grilling Sawyer, for another hour, until the crowd is down to half its size. Grace begins to gather up plates and trash, and soon we're all helping her clean our area.

"This is one of the cool things about Creek-ville," I tell Sawyer. "Everyone does their part, so it's barely any overtime for our two-person parks department."

He dutifully picks up trash, but I notice he avoids me and doesn't say much.

When everything is put away and the blankets are folded, my mom asks if we're going to Miss Lily's tonight for fireworks.

"It's better than being anywhere inside town limits," she says. "Who knows what Carter Blount is going to do with his?"

I'm about to accept. It's slightly different than the nature scavenger hunt I planned along the creek trail, but Sawyer interjects.

"Thank you for being willing to include me, but I'm ready to head back home."

It catches me off guard, and I shoot him a sharp look to see if anything is wrong, but I can't read his expression. He's smiling at my mom, who makes a sound of disappointment. "Well, all right, but I have to tell you, last time we were at Miss Lily's, Grace and Noah gave us a completely different kind of fireworks. You're missing out."

"Next time," he says, and it makes my mom beam and wink at me.

I do my best to return her smile, but my stomach is tightening, an acidic feeling that has nothing to do with Camille Lynch's annoyingly good vinaigrette. Sawyer's voice is too smooth. If anything, he's become more expressive as he's gotten older. So why can't I read anything from his tone now?

My stomach clenches harder as I draw the only logical conclusion. This has all been too much. I gave him real life, all right, but I served it up in a single giant bite. Who wouldn't feel overwhelmed by that?

I keep my smile pasted on as we say goodbye to everyone else and walk back toward Main Street. "Back to Oak Crest, huh?" I keep my voice light, trying not to let my worry show. We haven't even gotten to the third date.

"Yeah, if that's okay."

"Sure." We walk toward his car in quiet. Sawyer doesn't chatter, and long silences from him aren't unusual, but this feels so . . . heavy. So pregnant with things he isn't saying.

When we reach his SUV, I stop on the sidewalk. "Thanks for coming out today."

"Thank you for inviting me." He slides his hands into his pockets.

I don't know what to say. I want to ask if something's wrong, but I already know there is. Now is a bad time to have this talk with all the curious eyes marking us as they pass. "Text me when you get home and let me know you made it safely."

His forehead furrows. "You aren't coming with me?"

"Oh. I didn't think I was invited."

He closes his eyes and sighs. "We have a lot to talk about, don't we?"

I hate those words. I hate them so much. Even though it's usually me saying them, I still hate them. There's never a good side of this conversation to be on. But I have to hold it together like I did during every taping when my dad was in surgery or getting an infusion, and it was all I could think about.

"Definitely." I clear my throat when my voice sounds creaky. "Lots to talk about."

"So let's go."

But I can't stand the thought of two awkward hours in the car with him. "I better follow you. It'll be a lot easier for me to get back here later."

"I should have thought of that. See you over there?"

"Sounds good."

His arms twitch up like he's about to hug me but stops himself and unlocks his car, a sleek Audi SUV. I step back so he can get in, then wave as he backs out of his space and takes the road out of Creekville.

I turn and walk to my rental parked behind the store. I slide in, grip the wheel, and take a deep, calming breath. "This is going to suck," I say out loud. "But it'll be good for both of you."

I say the words. I'm not sure I believe them, but I try to. I start the car and put myself on Main

Street. But when it curves and turns into the state road, when I should stay straight for Roanoke and on to the camp, I take the left fork that will eventually wind back to Creekville.

I can't do it. I can't have this conversation.

Yes, I'm a chicken. But I put my *whole* self out there today, and it's my whole self he rejected. It sucks. It sucks, and I don't need to have a post-mortem on it right now. We can talk about it eventually in a civilized video call where we put this whole thing to rest for a final time. But I *cannot* sit civilly on his furniture while he tells me kindly why we're not going to work. And I *know* he'll be kind. I know it. Somehow, that makes everything worse.

I drive until I pick up the road back to Creekville and pull into my parents' driveway. It's empty, and I'm thankful. I need a quiet space to fall apart. I go inside to my room and flop on my bed, staring at my ceiling. Sawyer should be home in another hour, and when I don't show up shortly after, he's going to call. I need to think about how to have that conversation.

Around the time he should be pulling into camp, I send a text.

> **TABITHA:** Decided to stay home.
> Thank you for coming out today.
> **SAWYER:** What's up?
> **TABITHA:** Long day. Weird vibes.

My phone lights up with an incoming call, but I send it to voicemail and send another text.

> **TABITHA:** It's okay. I fly out tomorrow, but I promise we can have a mature FaceTime when I'm back in New York. I need to retreat.
> **SAWYER:** FROM WHAT

I have a big gross-feeling pit in my stomach. It feels more like being physically sick than anything, but I know this feeling; it's the same one I had when Ben delivered his message on the dock that morning. Sawyer sent his own message today. Withdrawing. Shutting down. Right now, I don't want or need the words.

I send Sawyer another text.

> **TABITHA:** I don't know what went wrong today, but tbh, right now I'm too wrecked to figure it out. Will check in when I get home tomorrow but turning off my phone now.

Then I get up, turn off my bedroom light, and stare at the ceiling, hoping sleep takes me before the fireworks start going off all over town. It doesn't. I've been listening to the dull boom of fireworks for half an hour when my mom bursts in.

"Mom? Is Miss Lily's party over?"

"No, honey. Tell me why you're here and not at the camp."

I struggle to sit up and lean against the headboard, rubbing my hands over my face. "Why would I be at camp?"

"Because Sawyer's there."

I stop rubbing and stare at her. "How did you know that?"

"I asked you a question first. Why are you here and not with him?"

I slump down and drop my head to my pillow. "I'm not even sure what went wrong with Sawyer today, but I do know our ratios are all off."

"What does that mean?"

"It means for every five times we spend together, one of them is bad. There's some drama or problem to solve. That's not good."

"Twenty percent, hm?" She pats my leg again. "Tab, if all I ever had with your dad was twenty percent of our best times and the rest were bad, I'd still feel lucky. Eighty percent good times is a pretty good rate of good times. And I'll tell you something else. It's good you're hitting a few rough patches now because it's going to teach you how to talk to each other, and when bigger, harder rough patches come up because that's life, you'll know how to navigate them."

I'm not sure I buy it. "You don't think it's a bad sign we're dealing with all of this so early?"

"You are and you aren't, right? Weren't you friends for two years before you dated and broke up?"

"Yeah."

"Until that breakup, what was the ratio?"

"That was the only bad time we had. But it was a pretty big bad time."

She's quiet for a minute. "Honey, I knew where you were because Sawyer tracked down Miss Lily's home number online, called her house, and got me on the phone. When I told him you weren't with us, he asked me to check if you'd come home and give you a message."

I sit up again. "He did? What?"

Her smile stretches into a grin. "You have exactly two hours and fifteen minutes to meet him at Moon Rock from the time I tell him you're on your way, or he's coming back to Creekville to drive you there himself."

"Wh-what?" It's so . . . so . . . caveman.

"I wouldn't test him."

I freeze, not sure what I should do. I know it makes me a bad feminist to run when a man crooks his finger, but . . . dang. It is *working* for me.

"If it helps," she adds, "he also said he thinks you read today wrong and he's going to set you straight."

"Like talk it out?" The way any sweet, cinnamon roll of a man would?

"No. Definitely 'set you straight.' " She plucks at her shirt like she needs cool air.

I *am* a bad feminist. I pause to see if I can rescue my principles, but nope. "I better get on the road."

My mom gives a small whoop. "I really like him, Tabitha. So yes, I really think you better."

CHAPTER THIRTY-TWO

Mom shoos me out the door with a hug and a promise to text Sawyer that I'm on the way.

"This is a huge sacrifice, you know." She holds her cell phone up. "I'm dying to see what would happen if he came out here to get you."

"Mo-o-o-om."

"Go, go." She sends me off with a swat on my bum.

I run every possibility through my mind of what Sawyer wants me out there for. And specifically to Moon Rock.

It could be bad. It could be he wants to dump me face-to-face. But wouldn't he have told me to meet him at the dock if that were the case? And besides, he said I'd gotten today wrong.

Which means . . .

Maybe for him it was good? And if it's good, and he doesn't want me running off again, and he wants me to meet him at Moon Rock . . .

My fingers tighten on the steering wheel, and I cruise fifteen miles over the speed limit all the way to camp, catching glimpses of fireworks now and then through the gaps in the trees.

I park by the main office and get out, hearing the sounds of a camp Fourth of July. Ben and Natalie—okay, Ben—have continued the tradition of letting the counselors put on a fireworks display for the campers by shooting them off over the lake. Tomorrow, the campers will each take a shift going out in the canoes to collect the debris, but the counselors make it a game, and they don't mind.

The regular camp lights all burn, but the buildings are dark, and I grab the flashlight my mom handed me on my way out of her door, per Sawyer's directions. I'm glad he remembered because I was so flustered when I left that I wouldn't have thought of it.

I pause at the Moon Rock trailhead, not sure I'm any less flustered now. Sawyer is up there. Up there waiting for me. And I hope—I *believe* he's going to say things I want to hear.

I start on the trail, listening to the sound of slight rustles in the underbrush and the crack of the lake fireworks. I focus on my breathing, keeping it even on the slight incline leading up to Sawyer.

Leading up to the man I love.

Leading up to the only man who can crook his finger and make me come running.

I force myself to stay at a brisk walk. A very brisk walk.

Ten minutes later, I step into the clearing. Sawyer stands in the center, waiting for me.

"Hey," I say, quietly.

"Hey. You ghosted me today."

"Tried to," I correct him. "But I'm here."

"Why did you do that?"

"You didn't seem into it today."

His eyebrows pull together. "What makes you think that?"

"You were . . . distant. No handholding. Didn't talk to me much at the picnic. Didn't want to go to Miss Lily's party. It seemed like you might be remembering how different our backgrounds are."

He scrubs his hands over his face. "You are such a frustrating woman."

"Me? *You* keep blowing hot and cold."

"I was trying to follow your lead today. I didn't hold your hand because I thought it's what you wanted. I spent all my time at the picnic talking to your family for the same reason."

"But . . . but you left as soon as you could."

"I turned down the invitation to Miss Lily's because I wanted to be alone with you, not because I wasn't having a good time! Your town is great. Your parents are great. I love your mom. If you won't take me back, I might ask her to adopt me anyway."

"Oh." OH. Oh my.

"Want to guess why you're up here under pain of threat?" It's fairly dim up here, but I can see a small smile on his lips.

My mouth goes dry. I know what I hope, but it feels like too big of a wish. I shake my head.

"You're here to fulfill the terms of your challenge."

"Um." My voice is a croak, and I clear it softly. "Which terms?"

"Come here, Tabitha Winters."

I do. As easy as that, I do.

He takes a step and reaches out for both of my hands, rubbing his thumbs over my knuckles.

"The terms of the dare you laid out were that I got three dates and a kiss. If I don't think there's anything between us after that, we walk away. Am I getting it right?"

"It was your challenge first."

"Tab." It's a calm warning.

"Okay, yes, that's right." I don't know who this suddenly assertive alpha male is, but I don't hate it.

"What was date three?" His dark eyes gather the faint moonlight and shine it back at me. "Tab? The third date."

I shake myself. "Scavenger hunt in the woods around Creekville."

He gives my hands a light squeeze. "I'm sorry I missed it. But what do we do now that we can't have our third date?"

I'm not quite sure how to read this yet, but I *am* sure Sawyer didn't blackmail me out here to dump me to my face. Past his shoulder, another shower of sparks explodes over the lake with a distant boom. I gesture in their direction. "There's a fireworks show happening right there we could count. We could walk down to the dock to watch it."

"Not bad, Tabby Cat. But if you don't mind, I have another idea."

"Okay . . ."

"I don't want this date to be on the dock where things ended."

"That makes sense." There's a delicious tickling in my chest.

"I want it where everything began." His voice has grown soft and low like it had that night forever ago. Like that night, he slips one hand around my waist to draw me closer. He slides his other hand beneath my jaw and gently nudges my chin up. "Here, at Moon Rock, where you were wise enough to name what I couldn't see yet."

This kiss feels even more perfect than our first real one had nine years ago, and this time no one stumbles up the trail to interrupt it. The contours of Sawyer's body have changed as he's grown into it, but while it's still new to me, he feels like home. His lips are sure, and I slide my arms up his chest and around his neck, drawing him even closer, losing myself entirely as he deepens the kiss.

He breaks away and leans his forehead against mine.

I give a soft sigh. "I don't know if I fell in love

with you again after three days in May, or if I never fell out of love in the first place."

"Just so you know, Tabitha Winters, you are not my backup plan. Being with you and your people today only made me love you more." I give an involuntary shiver at hearing the word "love." He presses me closer. "Yes. Love. I love you. You're everything I've ever wanted since I was twenty, but I didn't have the brains or guts to see it. But I see you now."

"I thought you didn't like my family or my town. Or it made everything too real, and suddenly you understood about the bubble. And you finally agreed with me at the worst possible time."

"Worst time?"

I pull back to meet his eyes. "Yeah. After I figured out that I never got over you, and I don't want to." For the first time since I stepped into the clearing, I sense tension in him, a nervous energy I feel as distinctly as an electric current. That old Sawyer magic weaves around me even more tightly, and it coaxes the words from me, the ones I sense he needs. "I love you too, Sawyer. And a word on logistics," I say, as his arms tighten around me.

A small puff of laugh stirs my hair. "Yeah?"

I free one arm enough to wave at the clearing. "Good call on location."

I hear a smile in his voice when he answers.

"We could have done this two months ago if you wouldn't have bailed. It's the perfect venue."

I freeze. " 'Venue' is a wedding word."

"It is. I figure ours should be the first one we host at Oak Crest."

I stay still, trying to figure out how that makes me feel. "Three hours ago, I thought we were through. That's a big U-turn."

"And? Can you honestly say there's a chance in hell either of us is ever going to marry anyone else?"

A firework explodes in a shower of golden sparks to punctuate his question.

I laugh and press another kiss against his lips. "That should freak me out completely, but it doesn't. 'First' is probably ambitious. We've got to figure out this long-distance thing, and—"

"Why?"

"Why?" I pull back slightly to see if he's serious. "Don't you think long-distance will be hard? Remember how Ben transferred universities when he and Natalie only lived three hours apart because they hated it?"

He shrugs. "I don't see what the big deal is. The lease I'm signing next week in Brooklyn is a pretty short commute to the Secaucus site."

"What?!"

He grins. "Does *that* freak you out?"

I gape at him, then fling myself on him and press kisses all over his face. "Not." Kiss. "At."

Kiss. "All." But I pull back for a second. "Wait, how many pets do you have?"

"None?" He's thrown by the question.

I give him another kiss, one of relief that quickly turns to one of joy and promise.

When I let him come up for air, he rests his forehead against mine. "So you're saying there's a chance?"

I burst out laughing. "Your odds look good."

"Time for the finale." He lets go of me and walks me over to the rock and flicks on a lantern I hadn't seen in the darkness.

Immediately, a chorus of answering flashlights light up beside the lake, dozens and dozens of them, forming the shape of heart.

"Oh my gosh, Sawyer, how did you do this?"

"I had time while I was waiting for you to drive out here. I love you, Tabitha. I always have."

"I love you too, Sawyer. And I always will."

EPILOGUE
FUTURE

I try not to roll my eyes, scream, swear, or otherwise melt down as my improvised "suite" full of women fusses over me. In twenty minutes, I'm supposed to get married.

I *will* get married. To Sawyer, the man I have not seen nearly enough of since our rehearsal dinner two nights before. I love these women. I do. But the "conversations" Sawyer and I have had in passing as we run from one part of the camp to the other this week getting it wedding-ready have not been enough.

Since he moved to Brooklyn last year, we've seen each other every day that one of us isn't on a business trip. I hate being in the same place and having so little time together.

I have no fear about walking down the aisle shortly, but I almost wish we could get it plus the whole reception over and reclaim our time with each other. It has gotten more and more scarce the closer we've gotten to today.

Why didn't either of us think to elope? Natalie's fussing over me, and I'm kicking myself for never considering Vegas.

"I don't know if there's such a thing as boho

glam, but if there wasn't before, you just invented it," Natalie says, stepping back from the tendril of my hair she's adjusting. Her six-month pregnant belly swells the front of her chiffon maid-of-honor dress. It's a color called terra rosa, which just means somewhere between copper and pink, and it's warm and perfect for a late September wedding. The color looks good on her and Grace both.

"You ready to see yourself?" Grace asks.

I nod. I've had a few fittings in New York, so I know what to expect in the dress, of course, but I haven't seen myself in it with all the pieces pulled together. "I'm ready. Mom, can you handle it?"

But she's already crying and waves a hand with a crumpled tissue to go ahead, unable to speak.

I pause before I turn to meet my reflection in the antique mirror we've brought into Sawyer's— *our*—house to convert one of the guest bedrooms into a "bridal suite" at my mom's insistence.

She's why. Her happy tears. Her deep delight in helping me plan this. And Paige and Natalie, who have transformed the room in his—our— Oak Crest house over the last few days, filling it with subdued linens and soft vintage colors to create a calm space for me, clearing out the bed and setting up several makeup stations.

And Evie and Juniper, who sit in front of one, Evie patiently, Juniper less so, while Paige fusses over them. Each of them is now wearing an adorable flower crown for their respective flower girl and ring bearer responsibilities.

And Grace who says, "Go on, look. Oh, wait, your bouquet."

These people I have loved for years plus the ones I've come to love more recently, they are the reason. Sawyer and I want to stand up in front of the people who matter to us most and move into the next phase of our lives together.

I take a quiet, calming breath, and remind myself of how grateful I am that each of these women is here.

Grace scoops my bouquet from a nearby table, her simple gold wedding band catching the light as she hands me the arrangement of bronze mums and Sahara roses. The ring is new, Noah having placed it on her finger only four months ago in a ceremony in Miss Lily's rose garden where they met. That's part of why Evie is so patient. This is her second stint as a flower girl.

Bouquet in hand, I turn and catch my breath when I see myself in the mirror. I chose a simple ivory dress for our twilight wedding in Sawyer's yard. It has a fitted and lightly beaded bodice with a soft V-neck and delicate spaghetti straps. The gauzy chiffon A-line skirt falls in gentle tiers to the floor, a small twelve-inch train behind it.

My makeup is simple, and so is my hair, the front in a loose side braid, the rest of my curls hanging long and loose the way Sawyer loves them best. But it's my eyes that I notice; they shine, and I've never found a product that could make them do that. Only Sawyer can. In a few minutes, we'll head out to the yard, transformed into a lush autumn floral scape, and my father will walk me down the aisle on the petals Evie strews ahead of me, to meet Sawyer under our wedding arch, with Lake Lupine as our back-drop.

Our officiant will marry us in front of a hundred of our closest friends and family. And then we'll belong to each other. There will be a million more details to sort out after the wedding, of course, not the least of which will be moving into the Brooklyn brownstone we're going to remodel.

But today, it's just about celebrating the incredible year and a half we've shared since we got ourselves straightened out. My life began to make perfect sense once I accepted that Sawyer and I were always meant to be.

A knock sounds on the door.

"That'll be your dad." My mom sniffs.

But it's Sawyer who calls, "Tabitha?"

My heart trips just like it did when I saw him at the airport that second summer back. That day I knew something between us had changed but I hadn't figured out yet that it was the change that would lead us to this day.

Natalie jerks the door open. "You can't see her yet."

"But I have to."

"Is something wrong?" I call, my palms turning damp.

"No, baby. Nothing," he calls back, then softer but still clear, he says to Natalie, "Don't you sometimes need to see Ben just because?"

There's a beat of silence, then a sigh. "Yeah. I get that. But you're coming in here blindfolded."

"Fine."

Grace, maybe because of her recent wedding, winks at me like she gets it. "Come on, ladies," she says. "Let's go start lining up outside. Our processional starts soon."

When the last of them files out, Natalie comes back in with Sawyer, who has been blindfolded with the sash Juniper refused to wear. She leads him to the chair my mom just vacated, and when he's seated, she gives me a pointed look. "Can I trust you to navigate him back to the door without letting him peek?"

"You can."

She leaves and closes the door quietly behind her. I can hear their muffled voices in the hall, but I shift all my attention to my fiancé, walking over to slide my hand in his.

"You okay?" I ask.

He squeezes it. "I am now."

"Not ready to change your mind?" I tease him.

His grip grows even more firm. "No way. You're not getting out of this."

I run my thumb along his, a soft, soothing motion. "I don't want to."

He relaxes his hold but keeps my hand. "It's been so wild. Hasn't it been so wild? The moving, the wedding prep, the guests. So many guests. Just really a lot of guests."

"I was thinking the same thing, wondering why we never considered Vegas."

"Because our moms would kill us."

"I came to the same conclusion. I guess we have to deal with being loved like crazy by everyone who knows us."

He reaches out for my other hand, grasping fruitlessly a few times until I realize what he wants, and I give it to him. He doesn't say anything, only holds them both and takes a deep breath, releasing it like it's the first clean air he's had in ages. "No one loves you like I do, Tab. I just needed a moment to be us together before the rest of this takes over again."

"All that out there?" I say, indicating with my head even though he can't see me. "That's just for today. You and me, we're forever."

He brings my hand to his lips and presses a kiss against the knuckles. "I'm ready now."

"Then let's do this," I say, pulling him to his feet. "I hear there's cake."

He smiles as I lead him to the door, and as

Natalie takes custody of him, my dad slips in to replace him. His eyes fill as he sees me standing in my wedding dress. "Oh, honey."

"Don't, Dad. You'll make me cry and then you'll be in trouble with Paige for ruining my makeup." I sniff.

"Dad's prerogative," he says, carefully gathering me in a hug. We stand that way for a full minute. "Your mother and I are so proud of you, Tabitha. God was good to us to send us you and Grace." He lets me go and presses a kiss to my forehead, then turns and holds out his arm.

"It's time, honey. You ready?"

With a smile, I accept and step into the hall to join the line of all the women I love so much.

"Ready," I say.

My attendants file out in order, Paige patiently guiding the younger girls. We walk out to the deck, which has been turned into a fabric bower leading down to stairs dripping with rich satin ribbon and my wedding flowers. We'll step out so I can make my grand entrance as I descend the stairs because it satisfies my mom's sense of drama. We pause on the top step, still hidden in the bower, waiting until we hear the single violin switch from the Bach processional song to Debussy's "Clair de Lune."

At last, the first dreamlike notes of the melody reach us.

"Your groom is waiting for you," my dad says, smiling down at me with misty eyes.

"Nine years was long enough. Let's not keep him waiting any longer." And with that, I tuck my hand into my dad's arm and go to meet my forever.

Center Point Large Print
600 Brooks Road / PO Box 1
Thorndike, ME 04986-0001 USA

(207) 568-3717

US & Canada:
1 800 929-9108
www.centerpointlargeprint.com